THE SCULPTOR

KRISTY MARIE

This novel is a work of fiction. Names, characters, businesses, places, events, and incidents are either the product of the author's imagination or used in a fictitious manner. Any resemblance to actual persons, living or dead, or actual events, places, and companies is purely coincidental.

First Line Editor: The Ryter's Proof
Proofing: All Encompassing Books
Cover Design: RBA Designs
Cover Photography: Wander Aguiar Photography
Interior Formatting: Champagne Book Designs

Copyright © 2022 by Kristy Marie
Published by Kristy Marie Books, LLC

All rights reserved.

No part of this book may be reproduced in any form or by any electronic or mechanical means, including information storage and retrieval systems, without written permission from the author, except for the use of brief quotations in a book review.

Dear Reader,
The Sculptor deals with sensitive themes—though very fleeting—in portions of the story. If loss—of any kind—could be triggering for you, please use your best judgment when choosing to continue. Otherwise, I hope you enjoy Duke and Ramsey's story.

Kristy

For my granny, the woman who taught me:
There is beauty in adversity.
Strength in endurance.
Power in prayer.
Freedom in forgiveness.
And dreams worth fighting for.
You are His greatest warrior.

She opens her mouth in wisdom, And the teaching of kindness is on her tongue. Proverbs 31:21 NASV

AUTHOR'S NOTE

The Sculptor contains villainous politicians. These congressmen are completely fictitious and do not represent or resemble anyone who has been or currently hold positions in Congress. At the time of this novel, there are no congressmen named Ford and Albrecht.

THE
SCULPTOR

I've never been to Norway or the Alaskan Frontier.
But I've seen the midnight sun.
Her otherworldly presence is as magnificent as her beauty.
I basked in her spring glow.
I lapped up her summer heat.
And loved the fall of her heart.
But when winter came...
I shattered her light.
My obsession stole her freedom.
My love smothered her hope.
My shame froze her warmth.
Heartbreak drowned her in the shadows.
I deserved her screams.
I deserved her absence.
I deserved the haunting memories of her extraordinary seasons.
The seasons when I loved the midnight sun.

CHAPTER ONE

Ramsey

"Lower," I whisper, fighting off a grin.

His eyes widen with surprise. "How much lower?"

I nod at his sweatpants—gray just like the sky outside this ratty motel. "Push them down until I tell you to stop."

His gaze is alight with mischief when he inches the material down his waist. "What exactly are you planning on sketching?"

I twirl the pen between two fingers. "Why do you ask? Are you getting shy?"

"I'm not shy." His voice is unashamed. "I'm being considerate."

"Oh, yeah?" I shift on the table, pulling my leg closer to reach my thigh. "And what are you being considerate of? My innocence?" I chuckle.

I smile at the color blooming on his cheeks and begin outlining, taking time to accentuate the sharp lines of his abdomen that I'm sketching along the skin of my upper leg—my favorite canvas.

Duke scoffs. "I'm being considerate of your..." His voice trails off as he fidgets with the strings on his pants.

"You're being a chicken is what you're doing." I belt out a laugh. "Yank them down, Potter. Don't make me find another muse."

I should have known that would have him snapping to attention. "Is that a threat?" He steps closer to the table, all the humor evaporating with my exhale. Grabbing my hand, he places it on his chest. "Because if you know what's good for your next model," his voice drops to a menacing tone, "then you'll beg him to keep his clothes on."

He places my hand on his waistband, his fingers curling over mine, forcing an immovable grip. "I am your only muse."

The soft material slips lower with the pressure of our hands. "Do I make myself clear?"

I swallow, my gaze drifting to the dip between his hips where the perfect Adonis belt awaits. I've never seen one so masculine, so sculpted. "You are perfection." I breathe along his chest, leaving goose bumps along his skin.

He lets go of my hand, bringing his up to grasp my chin in a firm hold. "And you're mine. Forever."

Forever.

The word sends tingles swirling in my stomach.

"Don't promise something—"

He cuts me off with a rough kiss, but I pull back, not falling for his distraction tactics. "Stop trying to—"

His lips are on mine again, but he's not rough this time. His touch is gentle as his arms wrap around me. "You wanted something, didn't you?"

With my grip firmly on his waistband, I nod into his chest. "Mm-hmm."

I can practically feel him smiling in victory above me. "Then all you need to do is tug a little low—"

"A little lower, sweetheart." The strange voice pulls me out of the memory faster than being doused with ice-cold water. "More toward the middle of the arch."

My hands move on autopilot as I work past the ball of my fiancé's foot, kneading toward the center as he instructed.

"That's my girl, right there. That's the spot."

THE SCULPTOR

I wish I would have hit the spot about twenty minutes ago and ended this show of fake affection earlier. Instead, I've spent the past half-hour on my knees, trying to ignore the dry patches of skin flaking off his feet and falling into my hand.

It's disgusting and quite demeaning, considering I'm dressed in nothing but a bra and a thong.

But that's how Langston Albrecht prefers his women—stripped and helpless.

He's a distinguished man of power.

A well-respected congressman.

And an evil man.

"Ramsey." His gruff tone pulls me back to the task at hand—his freaking foot massage.

"Yes, sir?" I blink, looking up at his weathered face and crinkled eyes. He's such a pompous old bird. "Am I doing it wrong again?"

The words taste like acid, but I force them out, anyway. Whether I like this man or not, he has the information I need. And that information is worth more than my dignity right now.

Langston fondles the auburn hair at my temple, twirling it around his stubby finger. "No, darling, you're doing fine."

That's shocking. Most of the time, I do everything wrong.

"I wanted to tell you we have a guest coming in a few hours." His tone hardens, and he tugs my hair, pulling me closer so he can grip me by the chin in a bruising hold. "I expect you to be changed and showered before he arrives." His gaze roams over my skin, settling on my thigh where I've drawn *his* eyes again. "You'll be serving us drinks."

His fingers dig into my chin, but I don't flinch away. I hold his menacing stare as though my life depended on this show of bravery. And most days, it does. If I don't get the information I need, everything I've dreamed of will be gone.

Unfortunately, Congressman Albrecht is my last hope.

"I want you focused," he chides, referring to last weekend when he found me outside in the cold, nearly hypothermic. "No drawing."

3

Because that's what I had been doing when he found me shivering and blue.

"You will not draw on yourself. It's tacky and unbecoming of a congressman's wife."

He says the last bit like it should mean more to me than it does.

But the truth is, I don't want to be Langston's wife.

I would rather die than marry him.

But I learned a long time ago that true love only happens once in a lifetime.

I found my soulmate.

And then I lost him.

"Do you understand me, Ramsey?"

Langston's voice sends shivers down my spine.

"Nod your head if you understand."

I nod out of reflex.

A smile that has seen many Botox injections tips eerily at the corners. "Good girl. I want the best for you, and those silly drawings only bring unnecessary gossip."

"Of course," I lie. "You always know best."

The key to surviving a powerful man thirty years your senior is always telling him that he's right. For some strange reason, they like making you believe that you cannot think for yourself and need them to guide your every step and decision.

Despite what Langston believes, I *can* think for myself.

My patience and self-control are unbreakable.

I have waited years for this chance to right my wrongs, and no amount of his degradation will stop me now.

I will survive this nightmare.

I will win in the end.

"That's right, angel." Langston chucks my nose like I'm a little kid. "Now, go make yourself look pretty."

Because my wavy, auburn hair, green eyes, and slim body are not what *pretty* is made of.

"Yes, sir."

I rise from the floor and kiss his cheek. Oddly enough, this simple act taught me how to control my gag reflex. While probably an attractive man in his prime, Langston is not a silver fox—nor does he have a fantastic personality.

I'm not saying men need a six-pack of abs and a lush head of hair, but I think they at least need to have a caring and compassionate personality. Langston is lacking in all regards—except for money.

But money means nothing, in my opinion.

I've seen first-hand how money corrupts good men, controls families, and drives even the most honest men to commit evil deeds—like breaking up a family.

I had a family once.

But it's been years since I've spoken his name aloud.

Because we were reckless.

We were in love.

And we set off the biggest scandal Texas had ever seen.

But like all great love stories, it ended in tragedy.

No one finds their soulmate at five years old.

And no one loses him thirteen years later.

Money and power created a weakness in my father. And my scandal provided him the solution—teaching me that life is but a series of moments. Nothing lasts forever. Not relationships. Not love. And indeed, not loyalty.

But hope—that's the one constant you can count on.

Hope for a chance to make things right.

Hope for one more moment when I can see him again—to tell him I'm sorry.

"Ramsey!"

Langston's fingers snap in front of my face, and I straighten. "I'm sorry, I just—"

Those beady eyes that transform into something kinder while in front of a crowd, narrow. "You're ignoring me. Get out of my face before my good mood dissipates."

Offering him a tight smile, I step back out of his reach.

I am a willing prisoner in a world I hate.

All because I made a mistake—a mistake that ruined my life.

Fortunately for Langston, that mistake ensures my compliance. I'll suffer through the bastard's wrath with a smile for a bit longer.

Because Langston Albrecht took something from me, and I won't rest until I get it back.

CHAPTER TWO

Duke

"Please hold for an important message from Vance-hole, otherwise known as your big bro, who needs a life and a lot more pussy."

I roll my eyes at the voice on the other side of the phone as Remington pauses, waiting for me to respond. "I'm not in the mood. Get to the point."

"Aww. You're projecting." My brother's teenage assistant snorts. "Did last night's date end in a restraining order, or did she use a stun gun?"

Sarcasm is my first language. This kid doesn't know who he's playing with.

"Actually, it ended with her on her knees, screaming out a new nickname, Double Bubble." I grin. "You know, because I always leave her cheeks sore." I chuckle. "But I didn't think you'd want to talk about the naughty things your mama and I do when you're not home."

The line goes silent for a few tense moments before Remington recovers, his voice casually collected. "Cute. Vance requests your obnoxious presence at dinner tonight." He pauses, and I can hear the smile in his voice. "Your daddy is in town."

Like my brothers, I loathe speaking with my father. "Can't," I respond casually. "I'm in Nevada for the week. Tell Vance to reschedule. Or cancel. The latter being my personal preference."

"Tsk, tsk, Dr. Duke. I don't get paid enough to give your brother bad news. Hold, please."

"Wait—" The office hold music comes on the line before I can explain. Not that I answer to Vance. I'm an equal partner in the plastic surgery practice I share with my two older brothers, Vance and Astor. Potter's Plastics, though, has always been Vance's baby. He eats, sleeps, and breathes this practice—just like our father did when he ran it.

But unlike Harrison Potter, Vance isn't a tyrant. Vance rebranded Potter's Plastics when our father retired and made it into something we're all proud of.

We were no longer pawns in Dr. Harrison Potter's kingdom.

We run our practice with a singular focus—our patients.

And that business mindset has served us well.

Potters Plastics is now the most distinguished and sought-after practice in all of Texas.

"Where the fuck are you?" The hold music is abruptly silenced with Vance's gruff tone just as I turn into the driveway of my destination and park.

"Oh, hi, honey, it's so sweet of you to call and check on me. I miss you, too."

I can feel Vance's annoyance drift through the phone. "You are supposed to be here," he clips, "in the office."

"Noooo," I drawl out. "I'm supposed to be in Nevada, playing nip tuck with the old geezers this week, remember? I left you a note."

I wait for him to rifle through the stack of papers on his desk and find the scribbled note he needs to move this conversation forward.

"Oh," he says after a minute. "Langston Albrecht." He pauses, the sound of him clicking the keys of the keyboard following as he likely pulls up the electronic chart in our system. "Since when did you start taking on politicians as patients?"

Since Vance was sued for malpractice and stopped doing surgeries for a year while he processed the death of his best friend.

After a few seconds, Vance sighs, understanding likely dawning on him. "Astor will be back at work soon, and I'm fine. You don't need to keep moonlighting for these celebrities. The practice has reserves. We're stable."

Maybe so, but our practice still took a hit financially over the last year.

Moonlighting and catering to the cosmetic needs of celebrities has proven lucrative so I'll give it up when I know our medical practice has stabilized.

"Speaking of Astor," I drawl, changing the subject. "Have you talked to him today?"

"Yeah, he and the baby are doing well." He doesn't sound so sure, but I don't know how you could be sure about Astor's current situation. Not when my oldest brother came home from a six-month-long mission trip and discovered he was the father to a newborn who lost her mother—Piper, Astor's long-time friend—to a medical complication.

"And Keagan? How is she?" I ask, referring to Piper's sister, who is here, helping Astor with Tatum, his daughter.

"As good as can be expected, I guess." Vance's words carry a weighted sadness, and I imagine he's stressing over the fact that he can't do anything but support Astor and Keagan through this challenging time.

"She'll be okay," I tell him. "Astor will make sure of it."

Out of the three of us, Astor is the more responsible one. I guess it comes with the territory of being the older brother, but unlike Vance and me, Astor has practiced patience. He'll make a great father, and he'll make sure Keagan is taken care of.

"Yeah." Vance sighs, pulling in a deep breath. "Anyway, Father called."

I groan. I don't want to talk about our father.

"He's in town and wants to have dinner with us."

I tap the steering wheel in agitation. "I heard. You're going to cancel, right? Tell him Remington has a bad case of mono?"

Vance chuckles. "I would, but that would mean I'd have to tell him about Halle *and* Remington." He makes this noise in his throat like he's annoyed. "And I'm trying to quit drinking so much."

Meaning, he can't tell our father about moving his new girlfriend and the teenager she befriended at a ratty motel into his house while sober.

He would need a healthy buzz to get through *that* conversation.

"Ah." I fight off a grin. "That's why you want me at the dinner—for distraction. Father didn't request my presence. You did."

"He's your father, too," Vance clips out, his mood tanking by the minute.

"Yes, but you're his favorite. He doesn't require the fuck-up or the philanthropist's company, just his pride and joy—ruler of the plastic surgery kingdom. His *super sweet* legacy."

I'm being sarcastic with the last bit, but the rest of it... one hundred percent fact.

Dr. Harrison Potter has no use for his eldest son, who would rather donate his services to charity than pour them into private practice, and he especially has no use for his youngest son, who is an utter fuck-up—his words, not mine. There's never been a time I've made my father proud.

Not that I give a shit.

"You need to be there." Vance has pulled out his I-know-better-than-you voice.

"No, *you* need to be there. You let me keep my daddy issues. Women like broken men. It makes them think they can fix us."

Vance snorts out a laugh. "Is that how you justify your commitment issues?"

"You're a fine one to talk," I snap, his words sobering me. "It's how I justify not going to dinner. Cancel the visit, Vance. I promise, as soon as I make grandpa look like a frozen Ken doll, I'll come back and spend some quality time with my big brother, who sounds like he needs a hug."

"Fuck you."

Ah, there's the brother I know. "Not today, sweetheart. You know the fall is off-season."

"You and your fucking seasons," he chides. "You could try dating a woman longer than a season, you know?"

"And you could smile once in a while. We all have pipe dreams, big brother."

With that parting remark, the line goes dead, and I'm left staring through the windshield at a set of cathedral-style doors, a little less pissed off than I was earlier.

Getting out of the car, I grab my bag full of Botox and stride to the door. Even the doorbell looks pretentious, with a lion's head poised above the button. I press it once and wait.

And wait.

It takes more than three minutes—yes, I timed it—for someone to finally come to the door.

Just long enough to add to my irritation.

"Good afternoon, Dr. Potter. Won't you come in?" I almost turn around and leave due to her tone. I remember that pompous pitch—it still haunts me from when I was a teenager. Though, I wasn't dealing with Congressman Albrecht back then. I was dealing with Congressmen Ford, a ruthless son of a bitch. I heard his wife had passed a few months ago. God rest her soul. She didn't deserve the life she suffered by his hand.

I flash the older woman with graying hair a smile. She can't help it. Her employer likely makes her speak with this intonation. "Thank you," I say, because that's what's expected of me. "Is Mr. Albrecht available?"

It wouldn't be the first time I've shown up at a wealthy client's home only to wait for their trainer to leave four hours later.

"Oh, yes, he's waiting for you in his office." She closes the door behind me as I step into the McMansion and take in the circular staircase, million-dollar chandelier, and marble floors.

Note to self: Stop making house calls.

Hell, stop taking new clients.

You have worked too hard to see clients in their offices and not yours.

Maybe Vance is right. Perhaps the practice is fine, and I'm worried over nothing.

My stomach clenches. Even if the practice is okay, Astor needs time to adjust to being a new, single father. And Vance, while he's much better since the lawsuit was resolved, I still worry he's one case away from another breakdown.

And I can't risk losing him again.

"If you'll follow me, Dr. Potter." The woman steps in front of me, interrupting my thoughts, and begins leading me down the hall. We pass several rooms, which I don't bother looking in. They're all the same: a grand statement of wealth. I should know; I was raised in this opulent society where it was more about the presence of power than the love of family. Children raised in these homes—at least in my experience—were merely props for the Christmas card. They weren't cherished additions to the family.

"Congressman Albrecht is right through here." The woman opens the door, and a thick stench of smoke wafts out through the opening.

"Potter, my boy! Come in, come in."

The stout man a few feet in front of me has a receding hairline and more wrinkles than a cotton sheet, which, I suppose, is great for long-term business.

"How have you been?"

He speaks to me like we've known each other for years and spent summers at the Hamptons together, not that I'm meeting him for the first time since his friend, Senator Lefroy, referred him to me two weeks ago.

I step forward and take his hand. "I've been well. Thank you for asking." I don't have time for pleasantries, so I stick to why I'm here. "Your secretary booked a consult and Botox injections."

The Congressman offers me a wicked grin. "Straight to business—a man after my own heart."

Spare me.

"I like my patients to get their money's worth," I lie.

He nods, almost giddily. "Sweetheart, come meet our guest."

Great. Another bored wife.

Pulling in a deep breath, I set my bag down on the floor at the sound of high heels clicking against wood, drawing closer.

Find your charm, Duke. Your give-a-shit. A paying customer is a paying customer. It doesn't matter if you like him or his wife. It's simply business.

"Come, darling."

I'm still staring at the ground when the congressman shuffles someone in front of me. And inch by inch, I take in her red shoes, my eyes moving up her form-fitting evening gown, as my body straightens to its full height. But it isn't until I get to her cherry-stained lips and wide green eyes that I stop breathing.

Every muscle in my body clenches at the mere sight of her.

Red hair that once fanned over my pillow.

Hands that gripped my cheeks and promised me forever.

No. It can't be.

She would never be here—not with Congressman Albrecht.

But then our eyes lock, and every memory I've tried to drown comes flooding back.

Holding her as she screamed.

Begging her to stay.

Waiting… when she never came.

I flash her a fake smile and hold out my hand.

"Sweetheart, I'd like for you to meet Dr. Potter," Congressman Albrecht says, unaware there's a turbulent history in this room. "Dr. Potter, this is my fiancée, Ramsey Ford—your new patient."

CHAPTER THREE

Ramsey

N^{o.} No.
No.

It can't be him.

It can't be those hazel eyes that hold memories of lying under the stars, our hands locked together like no one could separate us.

He called it the season of wildfire that year we fell in love. A time when we burned the brightest before everything fell down around us.

Though, I can't be sure, because this guy's shoulders are broader than the ones I remember, and his waist is more tapered than before.

But it's his ticking jaw that smothers the last of my hope that this is a stranger and not my childhood love—Duke Potter.

"My doctor?" I rip my eyes away from Duke and narrow them at my soon-to-be husband. "Since when do I need a plastic surgeon?"

Gah, why is Duke here? How in the heck did he find me?

It's too soon!

He can't be here right now. He can't get involved.

Langston chuckles, his gaze going from hospitable to threatening as he grits his teeth in an evil smile. "Since last month… when you agreed to be my wife." Heat blooms across my cheeks when he sweeps a dismissive look over my body, pausing at my ample chest. "Marrying me is quite the upgrade from living the life of a broke expat. And as a proper thank you, you'll look the part of a congressman's wife and upgrade those tits." He dares me to argue in front of our guest—the very guest with the hardened jaw, clenched fist, and previous history of having a severe white-knight complex.

I step in front of Langston, blocking Duke from doing anything stupid. I know him—or used to—and unless he's found an abundance of patience in the last two decades, this meeting will end poorly. "Oh, Langston. You sweet man. Here I thought this meeting was for you, and you surprise me with a boob job!" I try pushing excitement into my words as I cup his cheeks and attempt a loving gaze. "How did I get so lucky?"

Fury rolls off Duke in waves, but I ignore it. Langston requires my nauseating "gratitude" at the moment, and I can't be distracted, worrying about what Duke thinks of me. "You are too good to me, baby."

The devil of a man grins at the stupid pet name and relaxes under my hands. "You better not forget it either, darling. Now, be good for Dr. Potter, and let him make you pretty for me."

He grabs my shoulders and spins me around to face Duke, who has somehow managed to unclench his fists and fake a smile. But the lingering threat of violence swirling deep within those hazel eyes concerns me.

I'd recognize that look anywhere.

It's the same look Duke gave my father after he had ripped me from Duke's arms. But unlike last time, I'm not clinging to Duke, pleading my apologies.

I'm not the same helpless girl anymore.

I don't need Duke to hold me and promise to make things better again.

No one should hold the key to your happiness, not even great guys like Duke.

But Duke would have tried.

He would have tried to love me past the pain.

He would have sacrificed his career and relationship with his family.

And that kind of devotion deserves protection—even if it's from himself.

So just like back then, I protect him now. It's for his own good.

I turn and flash Langston a shy smile. "Are you planning to stay through the appointment?"

"Would you like me to?"

Gag. "I'd like to keep my transformation a surprise. If that's okay with you?"

Somewhere from behind comes a low growling noise, but I ignore it, keeping my eyes trained on Langston as he puffs out his chest and drags his knuckles down mine slowly, lingering in the sensitive space between my breasts.

I fight the urge to slap his hand away. "Such a good girl," he coos before looking over my shoulder at Duke. "Money is no object. Make her perfect—like someone you'd marry."

Have you ever heard such swoony sweet nothings come out of a man? Seriously, I can't put all the lucky stars in my pocket.

"That might be difficult," says Duke, his voice raspier than I remember.

Whipping around, I knock Langston's hand off my chest, training my heated gaze on Duke and the shitty smile he's flashing me.

"I like my women curvier… and mouthier, but I'll do my best with your…"

His smile falters—a tell-tell sign of his impending explosion—and manifests into an irritated jaw twitch.

Tick.

Tick.

But like a practiced aristocrat, he manages to pull his lips back into a smile that promises more than pleasantries. "…with your fiancée."

A deep belly laugh erupts from Langston. "Never pick the mouthy ones, boy. They always end in a messy divorce." He steps away, swatting me on the ass as he passes by. "Do what you can with her. I don't expect a miracle."

I close my eyes and swallow the urge to lose my shit on this man.

Remember why you're here, Ramsey. This man is a means to an end. Whether it's closure or a fresh start, Langston will end your pain, one way or another.

My eyes are still closed when I hear the soft click of the door, then silence. Langston has left.

Though, regretfully, even the relief of his departure doesn't quell the knot in my stomach.

I can feel Duke's penetrating gaze cut into my skin like glass, slowly chipping away at the walls I've built around myself.

Don't be a coward. Face him, but don't let him see past your lies.

Wrenching my eyes open, I face the only man I've ever loved. "I'll need your help to unzip my dress."

Just saying the words sends my heart pounding against my ribs in a frantic rhythm. "I wasn't prepared for an…" I swallow as his fingers tighten into fists at his side.

Be brave.

I straighten, standing tall, and square my shoulders.

This is Duke.

His disapproval might make me cry later, but not right now. Right now, I'm going to be strong and finish what I started. Duke being here doesn't change anything.

"I wasn't prepared for an exam." I tilt my chin higher, slowing my breathing to a steadier rhythm. "You'll have to forgive my evening attire."

The grandfather clock on the far wall is the only sound in the room. It's still—stagnant, like the air is too thick to breathe.

"Are you going to answer me, Dr. Potter?"

I mean, really. I expect him to say *something*, not just stare at me.

This is Duke Potter we're talking about—the king of sarcasm. He would never let me out of this situation without a snarky remark.

"Do hear me, Dr. Potter?"

My voice rises, and I allow all the irritation with this situation to bleed into my words, which probably is not a great idea since it seems to snap Duke out of his catatonic state.

"Oh, I hear you, Ms. Ford. Very. Clearly."

His scrutiny is not welcome, nor is his attitude, but my skin tingles under his sharp gaze anyway when he prowls towards me.

He's yet to allow his eyes to drift to my chest, where his attention should be during this consultation. Instead, they are locked onto my face, his jaw ticking with barely contained fury.

This is not the boy who held me as I cried and promised everything would be okay.

No, this is not the boy I once knew.

And it kills me.

I can't stand for him to think of me like this—like I'm the puppet I swore I'd never become.

"I know what you're thinking," I try explaining when he proceeds to circle me like I'm his prey.

"I doubt that."

His tone is enough to irritate the dead.

If I didn't need to behave for my ruse with Langston, I'd tell Duke Potter where he can take his attitude. Trust me; it's not anywhere ladylike. But instead, I call on the years' worth of debutante lessons and grit out between clenched teeth, "Let's just get this over with, then."

I need Duke Potter out of here, like, last year.

"Now, now. Is that any way to treat your guest?" I can feel his breath against my neck as he leans in. "Your *fiancé*," he spits out the word like a curse, "requested a consult, Ms. Ford. I'll be sure he gets what he paid for."

I laugh like I couldn't give a shit—so much for the debutante skills. "Whatever."

Langston might have something I need, but new tits aren't part of the equation. This isn't the first time he's requested such things from me, but he is easily distracted. A well-placed lie and fake infections do wonders in deterring him.

I just need to endure this stupid consultation and Duke's heavy—and very judgy—scrutiny for a little while longer.

"Whatever, huh? I don't believe that word is very becoming of a congressman's fiancée."

Oh, hell no. "Are you trying to pick a fight with me, Dr. Potter? Because I haven't forgotten how you like it."

I can practically feel Duke's smile as he presses against my back, his crisp suit searing my already overheated skin. To make matters worse, the scent of bergamot and patchouli saturates the air around us, igniting a familiar longing I've managed to smother for years.

"I think you've forgotten a lot of things, Ray." He grabs the zipper and tugs, dragging his fingers down my back as the dress parts from around me. "Like your spine." Chills break out along my skin, almost as if proving his point.

"Fuck you."

He chuckles. "Ah, ah." Fingering a lock of my hair, he moves it to the side and slides the straps of my dress down my arms, baring all of me. "We've done that already, remember? You walked away."

Oh, fuck him and the arrogance he rode in on.

I flip around, not giving two shits about my tits shoved against his chest. "I did not walk away!"

That sharp jaw of his works as his eyes harden, certainly remembering the last time we were together. "Oh, but you did." He lets out a scoff. "I bet Daddy is very proud of who you've become."

Did I say I had great patience? Well, obviously, I overestimated my ability, because before I can compose myself, I slap Duke across the face, his head snapping to the side. "Don't act like you know me." I shove his chest, and he steps back. "I am not the girl you used to love."

Redness blooms on his cheek, but he doesn't acknowledge the slap. Instead, his face remains stoic as he steps forward, crowding me. "You're right. The girl I *loved* would never let a man pick her out a new pair of tits."

Unfortunately, he's right, but he can't know that just yet.

"Do your job, Dr. Potter, and get the fuck out of my house." I tamp down the hurt at seeing the love of my life, who is frankly insulting me, and roll my shoulders back. He's here to do a job, and so am I.

"Don't fool yourself, Ray. This isn't your home. This is your prison."

A slow grin pulls on his face, and without another word, he grabs my arms, lifting them out to my side.

"I need to look at you," he explains, inhaling a deep breath like he's preparing to endure torture.

I can feel the anxiety radiating off his body. It takes divine strength to keep my arms up and not reach back to comfort him.

Unfortunately, my mouth doesn't have the same restraint. "Don't get shy on me now, Dr. Potter."

"I'm not shy." His breath ghosts over the shell of my ear, sending a flood of warmth straight down to my toes. My head follows the sensation, leaning toward his strength, seeking comfort and a kiss that never comes.

I close my eyes and will this nightmare to be over, my chin trembling as the past year catches up. I've been so alone—feeling so guilty for what happened. All I've ever wanted was to have this moment with Duke. To wrap my arms around him and tell him I'm sorry. To tell him the truth about Langston.

But that would mean tearing his life apart again, and I can't do that—not until I'm sure Langston can make things right.

But that doesn't make this any easier. It's excruciating being this close to him and pretending it means nothing—like all those years we spent together meant *nothing*.

Tears threaten to fall down my cheeks when suddenly, warm fingers clasp my chin, lifting it gently and offering the comfort I so desperately crave. "Open your eyes, Ray. We've done this before, remember?"

Before.

When he was mine and...

My eyes flash open, the memory of that night flooding back like it was just yesterday.

"Yeah, you remember." Duke grins. "Keep those pretty eyes on me—just like before, and we'll get through this."

I let loose a smile and straighten, my breasts fully displayed to a man who knows them all too well. "Tell me something, Dr. Potter," I goad, feeling bolder, locked in his penetrating gaze. "Do you hold all your patients this way?" I let my gaze drift to my hip, where Duke's hand rests like it's always belonged there.

Duke drops his hands and steps back, his demeanor changing instantly. "Don't act like you know me, Ms. Ford. I'm not the same man you once loved."

CHAPTER FOUR

Duke

I could listen to her laugh for hours. The tone—the lightness, the freedom contained within it—calls to my soul like a hymn.

"Hold still," I scold. "I don't want any excuses that this wasn't a fair competition."

Let's be real. I have no real chance of winning. I only wanted to get her naked.

"You're tickling me on purpose, though." She tries squirming away, but not before I move my hands to her back, holding her in place.

"Uh-oh," I say, feigning shock. "Look at what you made me do." Our gazes lock, and I let my hands drift down the curve of her back, smearing the paint, as I touch every inch of skin I can. "You better tell me when to stop, Ray. Otherwise, my hands will end up somewhere naughtier."

Her tongue sweeps out and wets her lips just as I get to the curve of her ass. I think she'll stop me, but instead, she presses her lips together.

It makes me smile.

And just because she's a bad girl, I'll torture her longer.

Stopping at the swell of her ass, I move around her hips, smearing the paint across her body to her naval.

"I thought you were going to be naughty," she says breathily. "Don't tell me you've changed your mind already."

What I've changed is the ability to stay away from her. Fuck my father. Fuck hers. This girl was meant for me and only me, and I'll be damned if her father leverages her as collateral for his political position. Ramsey Ford is destined to be a Potter.

"I've heard patience can be very rewarding." I drag my palms up her abdomen and cup the base of her tits. "And very inspiring."

Her head falls back with a groan. "Keep it up, Potter. I won't be so generous when it's my turn."

Oh, the sweet threats of someone with the self-control of a mustard seed...

"I don't recall saying you could drop your arms." I kiss the arm next to my head, which contains a bottle of paint. "Get it up, Sunny-Ray. I won't tell you again."

I knew calling her Sunny Ray would bring her back to reality. "Don't call me that. It's silly. I'm not your ray of sunshine."

That's precisely what she is. All that sarcasm and warmth hits me right in the chest. No matter the day I'm having, just seeing her brings life to my cold heart.

"You're stalling." I tip my chin at her breast. "I need more paint."

Her lips flatten in disagreement. "Trust me. You have enough color there to repaint a house."

"Who's the artist right now?" I move my hand up and roll her nipple between my fingers. "I think that's me, right?" Her head tips forward, her knees buckling, before she catches herself.

"Yeah," I tease victoriously, "that's what I thought. Now, be a good assistant, and give me more paint, like I asked."

Lifting her head, she levels me with a look that promises payback I'm all too excited to endure. "I can't even tell what you're painting."

That's because I'm not painting anything. I am merely rubbing as much paint on her tits as she'll let me. "You were the one who wanted me to paint you," I argue, like this entire situation is her fault.

"Yes, but only because you said you were tired of being my canvas!"

I flash her a smirk that clearly relays that I'm a sneaky bastard. When this woman asks if she can paint something on my chest, I can't get my shirt off fast enough. But that doesn't mean I won't take advantage of her generous heart and guilt her into allowing me to rub paint on her boobs.

After all, fair is fair.

"Can you blame me?" *I ask, catching the liquid paint she squirts just above my fingers.* "You were having all the fun. I wanted a turn."

I pinch her nipple again, wetting my fingers with the paint. She squirms but doesn't try moving away this time. Instead, she stands there, absorbing everything I do to her. Rubbing, pinching, cupping, I move the paint everywhere before I meet her gaze again. "Eyes on me, Ray. I don't want you to miss this."

Her throat bobs, and she nods like I'm about to do something seriously amazing. But I'm not an artist like her. I can only drag my finger over her heart and make two teardrops that connect at the bottom—a heart.

She looks down, and the most radiant smile emerges. "It's perfect."

She traces the heart with her finger and leans down, pressing her nose to mine. "I'll keep it—"

"I'll keep it a secret."

Her voice pulls me back to the present—my hands on her tits, but not in the same way they were years ago.

"What?" I don't even try to hide that my mind was a million miles away.

She flashes me a grin, seeming to grow bolder when my nerves increase. I might know every inch of these breasts, but the situation isn't the same as it once was. She belongs to another man now.

She's no longer my ray of sunshine.

"I said," she lowers her voice, "You don't have to do this. We can make up something to tell Langston. I can keep it a secret if you can."

My eyes narrow. "You, of all people, know I can keep a secret."

"I'm sorry. You're right." She sighs. "Just do what you need to do, Dr. Potter."

Her dismissal stings, but not as much as the flash of ink peeking out from where her dress is pooled at her hip does. "And what exactly are you doing, Ms. Ford?" I finger the fabric, noticing her body tightening with her slight inhale. "Because as much as you've changed, you didn't suddenly fall for the dapper congressman."

To prove my point, I yank the fabric out of the way, revealing the hand-drawn heart that looks much like the sloppy one I painted on her years ago.

"I'll keep it with me always," she had said back then, and fuck if seeing the proof doesn't mess with my head.

My grip tightens on her as she tries wrenching away.

"Is *he* forcing you to marry this bastard?"

I'm surprised her father waited this long to marry her off. But then again, men go through many wives in the circle her father runs in. For all I know, this is Ramsey's third fiancé.

"Let go." Her voice is all grit and hate. "This is none of your business."

I arch my brows. "But isn't it? Your chivalrous husband-to-be called me to your home to evaluate your tits—"

"Yes, just my tits." She smacks my hand away and pulls up her dress, concealing her drawing. "Not to perform an inquisition. Finish your measurements, Dr. Potter, and get out."

The way her chin quivers smothers most of my anger. She might be saying all the right words, but the heart on her hip and the tremble in her body tells me something is very wrong here.

Sighing, I stand and take the last few measurements—let's be honest, I don't plan on doing anything to this woman's tits. They were perfect years ago, and that hasn't changed.

"Alright, Ray. I'll let you have your little secret, but not your augmentation." I toss the measuring tape into my bag. "It was great seeing you again. Take care—"

"What?" She grabs my arm as I try walking away. "You have to do the augmentation or at least…" Her breath hitches as my brows rise.

"Or at least what, Ray? Lie for you?" I chuckle. "You know the rules of our game. If you want me to lie to your fiancé, then offer me something I don't already have."

She scoffs. "What the hell is that supposed to mean? You have everything."

I glance at the massive diamond on her finger—its mere presence disgusts me. "Not everything."

It's hard not to smile when she lets out this defeated whine. "What do you want?"

"Let's not start with what I want, but with what I don't have—your number." I grab my phone from my pocket and unlock it. "Put your number in and call yourself." I won't have her giving me a fake number.

"That's ridiculous." She scoffs. "I'm engaged to be married."

"And I'm a virgin," I pop back. "We're both lying. You're up to something, Ray, and if you don't tell me what that something is, then you'll have to cough up your number. Otherwise, I'm gonna tell grandpa in there that his dream of smothering himself in your double Ds is nothing but a fantasy."

"You wouldn't dare." Her eyes narrow.

I've always loved how confident Ramsey is in her skin. She believes bodies, in any shape or form, are works of art. It's why they are her favorite canvases. So, her standing with one hand on her hip with her perky tits on display has my cock pushing against my trousers in protest.

I take the last remaining steps between us. "Trust me when I tell you, Ray, I will do *whatever it takes*"—I push my phone into her hand—"to get what I want." I tip my chin, holding her glare. "But you already know that, don't you?"

Prowling around her back, I lift her dress, pausing to help her slip her arms through. "Give me what I want, Ray, and then I'll leave you to your… happiness."

She pulls in a breath, and I use the opportunity to touch her, gathering her silky hair in my hands and moving it to her shoulder. It takes an impressive amount of restraint to keep from kissing the exposed skin on her back as I zip her up.

"Fine." She shivers under my hands. "But don't make problems for me, okay? I can't afford to mess this up with Langston."

Just the sound of her speaking his name douses the flame burning inside me. "Always a pleasure, Ms. Ford." I take a step back and pluck my phone from her hands as soon as she's finished inputting her number. "I'll be in touch regarding a surgery date."

"Wait—" She reaches for me, but I don't give her the opportunity. Grabbing my bag, I fling open the door, finding Langston lounging in a leather chair right outside the door.

"What size did you go with?" he asks, rising.

I force a smile. "Let's just say you'll be pleased with the results."

Fuck him.

"That's my boy." He pats me on the shoulder like we just made a business deal and weren't just discussing altering someone's body which is already perfect.

Too bad I'm not so easily manipulated. Ramsey might have business with the congressman, but I don't. I couldn't give two shits about my popularity. I'm only in it for the money—but not at someone else's expense. Vance said the practice had reserves—that we don't need the money.

I hope he's right.

"I'll have my secretary call you and set a surgery date." I look at my watch like the surgery schedule is written there. "Right now, I'm booked out six months."

I flash a smile before allowing my gaze to drift behind him to a pissed-off Ramsey.

"What do you mean six months?" Is that irritation I detect in the congressman's tone? Aww. He must have thought I was an ass-kissing tool who worked for him.

"I'm a busy man, Congressman. I'm sure you can understand that."

I don't give a fuck if he doesn't. I promised Ramsey I would lie, not get down on my knees and make it easy for either of them.

"What about our wedding?" I jerk my eyes away from Langston and level a glare at Ramsey, who has decided to join the conversation and put her hand in Langston's. "Our wedding is in eight weeks. It's the week of Christmas! Can't you do something before then?" She smiles at Langston, and it takes all I have not to snatch her out of his arms. "I want to be perfect for him."

Oh, she'll be perfect, all right—a perfect liar.

I offer her and Langston a tense smile. "I could try a few things," I lie, narrowing my gaze at the woman who haunts my dreams, "but no promises."

Ramsey straightens, the loving pretense disappearing instantly.

"Sounds good," Langston says. "We appreciate anything you can do."

Oh, for fuck's sake.

Inhaling, I tip my chin in agreement. Could this day be any shittier? "Absolutely. Now, shall I do your touch-up before I leave? You're only scheduled for an hour."

The novelty of having new tits and a new wife is quickly replaced by greed. "Oh, yes. Absolutely. Excuse us, darling."

Ramsey smiles and steps away. "I'll be waiting for you upstairs."

All the blood seems to drain from my body, and nothing but pure-white rage replaces it as I catch Ramsey by the wrist. "And I'll be in touch, Ms. Ford."

CHAPTER FIVE

Duke

What does your fiancé say about your little heart drawing?

It's been a couple of days since I've seen Ramsey at the congressman's mansion, but that doesn't mean I haven't spoken to her. I promised I'd be in touch, and I strive to maintain excellent communication with my patients—even the ones who'd rather I didn't. The funny thing is, though, Ramsey seems to enjoy our virtual doctor-patient chats just as much as I do.

Ray: Not that it's any of your business, but Langston doesn't care about my art. He sees a lot of drawings on my body… They don't mean anything.

I smile at my phone. *Tsk, tsk, Ray. You're acting like I'm someone who doesn't know you.*

My fingers tap out my response quickly. *You're lying…* **Everything** you draw on your body means something. You would never waste such precious canvas with irrelevant art.

I know I've hit a nerve when she responds almost instantly. **I wonder how your girlfriend feels about you texting me, huh? I know you have one—you always do.**

This is the Ray I love—the one I yearn to bend over my bed and own and fuck the sass from. That fiery passion of hers has always been gas to my flame. **Is that so? And how would you know I always have a girlfriend? Have you been keeping tabs on me, Ray?**

She responds within seconds. **Please. The local paper loves the Potter brothers. You can't frown without them reporting it the next day.**

The more she responds, the more I learn that my Sunny Ray is a little stalker. **But you live in Nevada. Why would you still read the Bloomfield Times?**

Because she's a little liar, that's why.

Are you serious? My family still lives there, Duke. Not everything I do is about you.

I tap out a sentence and then delete it. It's a response that would likely scare her into blocking me. Instead, I go with: **If we're only telling half-truths, you should know I don't have a girlfriend during the fall and winter seasons.**

Because those seasons are sacred.

It takes her a minute to respond. The chat bubble appears and then disappears before I get another text. **Why don't you date during those seasons?**

My chest tightens at the memory—of her screaming as I held her, completely helpless and defeated. It's time I can't erase. I respond with: **You know why.**

This time, she never answers. The topic of discussion is something neither of us can speak of.

Tossing my phone in the desk drawer, I pause.

Don't do it, dude. This is seriously unhealthy. The therapist told you to move on. Looking at it would be the opposite of moving on.

But then again, keeping it is likely worse.

Fuck it.

Slamming the top drawer, I pull open the bottom one, passing a dozen files, and stop. There, still sitting at the very bottom of my desk and underneath an old pair of gym shorts, is the little black box I've had since I was eighteen.

Fuck. This is a terrible idea.

But I'm notorious for indulging in bad ideas.

I blow out a breath and pick it up anyway, lifting the lid.

It's been years since I've stared at this ring. The ridiculously small stone is set in a white gold band. It looks like something out of a cereal box and not an engagement ring. But that's precisely what it is.

Some guys have big plans for their senior year—mine was a little more unconventional.

I wanted to go to college, but I never planned on going alone. At eighteen, I knew Ramsey Ford belonged at my side. And I planned on running off with her before her father married her to one of his buddies.

It was a solid plan.

And we executed it perfectly.

But then winter came and destroyed us.

"What in the total fuck do you have?"

At Remington's voice, I snap the box closed and toss it back into the drawer like it was on fire. "What do you need?" I ignore the fact that he caught me with an engagement ring in my hand.

"Halle!"

I roll my eyes. "Must you always call for mommy?" Remington does not need to make everything an office affair by calling Vance's girlfriend, his unofficial mom.

Remington grins. "Oh, '*Mommy*' would have me by the balls if I didn't let her in on this little scandal."

"Whatever." I can lie my way out of this. It's not like it's Va—

"Halle already left to check on Astor and the baby. What's going on?"

Perfect. Vance is a little harder to lie to. He knows too much and is very familiar with what's in the box.

"'What's going on,'" Remington points at me, "is your little brother has bought an engagement ring." He thumps Vance in the chest. "Looks like one less lawsuit you'll need to worry about." He nods in my direction. "Who is it? Summer or Spring that finally tamed you? Should we start looking for a replacement at the front desk?" He turns to Vance. "Summer is the one who works out front, right?"

Vance doesn't answer Remington right away. His body has gone rigid, the lines on his face harsh with controlled rage. "A patient is waiting on me in room five," he says tightly, addressing Remington without ever taking his eyes off me. "Let her know I'll be there in a few minutes."

Remington frowns, looking from Vance to me. "What's *really* going on?"

I grin. "Aww. It looks like this is a conversation for the grown-ups." I shoo him with a flick of my hand. "Better do what Daddy says before he gets the belt."

Remington takes a menacing step forward, but Vance blocks him from proceeding with a hand to the chest. "Room five. Now."

Without another word, Remington turns and disappears down the hall.

The silence hangs between us while Vance stands there, blocking the door. "I thought you got rid of the ring, Duke."

It's not a question.

"Why would I do that? It's now an heirloom. Your future child might want it." I try infusing humor into the conversation, but when

Vance steps forward and closes the door behind him, I know it didn't work.

"Give me the ring."

"No." Vance will have to pry it from my cold, dead hands.

"It's not healthy for you to keep—"

Oh, for goodness' sake. "I saw her." I interrupt his lecture. I've heard it all before.

"What?" Vance's eyes widen, and he pulls out a chair, settling in for an explanation.

"Two days ago, when I had the appointment with the congressman."

I rake my hands through my hair. I'm a grown man. I don't owe anyone—especially my brother—an explanation. But this—my past with Ramsey—didn't just hurt me. Unfortunately, Vance and Astor were caught in the aftermath when everything went down. They didn't need to get involved, but they did because we've always been there for each other.

"Congressman Albrecht?" Vance asks. "What he'd do? Have her chained up in the basement?"

He chuckles. Like me, he knows Ramsey.

I shut the drawer containing the ring. "No, she lives with him."

Vance visibly twitches. "What do you mean, she lives there? Ramsey hates politicians."

"Not this one." I smile, but it lacks sincerity. "She's marrying this one."

Vance blows out a shocked breath and leans back, his gaze going to the ceiling. "Wow. I never thought Congressman Ford would follow through and force her to marry one of his buddies."

I don't admit that I think she's up to something. People change over the years, but Ramsey would never budge on this. She would never marry a congressman—even if her father pressed her.

My Ray would run before she did something she didn't want to.

Because she did once.

Unlike my post-senior year plans, Ramsey's didn't include a college education. Her future, per her father, was at a powerful man's side.

His name was Albert. He was forty-eight years old.

"I'm sorry this brings up bad memories for you, brother." Vance's voice pulls my head up. "Maybe it's time you got rid of the ring—especially now." His tone is gentle, but if he knew I was texting Ramsey daily, he wouldn't be so understanding.

"She's not happy," I argue. "I saw it in her eyes."

"You *saw* it in her eyes?" Vance scoffs and stands. "You sound like a kook. I'm afraid you only saw what you wanted to see, brother." He comes around the desk and pats me on the shoulder. "She's marrying someone else. Let her go. It's time."

I nod like I agree.

But it's not that easy.

I've tried to move on—every fucking spring and summer, to be exact. Everyone at the office thinks it's because I'm some playboy with commitment issues. And while it may seem that way, they should know every action has a scar behind it.

I attempt to move on every spring or summer because the pain of the fall and winter is suffocating. I would love to close my eyes and not see her smile, her hands roaming my body, her paintbrush tickling my chest as she paints her next masterpiece.

Trust me. I've fucking tried to get Ramsey out of my head.

I've tried to date women for longer than a season.

But then the season changes and brings the sound of her screams and the coldness of her tears. My brothers should know we all have demons—I've just hidden mine better than they have. Vance thinks he knows everything that went down between Ramsey and me, but I left out the part that keeps me awake at night—the part that keeps me waiting for her return.

"Astor needs us to watch Tatum while he helps Keagan with funeral arrangements this morning. Remington said you don't have any patients until this afternoon."

He doesn't ask if I'll come. He knows I will.

"We'll leave as soon as I'm done with my patient."

I nod. "I'll be ready."

Thankfully, Vance closes the door and leaves. I figure I have about half an hour before he's done with his patient and ready to leave for Astor's, who I need to check on, anyway. My eldest brother hadn't taken care of himself while on a mission trip overseas and collapsed when he returned recently. Astor swears he's fine now and has everything handled regarding the baby and Keagan, but we're Potters—we ignore our problems until it's too late.

So, just in case Astor isn't as fine as he would like us to believe, we'll keep a close eye on him and offer support where we can, which isn't much. But it's something.

As promised, Vance returns to my office immediately after his patient leaves. "Remington is handling the phones," he says by way of a greeting. "We'll take my car."

I'm too tired to argue. "Sure."

I grab my phone and keys, but not before locking my desk drawers.

Vance's brows rise. "Paranoid Remington might steal a fifty-dollar ring?"

"It was seven hundred dollars, smartass. But no, I'm not scared he'll steal it." I cast Vance a knowing look. "I'm ensuring he won't do your bidding while I'm gone." I know my brother, and if he thinks me having this ring is unhealthy, he'll get rid of it—no questions asked. He would claim it was for my own good, just like I did for him not long ago. So I put nothing past him.

Vance grins, not bothering to defend himself. Instead, he holds the door open and shrugs. "How about you donate it, then?"

"No."

He closes the door behind us as we walk toward the parking garage. "I hate to break it to you, little brother, but you can't use it again. Women frown upon second-hand engagement rings. Besides, you can afford something nicer now."

"I don't need to buy anything nicer since I never plan on getting married," I argue. "Let me keep my spank bank toys, brother, and I won't tell Halle about yours."

The thing about being ten months younger than your middle brother is that, at some point, you shared a room. In my and Vance's case, it was a college dorm.

Vance doesn't want to go to war with me over a bullshit diamond ring. It may have caused strife in our relationship, but he needs to know I'm not budging. I'm not parting with the ring.

"Are you threatening me?" Vance chuckles. "Fine, keep your little bauble. Just make sure your unhealthy obsession stays focused on *only* the ring." He cuts me a look. "Leave Ramsey alone, Duke. She's moved on. You should follow suit."

But I won't. I can't.

Because he's right, I have an unhealthy obsession, and it's not with the engagement ring. "I will," I lie. "It was just weird seeing her again after all these years."

Vance nods and claps me on the shoulder as we shuffle into the garage elevator. "How about you come to the house after work and have a drink?"

I'd rather not, but Vance's tone isn't all that negotiable. "Sure."

At my acceptance, Vance visibly relaxes, leaning against the elevator wall, all cool and casual. "Great. Just so there's no miscommunication, I'm not changing diapers when we get to Astor's."

I turn my head and grin. "I hope that's not why you insisted I come with you. I'm great at many things, but changing diapers is not one of them."

Vance grins. "We'll convince Halle to…"

My phone buzzes, and I tune out the rest of Vance's words.

Because there on my screen is a text that releases something in my soul.

Something deep.

Something everlasting.

Something like redemption.

Ray: If we're still only telling half-truths, you should know I don't love Langston. Because I can't love anyone… except you.

Relief pours through my body like a soothing balm, coating all the anxiety I've had since I saw her in Langston's arms.

She loves me.

She—

The phone is snatched from my hands, and all I can do is square my shoulders, facing the rage as my brother reads her message aloud. "Are you fucking kidding me, Duke?"

After years of living with his Hulk-like anger, I don't even flinch when he takes a menacing step toward me. "Stop this." He shoves the phone at my chest—hard. "You'll stop whatever this is right now. I won't let you do this to our family again."

I take the phone and shove him back, ready for an all-out brotherly brawl in the elevator. "Hear me, brother, because I won't repeat myself."

My jaw hardens as I back Vance up against the wall. "I will not play the good guy this time. I'm done bowing to tyrants for a bullshit cause. No one, and I mean no one—not even you—will get in my way. Ramsey Ford is, and always will be, *mine*."

CHAPTER SIX

Ramsey

Just so you know, I was drunk earlier when I sent you that text.

I've done some dumb shit in my life, but nothing as stupid as having a few shots and texting my old flame that I was incapable of loving Langston because I. Still. Loved. Him.

Heaven freaking help me.

What a mess.

And all because I couldn't resist Duke Potter's charm.

But I should have known I'd react recklessly. Duke has always had this secret door to my freaking heart. No matter how many times I've tried to board it up and barricade it from corner to corner, he keeps finding a way inside.

Like now, when my phone chimes with his response. **Remind me again. Is that the text where you said you loved me?**

See what I mean? The fucker is witty *and* charming.

I was drunk, I fire back. **I didn't know what I was saying.**

He doesn't keep me waiting long for an answer. **I'd believe you, Sunny Ray. I would. But I've seen you power through my chemistry homework after slamming back three tequila shots. There's no way you weren't aware of what you were doing.**

Talking to him is pointless. **Whatever. I just wanted you to know I made a mistake. I don't need things becoming more awkward between us the next time you're here.**

There, I did the right thing.
It's not fair to Duke to know my feelings about him or Langston.

My phone chimes again, alerting me to another text. I should have known Duke wouldn't end the conversation there. **Were things awkward between us? I thought I gave an Oscar-worthy performance, playing the old friend who hadn't eaten your pussy on the hood of his car.**

I feel a deep flush spread along my cheeks. **Now you're being inappropriate and crass.**

But despite my words, I grin. He did eat me out on the hood of his car—several times—and those nights were life-changing.

I'm serious, Duke. I text him once more. **I can't mess this up with Langston.**

I press send, and my chest aches in response. If Langston didn't have something I needed, I would lap up Duke's attention. It's all I've wanted for years. But nothing has changed my circumstances.

I couldn't pursue a relationship with Duke back then, and I can't now.
Duke Potter is too good of a man.
He doesn't deserve this broken version of me.
He deserves the woman who laughed in his arms and kissed him senselessly. Not the woman who can't let go of a past they once shared.

My phone buzzes, and I pull in a cleansing breath before I look at it. No matter what, Duke doesn't deserve to get tangled up with me or this business I have with Langston—at least until I'm sure my theory is correct.

Dr. Potter: And what is it, exactly, that I would mess up? Langston's unconditional love for you?

I can almost feel the smirk bleeding into his typed words, but before I can say anything, another text comes through. **I can't know for sure since I've only had one long-term relationship. Still, I'm pretty confident you are supposed to love everything about the person you're promising forever to—not upgrading their tits disguised as a wedding gift.**

My fingers can't move fast enough to blast out a response. **I'm not that gullible! I knew the tits weren't a gift, just like I know what I am doing marrying Langston! I don't need your input, Dr. Potter. I can take care of myself just fine, fuck you very much.**

I don't even have time to throw my phone before he texts right back.

Yet, you cower at his demands—I'm thinking that's hopelessly toxic, boo.

Rage blinds me. **Fuuuuuuuck You!!!!!**

Dr. Potter: Please! I wish someone would fuck me—it's been a while. But more than that, someone should probably fuck you. The congressman looks disappointing in the bedroom department.

I can't. I can't do this with him anymore. The more I text him, the more he keeps me hooked, making a simple apology—okay, more like an explanation text—turn into a whole conversation.

Me: Goodbye, Dr. Potter.

My phone dings. **In my professional opinion, this text is a cry for help. I can't ignore it.**

Not a moment later, the phone rings, but it's not just a call. It's a video call.

What a bastard.

I answer on the fourth ring just to make him wait. "What if I would have been in bed with Langston?" I prompt, trying—and failing—not to make eye contact with his amused hazel eyes.

"Then we'd have a far more interesting conversation," he snaps back. "But then again," he flashes me a heated look, "maybe we still can. Do tell, Ray. What is that little number you're wearing?"

Shit.

I toss the phone onto the bed and strip off the old T-shirt, riddled with holes and paint splatters, and find a nightgown Langston bought, slipping it on.

"Come on, Ray, don't be like that."

His infectious laugh makes me smile, and that pisses me off more than his words. Why do I let him get to me like this?

Because you love him, stupid.

"I'm sorry. I'll pretend I didn't see it. Cross my heart," he swears on the other end of the phone with a chuckle.

But the fact is, he did see it, and he knew instantly the T-shirt used to be his.

"Though, I'm impressed the shirt held up this long," he continues, undeterred. "Look at the tag and tell me the brand. I should probably buy more of them. What's it been, twenty years?"

Inhaling, I look to the ceiling for patience and pick up the phone. "Eighteen years, but that's not relevant." Ignoring the cutest, most adorable grin ever given to a man, I snap. "Why are you calling me?"

He shrugs, the movement drawing attention to the snug T-shirt, which then draws my eyes to his bulging muscles.

"I could flex for you. All you have to do is ask." He brings one arm into the camera, and I snap out of the lustful haze.

"Dr. Potter!" I need to put a stop to this. "What is it that you need from me at this hour?"

Duke drops his arm, his face turning serious. "I'm making sure my patient's mental stability is intact. Otherwise, I might have to push your surgery date back even further." He makes this pouty face. "No big titties for Langsty-poo."

Oh, for goodness' sake. "You don't even plan on scheduling my surgery in the first place."

Who does he think he's playing with? I know Duke Potter better than himself.

He laughs. "You're right. I will never give you breast implants, Ray. Call me sentimental, but I recall they fit perfectly in my mouth. I'd hate to destroy that memory just so Langston can dabble in a little breath play with *my* tits."

I sigh. "They aren't your tits anymore, remember?"

"No," he says thoughtfully. "Saying they aren't mine would imply that you somehow severed our relationship—which came with the free gift of titties."

"We broke up," I remind him.

"No, you walked away and never returned." He looks victorious with this insane explanation. "There's a difference."

"Duke."

"Ray."

"We're not together anymore." This day just keeps getting better and better. "I'm with Langston now."

Duke grins, lying on his bed, one hand behind his head as if this conversation is delightful. "I know. I feel like I'm supposed to react all alpha-male-ish and punch the guy for fucking my girl. As a matter of fact, shouldn't you be wearing a scarlet letter or something?" He makes this shameful noise. "But don't worry, Ray. I'll forgive you. People make mistakes. I know a great therapist that will have us back to fucking on my car in no time." He grins. "I have more than one now, you know?"

He jumps his eyebrows, and God help me, I can't keep the laugh contained. "You need to stop," I say through fits of laughter.

"I will just as soon as you tell me what you're really doing with Langston." His tone has turned serious again. "I mean it, Ray. Whatever it is, I can help you."

I shake my head. "This is one thing I won't let you help me with."

The devastation on his face has tears pricking my eyes. "I promise, Potter," I use the nickname I called him when we were kids, "I'm okay. Let me do this for u—." I've said too much already.

"Do this for who, Ray?"

"Goodnight, Dr. Potter. I'll see you at our next appointment."

"Tell me, Ray, or I won't let you have it."

He dangles the T-shirt over my head. *Why did he have to grow a freaking foot this summer?*

I jump for the shirt only to meet air and laughter. "Tell me."

"Duke, my shirt is ruined. Please give me yours." I've resorted to whining.

"I wouldn't say it's ruined," he fingers the sleeve and gags dramatically, "more like it's disgusting."

"And as my concerned and caring boyfriend, you shouldn't want me to continue to wear a shirt covered in bird shit."

Duke doubles over in laughter for the hundredth time in the last two minutes. "I told you not to sit under the tree."

"I was hot! It was the only shade around." I use his distraction and swipe at the shirt, but he's too quick and holds it out of my reach again.

"You could have jumped in the lake with me," he counters.

"And get bitten by a water moccasin? No thanks."

He narrows his eyes. "You saw one snake by the dock, and now you think the entire lake is filled with them."

I don't appreciate his sarcasm or the disappointed frown. "Where there is one snake, there are others. It's nature."

"It's nature, huh?" He circles me, holding his T-shirt hostage. "So, if we're using your logic, then the mounds of bird shit on your shirt is just nature, too."

Oh my gosh, he's utterly impossible and severely dramatic.

"Duke…" I actually stomp my foot like a freaking toddler. "Please let me have your shirt. I can feel the poop leeching through the fabric." Great, now I'm being dramatic.

"Only you are standing in your way. Say it, Ray. Say it, and you can be free of the bird shit."

"This is blackmail."

He shrugs, not giving a damn. "One way or another, you're gonna tell me—not my brother."

"Vance and I were fighting! It wasn't like we had some heartfelt conversation. He warned me to stay away from you, and I—" I stop myself, and it only serves to invigorate Duke's enthusiasm.

"And you said what, Ray? You…" God knew what he was doing when he blessed the man with that smile. I fall for it every time.

Stepping closer, I bat my eyelashes and gaze up at him. It's a shy look that he should know not to trust. "I told him too bad because I love you."

"You love me?" I swear he smiles wider.

I move in, feeling the heat of his body. "I do. I love you, Duke Potter—very, very—"

This time, he isn't fast enough when I jump, wrapping my arms and legs around his waist and smearing my very shitty shirt against his chest.

"Dammit, Ray!" He tries to pry me off, but I hold on, paying him back for torturing me.

"That's what you get for blackmailing your girlfriend," I scold, feeling pretty victorious for gaining the upper hand.

"All right, you win, Sunny Ray." He stops fighting and accepts his fate of being in a literally shitty situation. "I was wrong to blackmail you…. Just like I'm wrong for doing this."

"What?"

Dropping the T-shirt, this man holds me tighter and takes off toward the dock. "No!" I scream. "Don't you do it!"

"Do you still love me, Ray?" I swear he's running faster than he usually does, and that's not with him carrying another person.

"Yes, but—"

"But nothing," he cuts me off, already reaching the dock. "When you *love someone, you become one."* He hugs me closer. "Therefore, your shitty situation is now my shitty situation."

We're at the edge before I can adequately absorb what's happening. "No, my situation is not—"

"Watch for snakes. I hear they're everywhere," he teases.

And then he jumps.

I wake up drenched in sweat in the guest room of Langston's mansion, an unsettling feeling swirling in my stomach.

I didn't get bitten by a snake that day when Duke jumped off the dock.

I didn't even get the chance to haul ass back to the dock.

Because Duke Potter didn't let me go in the water.

Instead, he wrapped his arms around me and swore, "I'll always keep you safe, Ray—no matter what."

CHAPTER SEVEN

Duke

"Where are you headed?"

I glance up from my duffle bag, where I finished stashing the "unhealthy bauble," as Vance calls it. I don't trust leaving it in my desk anymore. Not after the heated conversation we had last week in the elevator.

"Vegas," I respond casually, holding Vance's accusing stare.

He hasn't brought up Ramsey since we kept Astor's daughter for the day, but I know it's only a matter of time before he revisits the topic.

"What's in Vegas?" Pushing his way into my office, he tries acting like he isn't surveying the room for clues—which he doesn't need. He knows I'm up to no good.

"What's in Vegas *other* than Ramsey, you mean?" Let's not pretend Vance cares that I'm headed to Vegas, where I've visited a million times. He only cares about one thing—being involved in another scandal.

"You're getting brave, little brother." Vance chuckles darkly.

"And you're getting nosy." I flash him a grin. "Don't tell me things have grown boring between you and Hal, and you now need to hear about my weekend exploits."

The fact that my brother doesn't threaten me about commenting on his sex life tells me his mind is preoccupied—with me.

"Is that what you're doing? Having an affair with the congressman's fiancée?"

I scoff. "I wish. But you see," I shake my head in mock shame, "Ray has this thing about being a good person. She wouldn't sleep with me if I begged her wearing nothing but acrylic paint."

And damn, if thinking about her upstanding morals doesn't make my dick hard.

Vance moves in front of me, holding my stare. "Is that what you're doing? Do you intend to beg Ramsey for scraps of attention? You're better than that, brother. You deserve a woman who wants to be with you—not one who leaves when things get rough."

I know he means well; I do. Vance and Astor were the only people who stood by my side when the news ripped me apart, and the school took back my scholarship. But neither of my brothers knows the story of what really happened that winter.

I'm not the man they think I am.

Sighing, I flash Vance a sarcastic smile. "Fine. You caught me. I was sneaking off to kill the congressman." I shrug. "My dick and I decided we couldn't settle for her scraps of attention."

I know the minute I've slipped past his barrier of patience. He slams his fist on my desk. "I'm serious, Duke! Leave this girl alone! She's already destroyed you once." His arm trembles, and his entire body vibrates with controlled emotion. "I won't watch her destroy you again."

Halle and Remington suddenly appear in the doorway, checking on their boy.

I wave them off and face the concern in my brother's eyes. "Ramsey did not destroy me. If anything, I destroyed her."

Vance snaps. "Is she the one I dropped off at rehab for six weeks?

Or was she the one who slept on my dorm couch when our father kicked him out?"

Inhaling, I try not to lose my calm. "You don't under—" He doesn't let me finish.

"I understand perfectly, Duke. I understand that she went back home with her father and left my brother, the valedictorian of his class, looking like a fool. Where was she, Duke? Huh? Where was she when you delivered pizzas to pay your way through school? When you could only sleep two hours a night without waking up screaming?"

The muscle in his jaw ticks erratically, and I know I need to stop this.

"You're right," I tell him. "Vegas is a bad idea."

"Damn right, it's a bad idea," he snaps, folding his arms and seeming to relax.

I nod like he knows best, even though he doesn't.

It's true. All those things did happen.

I did go to drug rehab and suffered from insomnia when I worked long hours through med school.

And you know what? I'd do it all again… for her.

Halle has finally had enough and steps behind Vance, wrapping her arms around his waist. His hands go to the top of hers, visibly calming down. "How about you come over for dinner tonight? I'm making Vance's favorite—chicken pot pie," she encourages.

I have no intention of attending dinner, but I won't break Halle's heart just yet. Maybe I'll call her from the car and say I have a patient emergency at the hospital. Vance will know I'm lying, but he'll keep my secret for his girlfriend's sake.

"Sure," I tell her, flashing Vance a grin and mouthing *pussy*.

He rolls his eyes—indicating that he agrees with my assessment.

"Dinner is at seven. Don't be late." With that, Halle tugs my brother from my office, finally giving me some fucking space.

Or, at least, I thought.

"Why does Vance-hole hate your girl so much? She spit in his bourbon or something?"

I groan and drop my chin to my chest. "Don't you have delinquent friends to meet or something?"

Seriously? What is up with this office being in my damn business?

Remington stalks forward, his brow cocked in amusement. "Sounds like my delinquent friends should talk to your friends. Rehab, huh? What happened? You have some little side hustle going on with Daddy's narcotic cabinet? No wonder you were more popular than Vance in high school."

He pulls out a cigarette and lights it up in my office with a chuckle. I don't even have the energy to stop him. Instead, when he gets it lit, I pluck it from his fingers and inhale deeply, allowing the smoke to fill my lungs and settle the stress.

"Well, well. Baby Potter isn't as squeaky clean as his big brothers." He snatches the cigarette back and takes a long drag, blowing the smoke in my face. "I'm impressed, Dr. Duke. Who knew you were more than just a fraternizing playboy?"

Dusting the ashes off my desk, I level an annoyed glare at my unwanted company. "Not that I don't appreciate being accepted in your demented circle of sin, but is there something you need? I'm on my way out."

"To meet Ray?"

I blow out a frustrated sigh. "No, to give your mom a little backdoor attention." I grin. "I hear you have to be home for dinner at seven."

Remington laughs around the cigarette between his lips. "You know, fuck it. I'll play."

He taps my desk with his knuckles. "Enjoy your scandal, Dr. Douche. I'm rooting for you."

I can feel it the second she walks in. Her anger shot straight to my cock as she approaches me with intention.

"What are you doing here, Potter?"

Strands of red hair fall onto my shoulder.

"Excuse me? Do I know you?"

Nothing brings me such pleasure as sparking her fury.

"Duke!"

I grin, feeling her breath against my neck. "Wait a minute." Reaching up, I grab the lock of hair and wrap it around my fist, holding my furious ex captive. "Ah, yes. Now this, I recognize." I rub the silky strands against my cheek. "It's been too long, old friend."

"Stop talking to my hair and answer me!" I can appreciate her trying to keep her voice down, but again, I'm not the man she used to know.

"Persuade me, and maybe I'll consider it."

I give her hair a gentle tug, and she whimpers. "Duke, please. You can't be here."

"Sure I can, darling." Unwinding her hair, I let it drop and stand, turning to face her full wrath. "This is an art class, is it not?"

I lean my back against the table, aware of the curious looks we're now attracting, which only notches up my grin. "Be careful, Ray. You're drawing a crowd."

Wearing nothing but a tank top and overalls, the woman who haunts my dreams narrows her eyes. "Leave. Now. I won't ask you again."

Glancing around the room, I note several people are quickly turning away as I offer Ramsey a threatening smile. "Sit down, Ms. Ford, before I show these people how I deal with your demands. You must have forgotten that I'm not Langston. I find your fight"—I step closer, my hips pressing against her softness—"alluring."

She sucks in a breath, her eyes widening from the evidence of just how alluring I find her right now. "Someone will see us and report it back to Langston."

I take her hand, the one with the wrong engagement ring. "Are you sure that would be a bad thing?"

"Yes." Her chin quivers, but she holds back the emotion, pulling her hand back shakily. "I love Langston."

The difference between a good and honorable man is knowing when to concede defeat.

I'm neither good nor honorable.

I'm relentless.

Stepping back, I graze my knuckles down her soft cheek. "You're never more beautiful than when you lie."

"I'm not ly—"

"All right, ladies and gentlemen. Now that everyone is here, let's get started," the teacher says, interrupting yet another lie. "Find a partner. We're going to continue working on last week's project."

Ramsey looks around nervously.

"If you're scared of your old man finding me here, I promise I'll take care of it." It's not my intent to break up sweet love, but I know what love looks like on Ramsey Ford, and what she has with Langston is not it. "Or you could just tell me what kind of trouble you're in with the congressman and let me help you."

Her gaze snaps to mine. "I'm not in any trouble. I'm marrying Langston in a few weeks, and there's nothing you can say or do to stop me."

"Spoken like a true con artist." I grin. "I have to say, Ray, I'm awfully turned on by your naughtiness right now."

Pulling out her sketchpad, she rolls her eyes. "You're ridiculous if you think I'm—"

A guy I don't know interrupts her. "You ready, Ramsey?" He has a sketch pad in his hand and a death wish in his eyes.

I snatch the pad from his hand, flipping through the pages until I find one of Ramsey's eyes—sad and haunted. "And you're both delirious if you think this little coloring session is continuing." I tear the page from his book and hand it back. "Find another partner. This one is taken."

Ramsey sighs and drops her head back to her shoulders. "Duke, you can't just—"

Every breath she uses to defend this stranger does nothing but ignite white-hot jealousy throughout my body. "I warned you, Ray." This time, I grab her sketch pad and flip through the pages, looking for the portrait of this obnoxious dude, but when I get to it, I stop cold.

There is no portrait of the guy in front of me. Just one of me, angry and seething from the last time I saw her at Langston's.

I blink at the image, at a loss for words.

She drew me.

Not just my eyes or the heart she carries on her body.

This is not the eighteen-year-old version of me. This is the man who saw her for the first time in years—whose prayers were answered and destroyed in a single moment.

Her hands slip the book from my hands. "You warned me, and I heeded your warning." She flips the pages slowly, allowing me to absorb each detailed image. "You still are my *only* muse."

I nod slowly, silently, taking in everything on those pages.

My happiness.

My anger.

My devastation.

She's captured each moment as a memorial.

To what we had.

And what we lost.

Lifting my head, I take in the tears welling in her eyes, but the trembled plea in her voice crushes me. "If you love me, if this means anything to you"—she holds up the book, her breathing uneven, as she finishes pushing the proverbial knife through my chest—"then you'll let me go."

I don't know what propels me forward.

Maybe it's the crushing weight of the finality in her voice, or perhaps it's the blow to my heart. No matter how she feels about me, she wants to be free. She wants to marry Langston, for whatever reason.

And denying her is the one thing I've never been able to do. "As you wish."

CHAPTER EIGHT

Ramsey

As you wish.

I can't get his words out of my head.

They've made me sick to my stomach, or maybe that's just Langston's feet inducing the nauseating reaction. "Put your elbow into it, Ramsey."

Honestly, I'd love to put my 'elbow' into it. However, I'd rather aim it at his crotch, not at the arch of his foot. But this is what I asked for, right? For the man I love to leave me with this serpent disguised as a man, all so I can get the information that will change our lives.

Maybe.

The information could blow up in my face and be nothing more than a nightmare that I'll never be free from. But it's a risk I'm willing to take. Because if my mother was right…

I shake my head, smothering the runaway thoughts of a different future.

Focus, Ramsey. You're so close. Duke will forgive you. He'll understand you did it for the both of you.

Unless Mom was wrong.

Then Duke will never forgive me, and I'll be stuck with Langston until he grows tired of me.

"Ramsey!"

I snap out of the thoughts racing through my head and look up at Langston, who is scowling, pointing to my phone on the table.

"Silence your phone," he snaps. "You know how I feel about being disturbed this late in the evening."

Yet he gets calls at all hours of the night, but whatever. I don't even care at this point. Jumping up from the floor, I wipe my hands on my pants and swipe my phone open, seeing a familiar number and a text that stops me cold.

Duke: Ray? This is Lads and Lagers—the bar. Mr. Potter asked us to contact you.

Oh, no. My heart tumbles in my chest as I sneak a peek at Langston, who is busy reading his newspaper.

Quickly, I text back. **How drunk is he?**

I don't have to wait long for their answer. **Well, we tried to call him a cab, but he couldn't remember where he was staying.**

Three little dots appear and disappear before the last part of the text comes through. **He said you knew where home was.**

A sharp pain hits me straight in the chest—my beautiful, broken boy who hides behind jokes and sarcasm. I thought he had moved on from our past. Unlike me, Duke has a wonderful family—well, brothers—who supported him through it all. He went on to become a surgeon and make a name for himself. He didn't crumble like I did. He was strong.

Until now.

Until I brought it all back.

The pain.

The longing.

The love.

And that love is something I can't let go.

Glancing back at Langston, I hurry out my response. **I'm coming.**

No matter what happens between Langston and me, or the information I need, I will always be there for the man I love more than anyone. The very man I'm doing this for in the first place.

"Gillian needs me," I lie to Langston.

"This late?"

I wave off his accusing gaze. "You know wedding planners. They work all hours of the day." I walk over and kiss the top of his head. "I'm sure it won't take long. I'll call you."

His lips turn down in a disgusted manner. "Don't bother. I'm off to bed. I'll see you in the morning."

Thank goodness. I'd hate to lie even more. I already fear for the integrity of my soul by just being in the presence of Langston.

But *he's* worth every lie—especially this one. "Goodnight, my love."

Lads and Lagers is an upscale Irish pub just outside the Vegas strip. It's low-key and the perfect place to keep from being seen by any of Langston's spies, which is fabulous, because Duke is absolutely shit-faced when I get there.

"I told you, Billy." Duke points to me as soon as I approach the bar. "There's no one more beautiful than my Sunny Ray."

Sitting there, with his pupils wide, a grin as big as the bar top, Duke reaches out to me, and God forgive me, I take his hand.

I did this to him.

I asked him to let me go—something neither of us could do, and he dealt with it the only way he knew how.

"Seems like we've been here before," I tease, letting him pull me between his legs, safe and familiar.

"You're right." He swallows, the alcohol-induced buzz fading in an instant. "But this isn't before."

Before.

When he left school and his family, choosing to give up everything and run away with me.

He drops my hand and pushes me back. "Go home, Ray. I'm fine."

There's something about how he turns away from me that I can't handle. I know I asked him to let me go, but I don't *actually want* him to let me go. I just need the information from Langston, and if I can get that information out of him before the wedding, then great, but I'm prepared to sacrifice everything—even my freedom—to get it.

That's how important this information is to me.

And once I have it—I can make things right for Duke. We deserved a different ending to our story. Duke didn't deserve to be shipped off to rehab and labeled a drug abuser.

We were mere kids when we had our futures ripped away.

Duke seems to be recovering better than I am, but clearly, he's not without scars.

And those scars—those wounds—call to me on a visceral level.

"Get up, Potter." I grab him by the upper arm—and damn if it isn't solid.

He goes nowhere.

"I made you a promise, remember?" he says, tipping back the last of what looks like bourbon. "I'm doing what you asked. I'm letting you go." He nods to Billy to refill his tumbler, which so isn't happening.

I smack the glass away. "While I appreciate the effort, I can't, in good conscience, let you drown yourself in bourbon."

"Sure you can, Ray." He tilts his head to the side, a flash of anger hiding behind his smile. "That's your specialty, right?" That fake smile morphs into a flat line—nothing but pent-up hatred behind it as he leans closer, whispering loud enough that Billy hears. "Because we've been here before, and you had no problem leaving me to drown back then."

The blow stings much worse than I expected. I knew what he

thought, and I've let him believe it all these years. It was easier that way—him thinking the worst of me. It assured me that he would look for someone better—someone who wasn't broken, who would fight for him harder. Duke would move on. He's more resilient than I am, and that's all I needed to know—that one of us would end up happy.

But now?

Hearing him give up on me.

This man has already broken once in front of me. I won't let him do it again without knowing the truth.

I place my hands on his cheeks, forcing him to look at me. "You're right. I did leave before, but not because I wanted to."

He tries to jerk away like a little kid, but I don't let him. "You want to know where home is, Dr. Potter? It's right here." Dropping one hand, I grab his hand and place it on my heart. "Your home is here. It's always been here. Even when I 'walked away' after my father forced me into a mental institution."

Duke flinches, his mouth opening, but I don't let him move. He's going to listen to me. I might have been forced to walk away, but I never let him go. "I walked away, yes, but I kept you here. I've never married—never even had a boyfriend—because I couldn't love anyone but you."

Duke swallows and removes his hand from my chest, holding my gaze. "Then why are you with Langston?"

I sigh. "I just need you to trust me."

I'm tired of fighting with him. He knows I'm up to something, so I might as well roll with it.

Duke chuckles and then motions to Billy for the bottle of bourbon, then takes a long pull, hissing out a breath through his teeth. "I should have known."

He shakes his head and takes another drink. "All these years... wasted."

Another drink.

"And for what? To know you didn't leave and that I would have to relive the pain of you leaving all over again."

Billy cuts me a look that says *one of us needs to take the bottle from him, and it isn't me.*

Great.

"Let me take you home, Potter." I tug at the bottle, but his grip is too tight.

"And how do you suppose you're gonna do that, Ray? Since home is there"—he points the neck of the bottle at my chest—"and you've locked me out of my home in the name of trusting you."

He's not making good sense, but he's probably drunk a third of the bottle of bourbon. Making sense is no longer in his wheelhouse.

"You know what I mean," I explain. "Let me take you back to your hotel."

This time, it's Billy who chimes in. "Good luck figuring out which one it is. All he can say is that it's the big one on the strip."

I chance a look at the mess of a man in front of me, the bottle poised at his lips as his throat works, trying to erase the events of today. He is hauntingly beautiful, even when he's trying to forget me.

"I think I can figure it out," I tell Billy.

If anyone knows Duke Potter and his favorite places to stay in Vegas, it's me. We might not have ever come to Vegas together, but that doesn't mean we didn't lay out under the stars and talk about all the places we wanted to go. Not to mention that I bet neither of them checked his pockets for a keycard.

Leveling a knowing smile at Duke, I tip my chin at the bottle in his hand. "Give Billy the bourbon."

There's always been this push and pull between Duke and me, so as soon as he hears the change in my tone to one more playful, he responds exactly like I knew he would.

His legs close around me, pinning me in place. "Convince me."

I grin. "Your heart," I drawl, "for the bourbon."

Duke groans as I finger the bottom of my shirt, indicating his heart is painted somewhere a little more scandalous than last time. "What's it gonna be, Dr. Potter? The bourbon or your heart?"

I know immediately when he's made his decision. His tongue wets his lips while his eyes become hooded with want. "I need to close my tab, Billy."

If Billy could give me a high-five, I'm sure he would, but instead, he takes the bottle from Duke and prints out his tab for him to scribble something that looks like a signature.

"Come on, Dr. Potter." I offer him my hand. "Let's find your heart." But then I think how ridiculous that sounds and add, "And your hotel."

For a moment, Duke just stares at my outstretched hand, and something primal passes through his eyes before he stands, his chest brushing mine. "If I were you, Ray, I wouldn't taunt me with my own possessions."

Leaning closer, his breath ghosts over my ear, the smell of bourbon invading my senses. "I might decide I'm no longer willing to share them with your congressman."

CHAPTER NINE

Ramsey

D uke magically remembered where he was staying as soon as we left the bar, but unfortunately, that's where his helpfulness ended.

"Hold still," I tell him for the thousandth time.

"I would, Ray," he chuckles, "but the aggression you're taking out on my pockets is torture." He leans back against the hotel door, not embarrassed at all that there's a raging boner tenting his pants.

"I'm looking for your keycard," I explain, which, apparently, is in a pocket he can't remember. Who knows if that's the truth or if it's just an excuse for me to shove my hands down his pants again.

But I've always loved it when he's like this—playful and unguarded.

It reminds me of before, when things weren't so complicated.

"No one told you to yank me around, Ray. You know what that does to me," he says with a flippant shrug, grinning like a fool.

I swear he makes me crazy—especially when I'm trying not to

laugh. "I'm not yanking on you. I simply asked you to turn around so I could check your other pocket."

"And I did turn around…" His brows rise mockingly. "Then you yanked me."

I swear to all that is holy… "You were falling! If I hadn't yanked you, you would have ended up on the floor."

"Tomato, potato."

This time, I do laugh. "It's tomato, tomahto."

This man is the cutest, most ridiculous person I know.

"Now, seriously, hold still." I slip my arms around his waist, trying to ignore the firm muscles of his ass, and lift his wallet from his back pocket.

"How many do you see?" I hold the leather wallet in front of him.

The grin that makes me stupid flashes. "Is that a trick question?"

And that means one wallet too many. "All right, Potter," I say, flipping open his wallet and, as I expected, finding his keycard. "Let's get you to bed."

A low and pained noise rips from Duke's throat. "Those words used to be more exciting when we were younger."

"Oh, yeah?" I tease. "Are you saying if I put you to bed like I used to, you'll behave? Perhaps even leave Nevada?"

His grin falters, but only for a second, before he recovers, his thumb going to the corner of my lips. "If you put me to bed like you used to, I'll happily leave Nevada."

Those beautiful hazel eyes dance with delight, and that fact alone should have warned me to retreat and not lean into his touch as his thumb drags across my cheek, his whole hand joining the excruciating warmth as it settles at the base of my neck, holding firm. "I'll gladly leave Nevada, Ray. The question is, will you leave Nevada amenable or kicking or screaming?" He leans in closer, the warmth of his breath ghosting over my skin. "Because either way, my love, you're leaving Nevada with me."

His words root me into place. "You promised to leave," I remind him.

"And you promised to marry me." He shrugs. "Guess we both are breaking promises."

"That isn't the same thing! I was a teenager when I promised to marry you."

This man seriously needs some sleep and a reality check—though the flutters in my stomach appreciate the sentiment that it wasn't just me that could never love again. It's one thing to accept that you would never be with the person you were meant to spend forever with, but it's another to know that person is far from accepting that fate.

Hope is a dangerous game to play.

"You should sleep." I place my hand on his arm and offer him a sad smile. "We'll talk about this when you're sober."

Duke drops his hold and steps back, allowing me to swipe the keycard and unlock the door to his room. The burst of cool air hits me in the face, graciously cooling me off from the heated exchange.

But it doesn't last long.

Immediately, I feel Duke's heat on my back, his body still hard in the most inappropriate places. "I think we've been here before, Ray," he rumbles, low and gravelly. "But last time, you were the villain."

I try snapping around, but Duke's hands grip my hips, holding me in place, while he towers over me, his voice in my ear. "Do you disagree?"

I swallow. "We were both virgins. I was not the villain."

He chuckles. "As I remember, you pulled me into that hotel room, too."

"Don't act like you weren't just as eager as I was." We were so in love that we couldn't stand not to claim all our firsts together.

Duke takes an intentional step forward, the momentum pushing me along with his actions. "Oh, I was eager, Ray. I'd even wager that I'm more eager now."

His hands grip me tighter, almost as if he remembers what it felt like to have me beneath him as he gently devoured all I had given him that night—my body and soul. I have never loved a man since Duke Potter. I haven't wanted to. Even if I tried, no one could compare. Duke might live in a world of sarcasm and jokes, but his heart is so big, so unconditionally pure, that it must be guarded at all times. He couldn't show just how deeply he loved or cared—not in the families we lived in.

Duke was different.

He wasn't cold and aloof like Vance.

He wasn't distant and detached like Astor.

He was warm and compassionate—so full of life that even death couldn't kill the joy he brought to others.

Duke might call me his ray of sunshine, but it couldn't be further from the truth.

The truth is, Duke kept us warm. He kept us alive—he kept me alive, even when I begged for death.

No soul is purer than his.

And when you have a taste of someone like that, there's no way you could ever love another.

Because you know what it feels like to be loved by nothing but raw goodness.

"One day," I whisper in the darkness, "when this is all over. I'll tell you what this moment felt like, being wrapped in your arms after all these years of longing and pain."

His arms tighten like he alone can prevent me from leaving. "I can fix the longing," he promises. "I will even try to heal your pain. All you need to do is stay."

Stay.

It sounds so simple.

So easy.

Heaven knows I want to, but staying would only be like putting a bandage over a gushing wound. The bleeding wouldn't stop. Sure, it'll slow it down, but it won't heal until I stop the source of the bleeding.

And Langston, unfortunately, holds the sutures I need.

I tug on Duke's hand, and he releases his hold of my hip, interlocking our fingers as I pull him to the bed. "You need rest." And I need to get out of here before I do something stupid like stay.

"I'm not tired."

Ignoring his lie, I turn and push him toward the bed. His legs hit the back of the mattress, and he plops down unceremoniously. "Your eyes say otherwise." I step between his legs and cup his face, stroking along his cheeks, feeling the day-old stubble.

His head leans into my touch as his eyes drift close. "I can't sleep—not since seeing you with him."

My heart—at least what is left of it—aches. "I'm not marrying Langston to hurt you. The last thing I want to do is cause you more pain."

He chuckles, his head dropping to my stomach while his arms loop around me in some half hug, which I return by rubbing my hands down his back. "You being away causes me pain. You being with him brings back the screams."

My hands still along his tense muscles, but he doesn't seem to notice. He simply continues confessing in the darkness.

"It took me years to quiet them, but one look at the pain in your face as he shamed your body, and it brought them all back." He pulls me closer, burying his face in my stomach. "You screaming and me helpless to stop it."

I don't know when I started crying, but the tears dripping onto his shirt are hard to hide.

"I want to stop the screaming, Ray," he mumbles. "I don't want to feel helpless again. I don't want to sit by and watch you marry Langston when I know you loathe him."

I rein in the tears and smooth a hand down his back. "You're not helpless, Potter. You never have been. This isn't the same as before."

Lifting his head from my stomach, I wait until he opens his eyes. "I'm stronger than before." I smooth the stress lines along his forehead. "This time, I can help you fight our battles. I just need you to trust me."

I offer him a smile that only makes his jaw clench while he struggles to keep his eyes open. "I don't want to trust you. I want to hold you until the screaming stops."

For years, I haven't broken, not since before.

But I break for this man—this beautifully strong man clutching me against him in a silent plea.

I break because I owe him.

I break because I love him.

He might think he was helpless while I screamed years ago, but his silent strength, his unwavering promise, held me together.

I might have broken that winter, but I took his hand and stood.

I stood afraid.

I stood broken.

But I stood.

And there's nothing I wouldn't do for the man who reached out and pulled me up in my darkest hour.

Cradling his cheeks, I lean in and kiss his forehead. "Close your eyes," I prompt, dropping my hands and allowing them to graze his shirt until I reach the bottom.

"What are you doing?" His eyes are wide open and much more alert than they should be.

"Close your eyes, Duke," I tell him again. "And let me make the screaming stop."

His hands close over mine. "No. I won't taint your morals, even if I don't believe you love Langston."

I can't smother the laugh that bursts out of me. "While I appreciate you saving me from myself, I don't plan on tainting my morals, as you call it."

He blinks slowly. "I don't understand."

His confusion is adorable. "I'm not sleeping with you," I tell him—though I leave out the part I want to. "I'm letting you hold me until the screaming stops." For both of us.

I test his willingness again and tug on his shirt. This time, he doesn't stop me. Instead, he holds my gaze and raises his arms above his head while I slip the fabric from his body, revealing a chest that has only been sculpted over the years. This is not the same body I drew at eighteen. Oh, no, this one is full of hills of muscle and valleys of tanned skin. This is the body of a man who knows no lazy days.

"You keep looking at me like that, Ray, and we're gonna have a problem keeping those morals of yours intact."

If this were before, I would respond that my morals are just as cloudy as his. He's the one who holds me on that pedestal. But this isn't then, and while I'd love nothing more than to feel the comforting weight of his body, I can't. Because I really can make the screaming stop for both of us.

I just need time.

Tossing Duke's shirt to the floor, I grin. "Do you want to sleep in your pants?"

"Are you gonna take them off for me if I say no?"

Do not smile. Do. Not. Smile.

"No, but fair warning, I don't sleep with pants on either." I push down my leggings, keeping my eyes on Duke, as he watches intently as I step out of his legs and crawl into the bed.

Taking the extra pillow he won't use and tossing it on the floor, I snuggle down into the crisp sheets and extend my hand invitingly. "Tonight, we'll rest."

Duke ignores my outstretched hand, and without warning, rolls me over and throws his arm and leg over me, pinning my back to his front. "Tonight, we'll rest," he agrees, his lips finding the soft skin of my neck. "And tomorrow, we'll lie."

CHAPTER TEN

Duke

Someone is staring at me.

But it feels judgmental.

"I've been told to ask if you are a toddler or a surgeon, but considering I was instructed to bring electrolytes and pain relievers, I think we all know the answer to that question."

Groaning, I pull the sheet over my head. I recognize that voice, and it isn't Ramsey's. "Go home, Remington."

"You see, I would love to go home. Better yet, I would love to spend my weekend not doing Vance a favor and checking up on his little brother, but I can't, since big bro loves to throw around threats when it comes to not getting his way."

Rolling over, I bury my face in Ramsey's pillow and ignore the rest of what Remington says. I don't care what my brother threatened him into doing; all I care about is how long Ramsey has been gone. How long did she lie next to me, soothing my soul? Hours? Minutes?

All I know is that it was long enough to keep her promise.

She stopped the screaming.

And I was able to rest while holding her, knowing she was safe in my arms. For the first time in years, I felt at peace.

"...and here I thought I had seen you at your worst." Remington is still talking, but thankfully, I miss most of his rant when I sit up and blink several times, trying to clear the blurry image of Remington from my vision. "What are you really doing here?" I ask.

It's not uncommon for my brother to grow nosy, mainly where Ramsey is concerned, but why now? I would be home later tonight, anyway. His sending Remington—even knowing where I am—is a little aggressive, even for Vance.

"Well, apparently, I'm here to witness what happens to a man who lets pussy rule his brain," he pops back from the chair pulled next to the bed.

"Pussy doesn't rule me." I don't owe Remington an explanation, but for some reason, I don't want him assuming my relationship with Ramsey is trivial, either.

Remington's lips tip up at the corner. "Are you sure?" He points at my chest. "Because that looks like you let someone get carried away with the hotel's pen. Don't tell me you were trying to bag a virgin." He makes a tsking noise. "I would have thought you knew this already, but you're a surgeon, Dr. Douche. You don't have to work that hard to score. The women will come to you willingly. You don't need to be a pussy and let them play third-grade art class on your chest. What is that even supposed to be?" He drags his finger through the ink on my skin. "A fucking heart?"

Throwing his head back, he lets out a boisterous laugh before pulling out his phone and snapping a picture. "Wait until your brother sees this shit. He already had me make you an appointment with the therapist this week." He laughs again. "Now, he'll want to offer up his slot, too. A fucking heart…"

Remington stands and walks through the room, yanking the curtains open as he goes. "I'm supposed to shout, 'What in the colossal fuck are you doing here, Duke?'" He turns back and grins. "And then drag you out of here—which I'm eager to do, but I'd rather you not puke on me, so… Get dressed, Romeo. We're fucking leaving. Believe it or not, the rest of us would like a weekend where we're not trying to keep you from pulling your dick out and scaring the congressman's fiancée."

I level a gaze at my brother's assistant. "Tell your boss I'm capable of getting home on my own."

Still looking out at the city, Remington nods. "I could, but where would be the fun in that? Besides, it's not Vance who's worried about you getting home safe."

I cock my head to the side, waiting for him to elaborate. Though, I don't know why. I already know the reason he's here.

"Next time, try not to cry in front of your forbidden lover, who was so worried that she texted your brother and asked him to look after you." He chuckles. "I can't believe you cried in front of a woman."

"I didn't cry."

He turns and walks toward me, his brow cocked. "So, you're saying the ink streaks down your chest aren't dried tears?"

I glance down at the inked heart on my chest. He's right. There are streaks. It was as if she was crying when drawing the heart on my chest. I stand up abruptly, ignoring the nausea, and look around.

"Looking for this?" Remington pulls out a piece of hotel stationery, holding it between his fingers. "Since I'm being paid by the hour, let me give your brother his money's worth." He opens the folded note and clears his throat. "Dear Dr. Douche," he starts with a grin, knowing good and damn well Ramsey didn't address me that way. "I promise to make the screaming stop. I promise we can rest soon." Remington's eyes widen. "Just what kind of shit were y'all doing last night?"

I reach for the note, but he jerks it away and continues reading. "I never did fulfill my end of the bargain and show you your heart. So, I left you mine. Let it be a reminder that I haven't forgotten my promise to you. Just trust me—like I trusted you. Because we've been here before, my love. But this time, it's my turn to save us." Remington's voice slows as he lowers the note, his eyes full of curiosity. "My, oh my. No wonder Vance-hole has been in such a delightful mood lately. His little bro is into some shady freaking shit."

I snatch the note from his hands. "You didn't read this note," I warn him.

"Oh, I definitely read this note—this bizarre and cringey love letter." He laughs. "Why does Vance dislike this chick so much?"

"One, she's not a chick. And two, Vance doesn't dislike her. He just doesn't understand what happened between us."

"And what exactly happened?"

"Well," I push past him, "that would be the time when… it was none of your damn business."

Remington chuckles. "You really love this girl, don't you? I can't blame you. The toxic ones are always more fun."

"Ramsey isn't toxic."

Remington looks down at his shoes. "Maybe she isn't, but I've seen what happens when you ignore the poison for too long." He looks up, and something dark passes through his eyes. "Spoiler alert: They both die in the end."

"I won't let her die," I promise him, with more determination than I've felt in a long time. "But it sounds like you didn't die, either."

Remington grins, his mask slipping back into place in seconds. "Perceptive, Dr. Douche."

"How'd you do it, then?" I ask. "How did you keep from dying?" I realize we aren't talking about physical death. The death of one's soul is much more catastrophic.

"Who says I didn't?" He taunts me with a secret. "Maybe I'm just an excellent liar."

His words hit me with such ferociousness that I step back, the memory overwhelming as it plays out like a movie in my head.

"Tell them, Duke! Tell them what you did!"

I don't answer her. Instead, I pull her closer as she screams and pounds her weak fists into my chest.

"Tell them, Duke!"

But I can't. I can't tell our fathers what I did in the cabin.

Because what I did doesn't matter anymore. All that matters is what I didn't do.

I didn't protect her like I promised.

Everything was not okay.

The truth destroyed my family.

More importantly, hiding the truth destroyed her.

"You're gonna be okay, Ray," I whisper into her ear, soaking up her last seconds in my arms.

"I won't be okay. Not without—"

"Come, Ramsey," her father barks out. "You've said your goodbyes."

Her cries grow quieter as she gathers her strength, keeping her face buried in my shirt, which allows her father to turn his attention to Harrison while he waits. "You'll keep your son away from my daughter, as we agreed. I will take care of the media, and you and your son will make this right for our family—for Ramsey."

Congressman Ford levels me with a look he reserves for the people he feels are beneath him. "Don't let your brothers suffer for your mistakes, son. You've ruined enough lives already. Don't make me take theirs to settle the score."

The congressman would never threaten murder, but I picked up the translation loud and clear. My brothers are at an Ivy League school. They are my father's pride and joy. One call from the congressman and their dreams of becoming plastic surgeons will vanish. No college will accept them if Congressman Ford makes a call. I've seen it before.

"I'm not a forgiving man, Duke. There are more ways to punish you if this isn't enough incentive."

His eyes track to his daughter in my arms. He has no problem using her as a pawn. Her being used was why we ran away in the first place. I have no doubt he won't hesitate to use her again.

"I can't breathe," Ramsey pants out between choppy breaths, drawing my attention back to her. "It hurts too much."

I wouldn't know—I haven't been able to feel anything since the screams started hours ago.

I couldn't feel my heart beating erratically or the grime on my hands.

Even now, as Ramsey's tears soak my shirt, I don't feel the wetness.

The coldness in my veins is the only reminder that I am still breathing.

"It won't always hurt," I promise Ray, smoothing a hand down her back. "As long as we remember, it won't hurt as much."

She nods her head. "I won't forget. I promise. I'll never forget."

It was then that Congressman Ford ripped her from my arms and shuffled her through the back exit of the hospital.

My father waits until they are out of sight, and then he levels me with a glare filled with nothing but hatred and threatens, "You will not speak of this. Not to your mother or your brothers. You will do as you're told while I clean up your mess. Do I make myself clear, Duke?"

The words sound like they come from someone else, but it's my voice I hear when I agree. "Yes, sir."

"You have disappointed this family for the last time."

"Dude." Remington shakes me, but I can't stay on my feet and slide to the floor, crushing the note in my hands. Vaguely, I hear Remington's voice worriedly talking on the phone—likely telling my brother I've lost it.

Maybe I have.

But the fact remains.

She didn't forget.

I asked her to keep our love alive.

Because I couldn't.

I failed us.

So, I asked her to remember a winter I vowed to forget.

A winter that killed my soul.

The winter where I became a liar.

CHAPTER ELEVEN

Ramsey

"I want four kids."

Duke's brows rise. "Four? Is my handsome face not enough for the rest of your life? You want me pent-up and broke, too?"

I laugh and point at him with my paintbrush. "I have faith you'll find a way to bang me with four children in the house. And we won't be broke because you'll be an amazing doctor by then."

Duke eyes me curiously, pulling the sucker from his mouth in this super sexy way that screams naughty promises. "And what if I don't want any children?" He sits on his elbows, his suit coat and shirt open, exposing his chest with the painting I just finished. "What if I want to keep you all to myself?"

I press my bare foot to his shoulder, easing him back against the windshield of his Range Rover. "Then I suppose I'll have to convince you how much fun sharing me can be."

"Sharing, huh?" Reaching back with one hand, he holds my foot on his chest. "I have to admit, Ray, I do not see the appeal in sharing. I'm already jealous of this dress." He tugs on the sequined fabric, bringing me closer.

Even in the moonlight, I can see the mischief in his gaze. "How does my homecoming dress make you jealous?" I swallow thickly, anticipation tingling under my skin as he studies me with intensity.

"This dress," he starts, yanking me forward on a gasp, "is touching what's mine."

I never imagined at eighteen years old that I would find my soulmate. But here he is living, breathing, and blowing off our homecoming dance in the middle of a field, savoring every minute we have left with each other.

In six months, we'll graduate.

In six months, Duke will go to college and become a doctor.

In six months, I'll spend the summer in France.

My father calls it traveling abroad. I call it a test run for an arranged marriage with his politician friend.

Half a year and both of our lives will change.

Duke and I will become the people our parents demand we be.

We'll give up our freedom.

More importantly, we'll give up each other—all for the sake of family.

So, this stolen moment, like all the others, is precious.

I lift the corner of the short dress tauntingly. "If this dress is touching something that's yours, maybe we should save it before you lose your temper and destroy it?"

That boyish grin appears as his fingers dance further up my leg. "I think that'd be wise. You know how I can get when it comes to my heart."

His heart.

He says the phrase so much that I can't tell if he's still referring to the drawn heart on my skin or if his heart is simply... me.

Am I his heart?

I'm not sure, but one thing is for sure: He's certainly mine.

Bunching the skirt of my dress, I ease it past my thighs and over my hips, revealing the heart I painted jade to match the dress's color.

"There it is," he croons, sitting up straighter, before placing a kiss on my calf. I should have been ready for what came next. Duke never just takes the inch you give him—he takes the whole damn journey.

The sucker poised between his fingers lands on my thigh, and I suck in a breath as the sticky substance touches my skin. "You're gonna ruin my painting," I say breathlessly. But the truth is, I couldn't give a crap that the painting on Duke's chest is cracking. All I care about is how his mouth closes over me as he licks the sweet path of his sucker while dragging it up my leg toward his heart.

"Duke."

My hands tangle in his hair as I fight to keep my balance on the hood of his car.

"I've been patient, Ray." The warmth of his tongue against my chilled skin is blissful torture. "I've sat still while you danced on my lap, tickling me with your paintbrush, until my cock was painfully swollen."

My head falls back as he sucks hard on the inside of my thigh. "And if that wasn't good enough, I allowed you to dance with my brother without killing him."

I can't focus on what he's saying. "You're driving me mad," I cry out.

"Good," he returns. "Now you can understand how I feel about anything and anyone touching you."

Mad.

It drives him mad to share.

I tug on the hair wrapped around my fingers, lifting his head. "Your brother told me to stay away from you again."

The smile Duke flashes me is not sweet. "Then you best remember my warning." He nips the sensitive skin that makes me yelp. "No one, not even my brother, will come between you and me, Ms. F—"

"Ms. Ford!"

I snap to attention. "I'm sorry, Lucinda. I promise I'll hold still."

Lucinda, the seamstress Langston hired for the wedding, casts me an annoyed frown. I'm sure she'd like to shake me since she's poked herself with a pin several times in the past hour because I was moving on the pedestal.

Unlike most women, seeing myself in a wedding dress doesn't bring tears to my eyes. If I had it my way, I'd rip off half of the excessively long train and burn it. I don't need miles of wasted fabric serving as a Swiffer duster to the church's hardwood floors. It's not that I can't appreciate a gorgeous train; it's just not my style or the husband I imagine myself marrying in it.

"You're restless," notes Lucinda. "Pre-wedding jitters?" She smiles, and I feel bad for lying to her. Lucinda makes a living making brides feel like real-life princesses on their wedding day, and here I am not giving two shits about how I look when I sign my freedom away.

But it'll be worth it, I tell myself. *You'll have closure.*

Inhaling, I relax and level Lucinda with a practiced smile. "Is it that obvious?" I chuckle. "I just want everything to be perfect for Langston."

The words settle in my stomach like lousy tofu.

"You'll be perfect," says Lucinda with an excited lilt in her voice. "I'll make sure of it."

I don't tell her Langston couldn't care less if every bead is in place or if the bustle looks like a cascading waterfall off my ass. He only cares that the plunging neckline highlights bigger tits than I have—which I still haven't figured out how to make happen.

It's been nearly a month since I left Duke in his hotel room. Four weeks of blocking his calls and texts. I knew he would be angry that I called Vance, but I couldn't leave him without knowing he would be okay. After all, I brought this mess to his doorstep—technically, Langston did. I had no idea Duke was his plastic surgeon. But the point is, I brought back the screams.

It is one thing for me to endure the pain of our past.

But it's unbearable to know Duke suffers the same.

I couldn't bring back his pain and leave him alone. He needed his brothers, even if it meant enduring Vance's disapproval. Though, when I called, Vance wasn't as hateful as I remembered. He simply thanked me for telling him and offered me a half-ass congratulations on my impending nuptials.

It wasn't the worst conversation I've had with him, but it was the only time I felt like I betrayed Duke by talking to his brother about us.

It was always him and me against the world, and I served him up to his older brother on a platter.

You would have thought I'd feel worse about marrying Langston than about telling Vance where Duke was, but I don't. Because I never intended to marry Langston. This marriage isn't about love. Therefore, my love and loyalty to Duke remain intact, as I promised years ago. Ideally, I would have already found the information I needed before the ceremony, but after multiple attempts to get into Langston's office safe, I have failed.

I need more time.

And the only way to get that time is to marry Langston. It's not a great plan, but if I can prove what my mother whispered to me on her deathbed, all this pain will have been worth an arranged marriage.

Because *he's* the only thing that matters.

Duke will have to forgive me for contacting his brother and blocking his calls.

I'm doing this for us whether he wants me to or not.

And I can't have him interfering or making me doubt my plan now. I need him safely away. Vance will make sure of that now. If there is one thing I can always count on is the Potter brothers protecting their own.

Vance thinks I'm bad news and fed his brother's drug habit years ago.

Which is certainly not true. Duke never had a drug problem. But Duke and I both promised not to dispute the cover story our parents concocted.

And I won't break that promise until I find the proof that will set us both free.

The wicked have prospered far too long at our expense.

We will not be shamed for our decisions.

And we will not bow to tyrants any longer.

The end is near for our fathers—for men like Langston.

It's time for the good to reign.

No more shame.

No more scandals.

Only a promising future.

"Excuse me. You can't be in here." Lucinda's voice snaps me to attention.

"Sure, I can. I'm here to make sure her tits are ceremony ready."

I groan, leveling a look at the man who shouldn't be here or occupying my thoughts just now.

Thanks a lot, Vance. Some help you were.

"Dr. Potter," I say sweetly. "I thought my fiancé agreed to the augmentation after the honeymoon?"

I honestly have no idea if Langston and Duke have been talking. I try to avoid speaking to Langston as much as possible.

Duke flashes me a cocky smile and pushes through the door, his eyes raking over me like burning coals.

The words he spoke years ago echo in my head. *"Then you'll know how I feel when someone touches what's mine."*

It drives him *mad*.

And that's exactly how he looks when he drags a chair in front of the mirror and sits directly in front of me.

"You're interrupting my fitting," I lie, trying to look anywhere but directly at his furious eyes.

"Your future husband disagrees." He levels Lucinda and me with a bored look. "You'll have to take the schedule up with him." He motions to the door. "I'll wait."

Dammit. He knows I won't ask Langston.

Sighing, I let my shoulders shrug in defeat. "Lucinda, will you give us a few minutes?"

"Thirty," Duke adds. "This won't take a *few* minutes, Lucinda." He lounges back in the chair, spreading his legs like he's settling in for a long argument.

"My apologies, Dr. Potter," I say through clenched teeth before turning to Lucinda, who looks more confused than agitated. "I'll reschedule. My apologies for the disruption."

With an audible huff, Lucinda grabs her bags and cuts Duke a glare that says if she were twenty years younger, she might whoop his ass.

But Duke doesn't spare her a glance. He can't take his eyes off me. And that's going to be a problem.

Duke's attention never ends well for my resolve.

When Lucinda finally disappears, I pull in a breath and face the fury that is Dr. Duke Potter. "You look rested," I lie.

He doesn't. Dark circles frame his gorgeous eyes.

"Where's my heart, Ray?" He doesn't bother with small talk. "Show it to me."

I don't know what makes me brave, but I refuse to let this man keep his attitude. He should know by now that if he wants a fight, a fight he will get. "No."

The corner of his lips twitch. "No?" He stands, circling the pedestal like a predator. "First, you call my brother. Then, you block my calls." He rounds my back, pulling something from his pocket. "And now, you deny me what's mine."

I swallow as he steps onto the pedestal with me. His eyes are fire and brimstone when he meets my gaze in the mirror, his hand settling on my hip, pulling me flush against him.

"What did I tell you, Ray?"

My skin is on fire as a scalpel appears at my shoulder, its blade shimmering in the lights. "You're here on business, Dr. Potter," I remind him, my gaze traveling down my wedding dress—the one I plan to marry another man in.

Duke smirks, and it's anything but friendly as the blade disappears behind my back. "You are my business, Ray. But it's not me who needs the reminder."

With the precision of a surgeon, Duke drags the blade down the back of my dress, severing the dress at the seams as the buttons scatter onto the floor around us.

"Duke!"

I grab the parting material, keeping a handful at my chest as he tosses the knife to the floor, his angry voice in my ear. "I'll ask you again, Ray. Where's my heart?"

You know what? Fuck it.

If he wants to see his heart, I'll show him.

Releasing the fabric clutched to my chest, I let the dress fall to my waist, exposing the painted white heart on the swell of my breast.

For a moment, everything goes silent.

I don't dare breathe, and neither does Duke.

He's a silent, immovable force behind me.

But then his hand tightens around my hip.

My eyes flash to the reflection in the mirror, but I don't find Duke staring at my breast. Instead, his gaze is locked onto my shoulder where—

I grab the fabric at my hips, but his hand clamps down on mine. "Don't even think about trying to hide this from me."

His voice is not to be fucked with. I've heard it before, and even as a teenager, it was scary. For all of Duke's charm and sarcasm, there's a territorial side of him that you don't cross.

"I fell," I lie, remembering Langston finding me rummaging through his desk drawers.

Duke scoffs. "You fell, and what," his fingers prod the bruises gently, "landed on five fingers?"

"It's not what it looks like."

It is what it looks like, but I'm so close to getting the information we need.

I'm so close.

"I just need you to let this go—for me."

The muscle in his jaw ticks, and I swear I can hear him grinding down on his molars. I can already tell he's going to say no. So, I beg. "Please, Duke. I've never asked you for much, but I'm begging you, please let me go."

His eyes close, and I know it's killing him from the inside.

This is not who he is.

Duke is a savior.

He helps people.

He's the one in the dark while you sob at rock bottom.

He's the only one with an outstretched hand.

And I'm slapping it away.

Not because I want to.

I'd love nothing more than to take that hand full of comfort and compassion and wrap myself in the security that is Duke Potter, but I can't. He deserves more.

And I can give him more… with time.

"Don't save me this time." A tear falls down my cheek. "I need to face the snakes on my own."

Absolute agony flashes when he opens his eyes and steps off the pedestal. I have to fight through the panic to avoid reaching for him and confessing everything.

But that would be a colossal mistake.

Duke might relent now, but he won't when he knows everything. There are only two ways he'd handle it. He wouldn't believe me, or he'd kill Langston.

Neither of those things can happen.

Not out of concern for Langston, of course, but because he still has what belongs to us.

Our real heart.

"All right, Ray. I'll let you drown, but remember who suffers when you draw your last breath." He steps forward and kisses my cheek, his heady breaths filling me with something otherworldly. "Don't let them take what's left of us."

Damn him and the bond we share.

Duke steps back, and I grab his arm to… keep him close? Tell him the truth? I don't know. But neither of those things come out of my mouth. "Langston plans on inviting you to his bachelor party next week. I respectfully request you decline."

A mischievous smile I've seen more times than I can count emerges on his face. "Do you now?"

"I do."

He pushes in closer. "Tell me how you really got that bruise, and I'll consider it."

I grit my teeth. "This isn't your fight anymore."

"Wrong answer, Ray."

His lips purse in this mocking pout. "Tell your beau that I take exception to property damage."

"I'm not your property."

He yanks me into his hard chest, his hands cupping my breasts, making sure the only part of me exposed is his heart painted on the underside. "That heart says otherwise."

His finger swipes over the paint, sending chills along my skin.

"Duke…"

He presses his lips to my neck, his eyes closing as he inhales deeply. "Please tell me why you're doing this."

He's begging.

My heart can't take it. Placing my hands over his, I offer him the only thing I can. Hope. "Hang on just a little longer. I promise I'll make the screaming stop."

With that, Duke's head snaps up, his eyes flashing with the same fury he had earlier. "Tell your fiancé I'll bring the cigars. I'm done entertaining you. I'll make the screaming stop myself."

CHAPTER TWELVE

Duke

I ignored her texts and calls.

All one hundred and twenty-five of them.

Let this be her reminder that my patience is not infinite. She's cute, and I love the fight in her, but I've waited nearly twenty years for her to return to me, and this is what I find. Her engaged to a pompous ass fiancé, who is currently lounged back in his leather chair, motorboating some college student's tits the night before he intends to marry her.

Yeah, no.

I'm drawing the line right fucking here.

"Tell me, Dr. Potter, have you ever enjoyed the tits you've sculpted?"

I puff on the cheap cigars Remington picked up for this special occasion—the boy knows how to impress. "I can't say that I have, Langs." I've resorted to unprofessionalism. It started when His Highness put his grubby hands on my girl.

Langston chuckles, not addressing the new nickname. "Don't tell me you're like your brothers."

I cock a brow. "Like them? As in respecting patients and protecting their dignity while in our care?" I nod, taking another puff and blowing out a ring of smoke in front of me. "Yeah, I guess you could say I am like my brothers—we have a problem losing those pesky morals."

At the mention of morals, Langston pauses his sloppy show of motorboating and leans around the woman on his lap to take a long, lingering look at me. "Be careful, boy. Some might think you're insinuating that you are above your present company."

Oh, that's exactly what I think, Langston. I think I am sitting among several dumpsters of trash claiming to be men.

"Not what I think at all, sir." I shoot him a look that says he's clearly overreacting and lean back in my chair, changing the subject to something more intriguing. "So... Ms. Ford. How did you meet her?"

I don't need Ramsey to spill her secrets. Her drunk fiancé will do it willingly, with bad cigars and tits. Ramsey had her go at him—whatever that was—and she failed. Now, it's my turn.

"Ah, Ms. Ford." He jiggles the woman on his lap, giving her ass a slap. "Her father, Congressman Ford, and I are friends."

Figures. Shit usually floats together in the same bowl.

"Congressman Ford"—I roll the name around like it's not familiar—"set you up with his daughter?"

Langston takes a sip of his drink and nods, pointing at me with his cigar. "It was the damndest thing. Out of the blue, he calls me and says his daughter is in desperate need of taming."

I chuckle. No one, especially a man, will tame Ramsey Ford. She is meant to be untethered. She's the wildfire burning out of control. Nothing will douse her flame.

Langston clears his throat. "I wasn't looking for wife number five yet, but I can never say no to the young ones with daddy issues."

I have to clench my fists to stay seated. Ramsey might have her issues, but she doesn't deserve to be put in a box. Humans aren't one thing. We aren't our political party. We aren't our fears and scars. We are living, breathing, evolving beings who break and heal. The past doesn't define who or what we become. We are freedom in the flesh. We are our failures. And we are our successes. Nothing can define us, but us.

"Interesting," I muse. "So, you guys fell in love quickly, then?"

Langston nods. "She was all over me, wanting to move in here just after a week of meeting."

That doesn't surprise me at all. I knew Ramsey was up to something. Whatever it is, she thinks Langston has it. The question is, what does he have that can end the screams in our heads?

The girl on Langston's lap moans, grabbing my attention.

"I can't wait for this wedding to be over." Langston groans, sucking one of her nipples into his mouth, and God bless the woman for acting like she enjoys it.

"Do you know how long it's been since I've felt the love of a woman?" he asks me.

I pause, acting like his comment didn't catch me off guard. "Are you saying your lady loves tradition?"

Please say yes. Even though I know Ramsey couldn't give eight shits about tradition.

Langston growls, and it sounds more pissed than tortured. "She wants to wait until we're married to have sex. She refuses to even sleep in the same room together."

That's my girl, Ray. Play dirty.

"Some women you just can't tame, Congressman."

I flash him a proud smirk. I've never tried to tame Ray. Instead, I added fuel to her fire and sat back, watching her flame burn out of control. And while I'd love nothing more than to see her burn down the congressman's kingdom on her own, she's too late.

I couldn't save her then.

But I can now.

"Oh, Dr. Potter. You have so much to learn. You don't tame women. You break them."

Yeah, not this one, Congressman.

I've broken her once.

And she rose.

She fought her way through the darkness and found her light.

I won't let you snuff the light from her again.

I won't let you destroy what's left of my girl.

Langston hoists the woman up on his lap as best he can, meaning she has to scoot closer so he can grind her into his cock. "Tonight is Ramsey's last night of freedom. She better enjoy it. Tomorrow is a new life—just like the one she desires." Langston chuckles. "No more separate rooms." He nuzzles the woman's neck. "No more fucking painting eyes and hearts on her body like a teenager. Ramsey Ford will know her place at my side, holding my…"

I don't hear the rest of what he says. All I can do is grip the sides of the chair as the screams take over—memories of the cold night I will never forget invading my brain like a monsoon.

"Squeeze my hand, Ray!"

"It hurts." Her body shudders in gut-wrenching agony, but she manages to find my hand, covered in blood, and squeezes. "I don't think I can do this."

"Yes, you can. You can do anything, remember? You're strong, Ray—so strong. Just look at me, okay? Keep your eyes on me—only on me."

She's so tired—so weak that I almost miss the small nod she flashes me. "Only on you," she finally agrees. "Us against the world."

"That's right. Us against the world. I promise, I'll make the pain stop. I just need you to give me one more big push," I lie.

We are so fucking fucked.

All the research. All the videos. All the medical supplies. None of it was enough to prepare for this moment.

A moment we hid from our families.

A moment we gave up everything for.

To birth our child in an abandoned cabin.

Alone.

Because we lied.

"Ow!" Ray screams, her hand squeezing mine in a tight grip. I manage to find my courage, placing a kiss to her hand. "One more time, baby."

I don't know if it'll take one more push or several, but I can see the head. It's almost over.

Ray braces herself, holding the backs of her thighs as I settle down between her legs.

And then she screams.

And screams some more as she pushes a floppy infant out into my arms.

Suddenly, everything is silent.

There are no cries.

Not from me.

Not from her.

Not from our newborn son.

Everything is just silent.

"Duke?"

She says my name as a plea, and I jump into action, placing the baby on the floor, using all the knowledge I learned to prepare for our baby and the delivery. I start CPR, clearing his airways, blowing into his tiny mouth, watching for his chest to rise.

Seconds pass, but he still doesn't cry. "Ray," I say between breaths. "I need you to reach for my phone and call an ambulance."

"No," she starts crying. "Don't say that. He's okay. Duke—"

"Duke—I mean, Dr. Potter." A hand lands on my shoulder, and I jerk to attention, smothering the lingering screams in my head.

"Yes?" I flash the woman carrying a tray of drinks a smile. "I'm sorry. You were saying?"

She offers me a drink, and I take it, downing it in one go before grabbing another and repeating the process.

"I asked if I could bring you anything else?"

I guess I look like I need a hug, and honestly, I do, but not from her.

A fiery redhead is the only thing I long to hold right now—the very one my host is marrying in a matter of hours.

"Anyway," Langston continues, speaking to his hoard of soulless colleagues, "once I'm back from the honeymoon, we'll discuss."

I have no idea what they were discussing, but I don't need to know.

I've heard enough.

He plans to "tame" my Sunny Ray.

And whatever Ray has gotten herself into, it's my duty to get her out.

I owe her that much.

Better yet, *I love her* that much.

Pulling out my phone, I open her unopened texts, not bothering to read any. I'm sure they are all variations of pleas and threats. Everything that will make my cock rock-hard in seconds. Best to let those texts stay a mystery.

Me: How are the strippers over your way?

It takes maybe two seconds for her to open the message before the chat bubble appears.

Sunny Ray: They're great. Mike has been very generous with his hands.

I smile. She's so full of shit I can smell it from here.

Me: Really? Did you tell him not to go close to the backs of your thighs? The pig snort when you laugh may scare him. He has a family to feed. He doesn't need a sprained ankle or months of therapy because you forgot to warn him of the danger zone.

Sunny Ray: I do not snort like a pig when I laugh.

Yeah, she does. Especially when she's not trying to be a proper congressman's daughter.

Me: I distinctly remember the time I thought pigs had invaded the den, only to realize you were watching an episode of "Friends".

Sunny Ray: Have you had too much to drink with Langston? Is that why you're suddenly so social?

I can feel the bitterness from here. I love it.

Me: Maybe. Maybe I just wanted to know you missed me.

Sunny Ray: Duke.

THE SCULPTOR

Me: Ray.

Sunny Ray: What do you want me to say? That I really do miss you. That I've missed you since the day they split us up.

I swallow. *Yes, that's exactly what I want to know. But more than that…*

Me: I want to know if you've forgiven me.

Her response takes longer this time, and something swirls in my gut—fear. It's not that I haven't wanted to call her since that winter. I tried. But every time, I feared what her father would say if he caught her speaking to me.

And then I just feared what *she* would say.

Once she went home alone.

Did she blame me?

I did.

I should have known that two kids couldn't deliver a baby on their own in some abandoned cabin with only the internet as a guide.

But we believed we could do anything back then.

It was us against the world.

We thought that, with enough planning and our collective knowledge, we could get through anything. Even lying to our parents that we had the abortion.

So, we ran away and lived off odd jobs.

We would have our baby and be a family like we always dreamed.

But that winter, I killed our dream.

Ramsey trusted me to keep them safe.

And I failed her.

I couldn't live with myself. I expected the same reaction from her.

I feared hearing the words come from her lips. Lips that I loved. Lips that read books to our son and sang hymns in the blistering cold.

I deserved to be hated. I still do. But I need to know if there's a possibility that she could set me free.

I need to know if she forgives me for killing our souls.

Glancing at my phone, I see her response, and something like a sob catches in my throat.

Sunny Ray: I never blamed you. I loved you.

It's then, reading her text for the third time, that I realize I'm at the wrong party.

Me: Then let me spend the last few hours with you. Let me remember what it was like to laugh.

To love. To cry. To hold you. Let me remember what it was like to love under the warmth of your sun.

But I don't say any of that. Instead, I sit tense and sick. But then the message appears, and suddenly, I'm free. I know exactly what I need to do.

Sunny Ray: Okay. 467 Crescent Blvd.

Langston Albrecht won't get the opportunity to tame my girl.
I've waited many winters.
Paid my dues.
Cried my tears.
Grieved my son.
I will no longer grieve his mother, too.
She is—and always will be—mine.
Because she promised me a life.
And I'm back to collect.

CHAPTER THIRTEEN

Ramsey

I stopped counting after the sixth Sangria.

"Hey, Ramsey. Are you in some kind of trouble?"

I flash Mike a severe frown. "Not for another few hours. Why?"

Mike, my bartender for the evening, pops the top of the beer in his hand and slides it to the guy next to me. "Because there's a guy by the door who's been staring at you for the last ten minutes, and he doesn't look very happy."

I grin. "Does he also look wealthy and pretentious but has this jawline that could crack the bar nuts without much effort?"

Mike rolls his eyes. "So, what you're saying is, you know him?"

I shrug. "Depends. Does this guy look more like he wants to hug me or more like he wants to throw me over his shoulder and run?"

Because if Duke is in alpha mode, this bachelorette party will be over before it begins. And I can't afford Duke to drag me out of here and mess up things with Langston.

I'm so freaking close.

With an awkward round of slow blinks filling the silence, Mike finally turns and says, "You know what? I don't get paid enough for this shit. Scream if you need me."

With that, he moves down the bar to help another customer, leaving me with the thrill of knowing my brooding Dr. Potter has arrived.

To spend my last hours as a single woman with me.

It shouldn't have come to this.

I should have found the information I was looking for, but nothing ever works out like it's supposed to. Duke and I know that all too well.

But this time is different.

This time, I have hope.

And right now, that's all I'm holding on to.

I can make things right.

I can restore our hearts.

I can lead us *home*.

"I believe we've been here before." I feel the warmth of his breath on my neck, wrapping me in a blanket of contentment as my eyes close on their own.

"Have we?" I smile, opening my eyes but not looking back.

"We have," Duke answers brusquely. "Recently even." His forearms suddenly appear at my sides as he cages me between his body and the bar. The restraint contained in his tight muscles is not to be messed with as he continues, his voice low and controlled when he says, "We have a problem, Ray."

I act like I don't know this territorial mood of his. "And what problem would that be, Dr. Potter?"

There's so much I want to say to him right now—so much I want to do.

But that's not the plan.

And the plan can't fail.

Not now.

Because Duke might hear my screams, but all I hear is his silence.

It lives in me like poison, running through my veins, killing me slowly.

I watched the light fade from Duke's eyes.

I witnessed the medics trying to shake the answers from his eighteen-year-old body as he fought to simply breathe.

He couldn't speak.

The doctors called it post-traumatic stress disorder.

I called it watching someone's soul die.

And I caused it.

I begged him to run away.

I begged him to lie.

And he did because he loved me.

He wanted to know if I had forgiven him, but the bigger question was, have I forgiven myself for pulling him down with me?

My current answer? No.

But if I can right my wrong with this thing with Langston? Yes. I think I can forgive myself for putting him through hell.

Because, this time, I can save him.

"The problem, Ray"—those strong arms of his move in closer, letting me know that running is out of the question—"is that we're in a country western bar, and you're not dancing."

I can't contain my smile. "That is a big problem," I agree. "Tell me, Dr. Potter, do you still suck at line dancing?"

His lips brush the shell of my ear. "Let's see."

Without warning, Duke hauls me off the bar stool, his forearms on full display as he leads us to the center of the bar, where a group of people are already dancing in their cowboy boots.

"I never thought you'd look out of place here," I muse as Duke tips his imaginary cowboy hat in my direction.

"Oh, yeah?" He grins, his feet moving in sequence with the other dancers without error. "You saying I'm not southern enough for you anymore?"

Oh, he's southern enough. He might not say y'all anymore or wear those flannel shirts, but here, under the chic barn lights, that southern charm shines brighter than I remember.

He grabs my hand, and I squeal as he dips me—dangling me over his arm like I weigh nothing. "Promise me something, Ray," he dares.

"What?"

I'm not that stupid. This isn't my first rodeo with Duke Potter. Never trust that smile.

"Promise you'll forgive me."

Oh.

I reach up, cupping the back of his neck. "I already told you. I've forgiven you."

His smile widens as he jerks me up, flush against his body. "Good. Now let's celebrate, Ms. Ford. Tomorrow, you'll be a married woman."

I should have known better.

I sprint to the only open door I can find in the strange hotel room and drop in front of the toilet, heaving violently.

I don't know how many drinks Duke and I had, but apparently, it was enough to be classified as one of those blackout nights, which isn't all that upsetting. I wanted to forget I was marrying Langston and leaving the love of my life for an unknown amount of time—again.

But I wanted to remember what it was like to dance in Duke's arms and have him tease me mercilessly about stepping on his shoes. More than that, though, I wanted to enjoy just being with him after all these years of longing.

If I was ever unsure about the void Duke left in my heart, last night answered that question.

I was fulfilled—more whole than I've been since that winter when I lost them both.

"I have a feeling I made some really poor decisions last night," I mutter to the toilet, resting my head on the edge.

"Depends on how you look at it."

A familiar hand appears at my side, clutching a towel, and I don't even question why he's here. Because all I can think is… *oh, fuck*.

"What is that?" I point at Duke's hand as it offends me.

"Well," he says with a smirk, "it's been a while since I've seen one, so I can't be positive, but I think it's a wedding band."

Fear settles in my stomach, churning up more acid—but that might be the brandy from last night's sangrias. "And why is a wedding band on *your* finger?"

Duke holds up his hand as if enjoying this exchange, carefully inspecting the titanium band like it's a prized treasure. "I think it's probably the same reason why there's one on yours. We got hitched, Ray. And I must say, you sure know how to woo a man."

Nausea forgotten, I whip my hand between us and… sob.

"Oh, my gosh," I cry at the sight of the ring on my finger.

It's not just any ring.

It's *the* ring.

The one he proposed with all those years ago. "You found it," I say softly.

And he kept it.

Duke's throat bobs as his words betray his emotions. "I couldn't leave it."

Because I had taken it off when my hands started swelling in that final month, leaving it at the cabin when emergency services took us away, leaving Duke to handle the questions.

I nod my head, understanding the pain in his voice.

He couldn't leave it, just like I couldn't leave him. They had to force me from his arms that night. He was in shock. Even at eighteen, I knew that. He wouldn't speak to me—he could only look at the infant in my arms—his son.

The son he breathed life into.

The son he saved.

And the son he inevitably lost.

This is no ordinary man.

Duke Potter is no Langston. He's not even an Astor or a Vance.

Duke is something wholly different.

And there is nothing that I won't do for him.

He says he couldn't leave it behind.

Neither could I.

But I'm not talking about a ring.

"It's still as beautiful as I remember," I muse, tracing the heart-shaped gem.

His heart.

It had become our thing, and he made sure I never forgot it by sliding this ring on my finger that winter.

"Oh my goodness, Duke! What are you doing? Are you getting on one knee?"

I don't know if it's panic or excitement or the fact that I can't see past my belly that has me asking such silly questions, but what I know for sure is that I love Duke Potter with every shallow breath I take.

"You're ruining this for me, Ray," he teases. "I practiced and everything."

Because that's what he does—he prepares.

"I'm sorry," I say, waving my hand between us, "please continue."

The grin he flashes me would get him pushed if I could move faster. "Are you sure? I can wait a little longer. Maybe when we retire will work?"

"Shut up and ask me like you rehearsed."

Because I love nothing more than knowing he wanted to get this just right—even if I ruined it by asking a dumb question.

Duke clears his throat, his expression turning serious as his gaze rakes over me with those beautiful hazel eyes full of silent promises. "Ramsey Ford. I can't offer you kingdoms and diamonds."

Tears are already streaking down my face.

"But what I can offer is all I have—love."

He pulls out the box, cracking it open and plucking out the ring before I can see it.

"I know I've placed such a burden on your shoulders this year. You were supposed to enjoy senior year like all the other girls in your class—not snowed in a cabin, concealing a pregnancy."

I want to stop him right there—to take away his guilt, but it would be useless. This is not an argument I've ever been able to win. Duke feels responsible that I got pregnant—but it took both of us to get here, and I don't regret a thing.

I stroke the side of his smooth face. "All I've ever wanted is to be with you. Don't let guilt cheapen what we have." I rub my belly, feeling our child squirm under my touch. "Because what we have is real."

Swallowing, his hands come up and lay over mine, caressing the child we created together.

"Okay, Ray. We'll do it your way."

He kisses my bare belly where I recently finished painting a heart. "Ramsey Ford, I promise you my life and future. Marry me, and let's build a life worth fighting for."

Because that's what we've done.

We've fought for our lives.

We've fought for our baby.

And we've fought for our family.

I hold out my hand and nod. "I promise you my life, Duke Potter—and a future we deserve."

Boys like Duke don't deserve a simple yes. They deserve a promise.

When he grins and slides the ring on my finger, I know I will spend the rest of my life with the honor of carrying his most prized possessions—his heart and his child.

I choke on my tears, remembering the day that felt like magic was in the air. We made declarations and voiced our dreams, and then he sealed them inside me with his sweet love, willing them to come true.

It was a night I wouldn't forget.

And apparently, neither did Duke. "Who knew you could be so convincing, Ray?" he continues, unaware of my trip down memory lane. "Here I thought you wanted to marry the congressman." He looks smug and not nearly as hungover as I am. "But instead, you marry me on the eve of your wedding night. What's a man to think?"

"A man is supposed to—" I stop, sudden realization setting in. Duke seems mighty cool about all of this for someone who should be hungover and in shock. "You did this on purpose, didn't you?"

He doesn't react. The steady tic of his jaw is the only indication he's even breathing.

"Yeah, you did." I press my finger into his chest, standing. "Tell me, Duke. Was I the only one drunk enough not to realize what I agreed to?"

"You agreed years ago," he snaps, snatching my finger and clutching it to his chest instead. "You promised me a life, and I collected."

"You collected?" I scream—full-on scream—in outrage. "I'm not some trophy you collect at the end of a game, Duke!"

"You're right," his voice rises. "You *are* my fucking life, and I want it back! I will not have you jeopardizing your safety on some hair-brained revenge pact—or whatever it is you're doing with Langston."

"It's not a stupid revenge pact!" Tears fall down my face in waves. "I'm doing this for us!"

"Doing *what* for us, Ray?"

I snap my lips together. This cannot happen—all this work, all the time, only for it to end like this. "I'm so close," I cry out. "We can fix this with Langston," I chant erratically. "We'll apologize. He'll keep it out of the media, annul the marriage, and the wedding can move forward as planned."

Duke goes tense under my hand, and I'm not prepared for his threat. "I'm not *fixing* anything, Ray. You owe me a life. You can file the annulment paperwork if you decide that's not enough for you anymore."

Dropping my hand, Duke steps back, disappointment drowning the sharp features of his face.

"But know, if that's the route you choose, I'll make sure my attorney buries you in motions for months. By then, your congressman will have moved on to a new punching bag. But guess what, Ray?" He smiles, but it's wicked. "It won't be you."

I can already feel Duke's absence before he leaves the bathroom.

Cold.

Distant.

Detached.

I've finally severed the last line to his heart.

He's letting me go.

And there's nothing worth that pain—not even the secret I'm keeping.

I reach for his shirt, barely grabbing on as he backs away. "Langston knows where he is!"

Duke pauses, silence filling the small space around us. "Langston knows where *who* is, Ray?"

"I tried to protect you. I wanted to be sure before I brought you into this fight." I drop his shirt and crumble to the floor as gut-wrenching sobs take over. "But you just couldn't let it go. You couldn't trust me."

"What are you protecting me from, Ray?" His voice sounds softer, comforting, like he's handling someone unstable as he squats down.

Maybe I am unstable, but the fact remains the same. "You saved our son that night," I say carefully as Duke springs up, already backing up like I spit on him.

"No, I didn't," he argues. "He died at the hospital."

Tears streak from my eyes as I watch him battle the images we both lived with. The doctor coming out and shaking his head. Me falling to the floor. And Duke... standing motionless.

I reach out for his hand, but he doesn't take it. He's looking at me like I'm a stranger, not the mother of his child or the love of his life. "No, Ray. You're wrong. You're confused. Jude died."

"I'm not wrong," I tell him, with every fiber of my being. "Our son is alive, Duke. And Langston knows where he is."

CHAPTER FOURTEEN

Ramsey

"I know what you're thinking," I plead as he steps back, shutting me out with bitter coldness. "And I get it. You have no right to trust what I'm saying or the source of this information. We both know I didn't have a good relationship with my parents."

I hated my father for forcing me to be his political prop and my mother for allowing it.

"But you should know that I kept your promise."

Tears streak down my face as I follow Duke into the room. "You asked me to remember, and I did. I remembered the family we had and the family we lost."

I hit my chest with my palm—passion coursing through me like a tsunami. "I remembered, Duke! Me! I didn't move on. I didn't quit because I remembered!"

I'm breathing heavily, watching the twitch in Duke's hand. I can't tell if he wants to reach for me or cover my mouth. Either way, it's my turn to talk.

"I came back for you!"

This time, I scream. "I played the part of the congressman's dutiful daughter. I showed up. I smiled and shook hands, but I never forgot. When you were in rehab, I was with you!" I tap my chest. "I was with you here. I never left you—not once. But your brothers…"

I shake my head, remembering Vance's stern warning. *"If you love him, let him move on. Your presence will only remind him of his addiction."*

Vance had thought Duke was in rehab for an addiction to pain meds that he reportedly stole from his father's office. But he wasn't. We did steal supplies and medicines, but it was never pain medication or an addiction. We only took what we thought we might need to deliver a baby on our own: fluids, antibiotics, and the like. The pain med addiction story was concocted by our fathers to account for why we missed the last few months of school and ran away.

Two drug-addicted kids getting high apparently made better headlines than two teenagers running away to have a baby alone because they lied and told their fathers they aborted it.

"Vance thought me coming back into your life would set you back," I tell him, "but still…" I suck in a breath, gathering my strength. "But still, I stayed with you through the winter, painting you from afar. You delivering pizzas. You studying for finals."

I was a super stalker back then, watching Duke in college.

But that's what you do for the people you love. He was hurting. So was I. I only wanted to be close to him.

A tear drips down my hand. "I was with you—until the spring."

I swallow, remembering the blonde who started showing up to sit with him, helping him study. He never spoke, but then it happened— he smiled at her.

"I knew Vance was right. You would never move on when I constantly reminded you of what you lost." Shrugging, I offer Duke a sad smile. "So, I decided I would set you free. I moved to France that spring, and I never returned until a few months ago, when my mother fell ill."

I don't know when Duke stepped closer, but he's moved, though he's yet to speak.

"In her final weeks, I sat by her bed drawing—painting you—sketching *our son*. What I thought he would look like if he had lived."

Duke flinches, and I quickly continue. "And on her final night, my mom started sobbing. Telling me so many things she regretted—secrets that killed her to keep." I fight the twitch in my lip. "She thought she was doing the right thing by giving us a second chance at a future. She thought we would recover and move on, but I didn't. I couldn't. Because all I felt was lost without you both."

My gaze drops to the ring on my finger. "She told me my drawing was wrong. That his eyes were brown, his cheeks chubbier than how I drew them." I wipe away a tear. "We sat that night, and she told me everything she could remember. What he looked like—how he sounded. I drew twenty-three versions of him, writing down the only information she knew: Langston had handled the adoption."

I can't stop the tears now. They fall in droves, relentlessly purging the painful secret. "She said she held him, rocking him to sleep until Langston came and took him away."

I chance a look at Duke to see if he's even breathing and instead, see wetness on his cheeks. "She said Langston knew a couple who wanted a child badly—so they—" I choke on a sob. "So, our parents forged our names, and Langston covered it up."

Holding my head up, I face the only man I've ever loved. "You want to know why I would volunteer to be Langston's punching bag? To marry such a shitty human being?"

With everything I have, I grit out the words. "Because he has our son! And I'm done asking for fucking permission. I want my boy, and I will crawl through hell to get him. There's nothing I won't do to bring him home."

Cautiously, I take a few steps forward and take Duke's hand. "Let me finish this. Give me the annulment, and let me bring our son home. I promise I won't fail."

At that, Duke seems to snap out of it and jerks his hand from mine.

He takes a shaky breath and gives me one last lingering look. And then he leaves.

It's been half an hour since Duke returned to the hotel room, threw two bottles of water and pain relievers on the bed, and locked himself in the bathroom.

I'm no fool. I know those waters and meds are his way of apologizing.

He didn't need to say no to my plea for an annulment. I could see it in his eyes. I know the boy behind those eyes. The way he clenches his jaw when he's determined. And the finality of his voice when he won't change his mind.

And that look he flashed me before leaving—the one that said, *I hear you, but it's too late*—was evidence enough.

He had made his decision.

The thing is, I'm not even surprised by it.

I knew Duke wouldn't annul the marriage. That's not his style. Mistake or not, Duke is committed. Where I take issue is him ultimately not including me in his plans.

I searched online this morning, and nothing has been mentioned about our impromptu marriage.

That means we have time to act before Langston hears about it. I don't know if Langston knows I am looking for my son, but something tells me he's not that stupid. That's why I endured everything he dished out. I wanted Langston to think I was broken—to believe I was nothing. With time, he would have dropped his guard, and I would have found some evidence of where he sent my son.

Or, Langston could be that stupid and doesn't even remember my son or me. Worst-case scenario, he has nothing to point me toward who adopted my baby.

Either way, I have to know.

Duke needs to know.

He deserves to move on truly, not only with a fancy car and medical degree.

I need him to see past his pain right now.

"Duke?" I finally gather the courage and knock on the door. "Can I come in?"

He doesn't answer, which concerns me more than usual.

This is precisely what I was afraid of. I wanted to protect him—I did. I didn't want him to be part of this until I knew what happened to our son.

Cracking open the door, I find the shower running, and there, forehead on the tile, water pelting down onto his back, stands the most beautiful, broken man I've ever seen.

I don't ask if I can join him.

I don't know if he would even hear me in his state.

This is not the Duke full of wit and charm—this one hides behind the snark and smiles, crumbling amongst the screams.

This Duke doesn't need an argument. He needs silence.

And I can give him that.

Slipping off my clothes, I step around his discarded phone and open the shower door, easing in behind him.

He never acknowledges me, even when I press against his back and loop my arms around his chest. For a moment, all we do is breathe.

In and out.

In and out.

Something that should be instinct.

But not now.

Not since everything has changed.

"Let me suffer with you," I beg him quietly.

Because that's what we've done since we've parted.

We've suffered alone—loving each other from afar as we've battled our demons and grieved the family we could never have.

"Let me quiet the screams."

Duke turns in my arms, his eyes vacant and streaked with red. He doesn't speak, but he doesn't need to. Nothing needs to be said—he needs to feel.

He needs to know that he's no longer alone—neither of us are.

Taking his hand, I move it to the heart on my chest.

His heart.

The one I've kept all these years is the one I refuse to give back.

"You should know," he says, his voice husky, "I won't give you an annulment."

I chuckle, placing my hands on his wet cheeks, moving the dark hair off his forehead. "I know."

I gently kiss his lips, feeling him for the first time in years. "But that's not what concerns me right now."

He does.

His forehead comes to rest gently against mine. "Hey," I say softly. "Look at me." As he told me all those years ago, I remind him, "It's just you and me."

Slowly, his head tips back, his eyes finding mine under the spray of water. "It's just you and me against the world."

It's always just been him and me.

Suddenly, like a weight being lifted, Duke sucks in a deep breath.

"Yeah, that's it," I coax. "Breathe with me."

And he does, letting his hand drift down from my chest to the few faded stretch marks on my hips. Lingering there, he traces the lines as if memorizing them, but then he lowers to his knees.

At first, I think he's collapsing, but then his hands grip my hips as he leans forward, kissing the faint marks. My hands go to his hair as he drags his lips over the scars I bear from carrying our child.

He kisses the top one, his hands trembling around me.

"Breathe, baby," I remind him, trying to step back and out of his grip.

But apparently, he doesn't need my help.

His hands lock around me, and suddenly, his mouth is at my center—at my core—when he growls, "You remember to fucking breathe."

It's the only warning he gives before his mouth closes over me.

CHAPTER FIFTEEN

Duke

I don't give her time to prepare before I steal her breath, shoving my tongue so far into her tight pussy that the only thing she can do is hang on as I stretch her open.

I'm done having pieces of her.

I'm done not being inside her, soaking up all her goodness.

All this time…

All the hope…

All the pain…

She carried it all.

For us—for our family.

Even when I wanted to block that winter from my memory, she remembered.

And now, she'll pay the price by binding her life to mine—forever.

"Duke," Ramsey all but moans. "We should talk about this."

Yeah, no. We're done talking.

"Go ahead," I tell her, thrusting two fingers inside, feeling her clench around me. It's the first time I've genuinely smiled since waking up this morning. "But, we both know how well you do with multitasking."

Scissoring my fingers, I nip at her clit, sucking the sensitive flesh with a vengeance. If she manages to speak through this, I'll beat my own ass.

"You're."

She moans.

"Not."

I suck harder, rocking my hand against her faster until she whimpers, pulling at my hair in frustration.

Yeah, now she's done talking.

We're *both* done talking.

There is no negotiation. No further conversations. Nothing will change my mind. This woman is done.

Ramsey Ford's fate is sealed.

She. Is. Mine.

Feeling her concede, I ease up, kissing a path up her stomach until I meet her gaze. "I'm okay, Ray," I assure her earlier concern.

Just knowing Langston won't put his hands on her quiets the screams.

Nodding, she threads her hands gently through my hair. "What can I do to help you, then?"

Closing my eyes, I remember the last night I spent loving her. "You can let me make love to my wife."

It's the most open and honest thing I can say right now.

"Will you give me that, Ray? Will you let me love you?"

Loving her will never be enough for what she's done for us, but right now, when I'm broken and vulnerable, I just want to bathe in her strength and not think about our pain.

Her hands smooth down my face, cupping my cheeks. Those brilliant green eyes lock on to mine and like the seasons never passed between us, she smiles. "Love your wife, Dr. Potter, and claim the life you're owed."

It's everything I need to hear as I hitch her up my waist and turn off the shower, watching as the water drips down her forehead.

For a moment, all we do is stand there, just breathing—taking each other in.

"I want you to know," I finally say, breaking the silence, "I never stopped loving you."

She smiles, and I've never seen anything truer. "And I you."

We don't make it to the bed.

Slamming her back against the tile, I apologize. "I wanted to love you sweetly," I admit. "I wanted to move slow—reclaim every second we were apart."

She shakes her head like she couldn't care less, reaching between our bodies for my cock. "We have forever," she assures me, lining up my bare cock with her opening. "But for now, Dr. Potter…"

I fight the urge to surge forward as she continues.

"You should know I've only *ever* dreamed of being Mrs. Potter. Not an artist. Not a mother. Just your wife."

Yeah, fuck being a gentleman. Her declaration severed the last of my resolve.

I thrust forward, ramming my cock to the hilt and stealing our breath.

Ray shifts, trying to alleviate the ache, but I clamp down on her hips. "Don't," I bark. "Let me feel everything." I've been deprived of her for so many years. I want every stretch, every bite of pain, as her body remembers where it belongs—around me.

We are two halves of a whole.

We haven't thrived.

We haven't grown.

But not anymore.

Now, we are complete.

And for the first time in nearly two decades, I lean forward and kiss my Sunny Ray.

Her lips part on an exhale as my tongue sweeps in, claiming, memorizing, taking all that she has.

I take the moment when my lips touched hers all those years ago.

I take the moment when we decided to run away with our son.

I take the fall and winter we spent in a cabin, watching her belly grow.

I take the moment she birthed our son.

But ultimately, I take the seasons when she stayed—loving me from afar.

This is what it was supposed to be like all those years ago—her in my arms, my cock buried inside her as she opened around me. Her soul was meant for mine—the missing warmth that created contentment.

I've never felt more loved than I have under this woman's smile.

Inching forward, I try burying myself deeper inside her. It's torture—I can't get close enough—and by the bite of her hold, she knows it, too.

"Duke," she says breathlessly, pulling back, "you gotta move, okay?"

I grin, but it's pained. All I want to do is crawl inside this woman and claim every inch. There will never be another Langston. No one will ever get close to taking this woman from me again.

I don't know if she sees the resolve in my eyes, or she's just saving herself from being a cock decoration, but her hands move to the back of my neck, her eyes gleaming with mischief when she leans in, parting my lips with another torturous swipe of her tongue.

I groan, readjusting as I hitch her up, inadvertently moving her up and down on my cock.

The motion sets off something chaotic inside—a need to claim.

"Oh, yes," she chants.

I slam her against the wall, the muscles in my arms engaging as I thrust her up and down on my cock as she matches the rhythm against my mouth.

It's sloppy.

It's uncoordinated.

And it doesn't last nearly as long as I hoped.

"I'm gonna come," she screams, which I ignore, keeping with the punishing pace. I'm there, too, but I fight off the urge to release into her sweet center.

"Duke." Her hands hold my face, forcing me to look at her. "Let go, baby," she says softly. "We have forever now."

She kisses my lips, and I taste the sweet goodness I've mourned for many years. It washes over me like a cleansing rain, showering me with new resolve and hope for the future we lost.

And when I finally let go in a random hotel shower, all I can think is…

We've been here before.

But this time, no one will pry her from my arms.

"You don't need to take care of me," I fuss as she dries my hair with a towel.

After we made love, or whatever that was in the shower, she convinced me to get out and dry off.

I thought she meant so we could have dry sex, but that hasn't been the case. Yet.

"I know I don't need to take care of you," she responds, "but I want to. Will you deny me the right to care for my husband?"

Well, fuck, not when she turns my words against me. "I suppose not," I agree. "But you could at least put me inside you while you do it."

She doesn't need her pussy to dry my hair.

"Will that help you talk about what we're going to do about Langston?"

I shrug, lying back against the pillows, naked. "We can always try and see what happens. You never know what might make me chatty."

She laughs but climbs over my hips, hovering just where I want her. "Now, tell me what's going on in that pretty head of yours, Dr. Potter."

Gah, her tits really are perfection—smooth, pear-shaped globes with pretty pink nipples, which are currently at attention for me.

Langston was such a fucker, wanting to change them.

I reach out to stroke the nipple that is now mine, but Ray stops me, catching my hand before it can take purchase. "We need a plan, Duke. What are we going to do about Langston now that you refuse…"

I grin. "Now that I refuse to share?"

I smack her hand away and grab her hips, yanking her up my chest, her pussy hovering dangerously close to my greedy mouth.

"Yeah." She breathes heavily. "He'll come for your practice—for you. He won't take it lightly that you made him look bad."

I did more than make him look bad. I married his fiancée.

Inhaling the scent that is my wife, I grin. "Gah, I really fucking hope so."

She slaps my chest. "I'm serious, Duke. What are we going to do?"

At that, my face turns serious. "*We* aren't going to do anything. You're tapping out of this fight."

"I'll be damned," she says with outrage, trying to wiggle off me, but my grip is too tight.

"You did your part, Ray. You carried this burden and fought with honor. You kept our family's memory alive." I secretly love the glare she pins me with. "Now, you have to share the battle. It's my turn."

"This is our battle. *Ours*, not yours alone," she insists.

Sitting up, I hold her angry fists to my chest. "Tell me something, Ray."

I wait for her to calm down and relax before I continue.

"What happens if we find Jude, and he's had a wonderful life with his adopted family?"

She shakes her head, but I keep moving forward. These are hard questions, but ones we must ask ourselves before we pursue this adventure—Langston's involvement or not.

"What if he doesn't want to see us? What if he doesn't know he's adopted or wants nothing to do with us? What will you do then?"

A tear streaks down her face, and we watch it fall to my stomach. "Then I'll let him go, knowing he's happy and lived a good life, despite not knowing us."

I arch a brow.

"What?" she snaps. "You don't believe me?"

"I didn't say that. I just want to know that once this is over, and we find our son one way or another, will you still feel the same about *our* relationship if we walk away without Jude?"

She may have held on to a dream all these years, but what happens when that dream doesn't become a reality?

"Because I won't set you free, Ray. I'm selfish enough to keep you in either scenario. But I want to know if there is hope that you could love me without him in our lives?"

Because I've seen his death certificate.

I've seen where his ashes are scattered.

Holly Ford might have lived with guilt over her relationship with her daughter.

But did she really conspire with Congressman Ford and Harrison Potter?

Did they really decide for us?

Did they sell our son for the sake of a predestined future?

I wouldn't put anything past them.

But hope is a dangerous thing, and the last thing I want to do is put Ramsey through more than she's already endured.

"Oh, Duke." Ramsey's voice pulls my gaze up to hers. "In no world will I ever not love you." She leans down and kisses my mouth. "Whether we find Jude or not, my heart will always belong to you."

Leaning over, she grabs the hotel pen from the nightstand and pushes me back against the pillow. "Is forever still enough for you, Dr. Potter?"

I nod, carefully watching her hand descend to my chest. I don't need to see what she's drawing. I know it's my heart as soon as she finishes and places the pen in my hand, guiding it back to her chest.

"Claim our future," she demands, "no matter what it is."

And I do, drawing the same shitty heart I painted onto her chest years ago before throwing the pen to the floor and flipping her beneath me.

"Promise me," I tell her, settling between her hips, "that you will not see Langston without me."

I cut her a stern look—one that says I have no reservations about tying her ass up if need be. "You can stay in this fight, but you're sitting this round out."

She glares at me under her long lashes. "And if I don't?"

Really, she doesn't have a choice, but being the gentleman I am, I sheath my cock inside her for added clarification. "Then you better get used to my company." I thrust forward so she knows I plan to keep her very busy.

"Are you threatening me with sex?" She laughs. "Spoiler alert, that's more like a consolation prize."

I grin, leaning down and sucking one deliciously pert nipple into my mouth. "Not sex, sweetheart—a honeymoon."

Because I already set off the shitstorm of the century.

She just doesn't know it yet.

CHAPTER SIXTEEN

Duke

Dear Congressman Albrecht,

You have something of ours, and if you want to keep his mother's heartbreaking Christmas plea off the national news, I suggest you provide us with the documents sooner rather than later.
As you know, my wife and I love nothing more than a juicy scandal.

Merry Christmas,

Dr. and Mrs. Duke Potter

It is a straightforward email—one that I hope Langston will take seriously, considering he was likely standing at the altar, awkward and alone, while Ray and I were on a flight back to Texas, settling her into her new home. But since I'm not dealing with the most moral of men, I doubt embarrassment and threats will make much of an impact. Still, I hit send on the email all the same. Hopefully, with only a few days until Christmas, Langston will have plenty of time to catch up on his emails and figure out where the hell his fiancée is hiding.

It's his move now.

And my move, apart from buying out the paint store and threatening Ray an obscene number of times to stay in the house, is to go to the office on the week we are closed for the holidays and ruin my brother's Christmas.

Vance and most of the staff are here, catching up on filing and inventory before we close for the Christmas holidays. Vance might be a workaholic, but even he has a small amount of holiday spirit, which I'm hoping is more abundant today.

Because telling him I'm a married man will undoubtedly bring out the grinch.

Fortunately, I've been here for two hours and have yet to cross paths with Vance. He's been suspiciously tied up in the operating room, counting "inventory" with Halle, per his unhelpful assistant, Remington.

With Astor still on paternity leave with his daughter, things here at the office are relatively quiet—meaning no one is working, including me.

"Are you naked?" I ask conspiratorially, holding the phone closer to my ear.

Ray laughs. "No. Are *you* naked?"

"Not yet, but the day is young." The minute I make Vance blow a blood vessel, I'm out of here, begging my poor wife to make up for a shitty day with naked time.

I'm not seeing a downside to marriage.

Granted, it's only been forty-eight hours since becoming a married man, but so far, I can eat, sleep, and fuck my wife whenever the mood strikes—which has been considerably often. As in hourly.

"Is that what you do before the holidays? Get naked at work?"

I stare at the inside of my forearm, where I woke Ray up at four a.m. for her to draw her heart somewhere I could see it. There's a tiny *Fucker* written underneath it, but I think it only adds charm. She didn't need the sleep. She needed to be tired so that any idea of leaving or calling Langston would seem exhausting at the mere thought.

I'm nothing if not thorough.

But still, just in case, I deleted Langston's contact information from her phone and put a tracking app on it instead. That doesn't mean she can't find his email or call someone else, but I'm hoping she won't. I'm praying her good morals will prevent her from reneging on her promise to sit this one out—which she only agreed to after I showed her the email I sent to Langston.

There is nothing she can do at this point but wait—and paint—and make love to her husband. Let's not forget that last one. We have nearly two decades to make up for.

Besides, if Langston has documents that contradict Jude's death certificate, then we'll really have an issue.

But right now, I don't know what the real issue is.

I don't know the truth. There are so many possibilities that could have happened.

Langston might not have kept any record of the adoption. Worse yet, even if he did, our son might not have made it in this thing called life, anyway. For all we know, he could have died in a car accident or something else terribly tragic. Hell, Ray's mom could have been delirious and given her inaccurate information.

The possibilities are endless.

But one thing is certain right now: My wife is safe and healthy, and I can promise her that we will be reunited with our son, even if it's only through closure.

"Duke? Are you still there?" I shake off thoughts of Jude and try to put the smile back into my voice. "I'm sorry, I was just thinking of what I wanted for dinner."

"Stop." She chuckles. "I can barely move. I'm so sore from all your 'dinner requests.'"

This statement only makes me feel slightly bad. "I'll give you a massage when I get home."

"No thanks." She lets out this unladylike snort. "I know how massages end with you."

I grin.

"You spend ten minutes undressing me, five minutes lathering me in oil, two minutes actually massaging, and forty-five minutes fucking my brains out."

She acts like we've done this a few times.

"Fine." I chuckle. "We'll soak in the tub together. I'll bring home some bath salts." Which will still end up with her naked on my dick, but she doesn't need to know that. We'll let her live with that romantic dream of actually being cuddled without penetration.

"You lie, Duke Potter. But at least you're adorable about it."

"I try." I chuckle. She isn't falling for my bullshit. "But for real. I really do know what I want for dinner—in addition to your pussy."

"I need to see Dr. Potter!"

I pause, hearing the familiar voice out in the hallway.

"Oh, my gosh! Is that Langston?" Ray whispers on the phone like he's going to hear her.

"I need to call you back, sweetheart," I say, eyeing the red-faced man in the doorway. "Try not to paint anything pretty on that body until I can blow it dry."

"Duke!" Ignoring her pleas to know what's going on, I hang up.

She'll have to forgive me or punish me later. I'm down for either. Now, to deal with this asshole. "I'm sorry—"

"I'm sorry. Dr. Duke is in a meeting." Remington appears in front of my office door, cutting me off. "You'll have to see his assistant and schedule an appointment."

Langston balks. "I see him right there." He points at me, which doesn't faze Remington whatsoever.

He simply lights up a cigarette and takes a long drag. "I don't see anyone here except you."

Langston's face reddens, and I swear he's seconds from grabbing Remington, who, if I'm honest, looks like he wants him to.

"Dr. Potter," Langston addresses me over Remington's head, "I respect your stature in this community, and because of that, I'm giving you a chance to make this right."

He clears his throat, still blocked from coming into my office by the unruly teenager. "All you need to say is my fiancée is an intoxicated, gold-digging whore who fed you a lie and tricked you into marrying her."

Remington's brows rise. "A whore *and* a greedy bitch?" He casts me an amused smile. "Does she have a younger sister?"

I fight the urge to laugh. Instead, I focus on Langston being just like Congressman Ford when he found Ramsey and me that winter. It's always about their reputation. Women are props to them. They use them as sacrificial pawns to keep from tarnishing their name.

Standing, I walk around and lean against the front of my desk. "I'm afraid I can't do that, Congressman. While I loathe your offer, I'd rather face the consequences of my actions than lie and say *my wife* is anything but the incredible woman she is."

I look down at my hands, where the titanium band rests on my finger, a symbol that has no beginning or end. It's infinite, just like my love for Ray. "I married your ex-fiancée because she's *mine*. I sent you that threat because killing you for bruising her wouldn't give us the necessary information. My wife did not trick me into anything, sir. If anything, she saved your life. You're only as valuable as the time it takes me to find the answers I need."

Remington's eyes grow wide. "You like it rough, huh?" He moves in closer, chest to chest with Langston. "Funny, so do I."

I reach for the idiot and put my hand on his shoulder, feeling the vibration in his body. The last thing I need is us both causing more trouble for Vance. "My apologies for how things played out, Congressman. Ramsey and I wish you all the best. But the clock is ticking. I will follow up with my threat—and I think we both know media attention won't bode well for you."

Langston fumes, his body vibrating with fury, as spittle flies out of his mouth when he barks out, "If you think you can embarrass me by having my fiancée stand me up on my wedding day then you are sadly mistaken, Dr. Potter. Your threats don't scare me. I'll make sure you Potters never—"

"Hey, Hal!" Remington shouts over Langston's head like: A.) we aren't in a physician's office, and B.) Langston wasn't just threatening us from a foot away. "You wanna grab lunch?"

I can't hear what Halle says, but she must agree since Remington grins and refocuses on the man before us.

"Langford," he inhales, blowing the smoke back into our guest's face, "if you'll excuse us, we don't actually give a fuck what you do. But if it makes you feel better, I'll make a note for Dr. Duke to cry tonight while he's fucking your ex-fiancée."

He taps his cigarette, scattering ashes on Langston's suit. "Have a good day, and thank you for visiting Potter's Plastics. The ladies out front will stamp your parking ticket."

"Remington!"

Vance's voice booms down the hall, and Remington's smile rises. "He missed me."

This time, I can't stop the chuckle from escaping when Vance approaches us, his eyes scanning the threat in front of him. "Can I help you?"

"You sure can," Langston replies. "You can warn your brother that going to war with me will not end well for *any* of you."

"Oh, geez. Well, that fucking changes *everything*," Remington says sarcastically. "Give him back his fiancée, Duke. You can't play with her anymore. Otherwise, it'll end badly for *all* of us."

He shivers dramatically, which earns an eye roll from Vance. But then he realizes what Remington said and snaps to me. "What fiancée?"

Remington's brows arch, his gaze volleying between Vance and me comically.

"Congressman Albrecht is referring to his previous fiancée," I tell Vance truthfully, "otherwise now known as my wife."

There was no easing Vance into the idea. He has his reservations about Ray, and that's fine. I know the lies he was fed, and one day, when this is all over, I'll set the record straight with him.

Until then, all he needs to know is that Congressman Albrecht no longer has a fiancée.

"You married her?" His jaw ticks as he steps closer. "Ramsey," he clarifies. "You married Ramsey Ford."

I nod. "It's Ramsey Potter now, but yes. I married her."

"It seems like you boys have much to discuss." Langston points at me with a vicious smile before addressing Vance. "Dr. Potter, if I were you, I'd speak with your partner about threatening men in power." Langston's face changes to one that is wholly evil. "I'd hate for your patients to learn their precious surgeons hide away wicked deeds."

Meaning that Langston would have no issue making up something and leaking a lie to the public to take down Potter's Plastics.

"And we'd love nothing more than to shove that silver spoon up your ass until you choke on it," Remington adds, stepping up and shoving Vance back. "You don't want to threaten us, Langford. We eat that shit like pussy."

"Remington!" Vance explodes. "Leave, now!"

Remington manages to flash me a wink before knocking into Langston's shoulder as he pushes past him, disappearing down the hall.

"Congressman, is it?" Vance asks, his tone careful and controlled.

"Albrecht," Langston adds. "Congressman Albrecht."

Vance nods like he actually gives a fuck what his title is. "Well, Congressman, I'm not sure what misunderstanding you have with my brother, but let me assure you, if you so much as step foot in our practice again, I will make sure all my 'wicked deeds' begin at your doorstep. I don't take kindly to threats or assholes. Now, if you'll see yourself out before I lose my patience."

I offer Langston a parting smile. "I look forward to reviewing those documents, Congressman," I tell him, earning me a pointed glare from Vance.

"There are no documents, Dr. Potter. I told you, your wife is a liar."

CHAPTER SEVENTEEN

Ramsey

"You don't have to do this with me."

Duke whips around, his hair sticking up in several spots from where he's been pulling on it for the last half-hour. "Don't start with that shit again. I'm not in the mood to argue."

I sigh. "I'm not trying to fight with you. I just want you to really think about this. You have a future, Duke."

He snaps. "And you don't?"

I offer him a smile. "Being the future wife of a congressman isn't as exciting as saving lives. I think the world could live without my contribution a little more than they can yours."

I swear if I wasn't crumpled up on the bathroom floor, feeling like death, he would shake me. Instead, he squats down and takes my chin in his hand, forcing my eyes to his. "Every future is a contribution to this world, Ray—especially yours. Don't belittle your value. Your spirit brings more to this universe than any degree of mine could."

And this is how I'm pregnant with his child at eighteen years old.

"You're such a charmer, Duke Potter."

"Don't try to change the subject."

He's in no laughing mood. Got it.

Not that this moment calls for laughing, but still. His serious expression concerns me.

"I'm not changing the subject," *I say, tugging on his shirt, a subtle hint that he needs to come closer.*

He sighs but does as I want, sitting down and tucking me into his side, where this conversation should have started in the first place, but... morning sickness.

"You're meant to be a doctor, Duke. If you do this—if you run away with me—you might never achieve the future you've dreamt of."

His hands tighten around me. "You're the only future I dreamed of."

"Duke."

He's being ridiculous again. It's been an ongoing issue in this conversation.

"Ray."

"I'm serious," *I try again.*

I can feel him shrug. "So am I. I'm not leaving you, Ray. No matter how many times you give me this martyr speech. My future is you. We started this journey together, and together, we will finish it. You're not running away and having our baby without me."

Tears well in my eyes. I don't know what I did to be worthy of such a good man, but I know I will forever be grateful for him. "What about your brothers? Your father?"

"Fuck my father," *he whispers in my ear, tickling the hair at the back of my neck.* "And my brothers will understand... one day."

"You'll ruin your relationship with them, though."

Duke and his brothers are all so close in age. There's less than a year between each one of them, and their bond is as close as triplets. They connect on such a deeper level than any other siblings I've ever seen.

"They'll understand," *Duke repeats.* "Don't worry."

But I do worry.

I don't have siblings, so I don't have a bond like he has with Vance and Astor. But I know his brothers are important to him, and I'd never intentionally do anything to come between them.

"And if they don't, one day, understand?" *I try reasoning with him once more.*

"Ray." *He groans.* "I really don't want to have to put you in the trunk of my car. I'm sure fumes aren't good for a baby, but I will if you don't shut up."

I tip my head back and let out this deep belly laugh. This freaking man... "You're impossible."

He kisses my neck. "But you love me, anyway."

"That I do." *Sliding my arms over his like a united front, I ask him one last time,* "Are we really doing this?"

Those hazel eyes grow serious. "Yeah, Ray. We're really doing this." *He presses a kiss to my forehead.* "We're having a baby."

There are two ways to get information out of Duke Potter.

One, get naked.

And two, get *him* naked.

However, neither of those things are currently working.

"What did Vance say when you told him about the wedding?" I narrow my eyes. "The wedding I don't even remember."

Duke offers me a sad smile. "I'll make it up to you. Promise."

I swear if he didn't seem fragile right now, I would shake him, but instead, I'm sticking with what I know works to pull him out of this mood.

The ridiculously large fireplace in his den is lit, music is playing, and he's lying naked on a rug, like a good little muse, while I paint on his chest.

Oh, and we have bourbon.

One of these things is bound to loosen his lips.

"I don't want you to make it up to me," I snap, pointing at him with my paintbrush. "I want you to tell me what fucking happened with Langston and Vance today!"

We'll deal with the conscious wedding thing another day. Right now, I have more important things on my mind. Like knowing what went down between the three of them.

"And I already told you. Nothing happened." He downs the rest of his tumbler like the sexiest liar in the universe.

If I had thought he was going to be this difficult, I would have hitched a ride to his office and listened for my freaking self!

"Do not make me stab you," I threaten, holding the brush up like it's a real weapon. "I'd hate to damage something so beautiful, but I will."

My patience is fleeting.

"Aww. You think I'm beautiful, Ray?" He grins up at me through his long lashes that he should not have out of pure principle.

"I think you're a beautiful liar," I say instead. "And if you don't tell me what happened today, I will call Vance"—I cast him a *try me* look—"or Langston. Either way, I will get the truth."

I agreed to sit out a round in this fight, not get kicked off the team because my husband has some kind of hero complex.

"Don't threaten me, Ray. I've heard enough of those for one day."

He leans up on his elbows, and the motion jostles me forward on his hips.

I grin. "Langston threatened you?"

This is progress, so I brush his cock with my center to keep him talking.

It works, but he shoots me a disappointed look, anyway. "Yes, but it was an empty threat. All Langston can do is tarnish the Potter name—nothing catastrophic."

I scoff. "That is a big deal, Duke!"

He shrugs. "You and I both know that's just our pride talking. At the end of the day, I'm still the same person I was before. No matter what Langston says about me."

He lies back on the rug, taking me with him. "We've been here before, Ray," he chides, plucking the paintbrush from my fingers and tossing it to the floor. "And just like last time, we'll stay calm and let them talk. We know who we are. We know the truth. Our 'good' name is merely a perception of who people *think* we are. A reputation—good or bad—does nothing but fuel an opinion. We don't need it."

"I know," I argue, but it comes out feebly, "but you've worked so hard to restore your reputation with your family."

He offers me a sweet smile. "A reputation that only means something to them. I know who I am, Ray. I know the kind of person who lives in here."

He places my hand over his heart. "That man is faithful and honorable to the woman he loves."

Here he goes, playing with my ovaries again.

"I don't need to earn the respect of others," he continues. "I live for an audience of one."

Me.

I fight back the tears and snuggle closer, inhaling the scent of soap and bourbon.

"Don't worry about the Potter reputation, Ray. The truth always finds its way to the surface."

I get it. I really do, but should we just sit idly by and let some asshole destroy everything we've worked for?

I'm thinking no.

"As incredibly sweet as that is," I tell him softly, sliding my hands through his hair, "shouldn't we at least try to do some damage control? At least for your brothers' sake? Should they suffer Langston tarnishing their good name, too? Are we allowing the innocent to pay for our war?"

"Are we not innocent, too?"

Gah, this is not coming out right. "Yes, we are, but Duke…"

"But nothing, Ray. This might be our war, but we're not alone. The good will always answer our call and prepare for war. No matter what Vance and Astor believe, they know me. They know the value of family. Even if I asked them to sit this one out, they wouldn't. Because they know I would do the same for them. No matter the casualties, I would fight for my brothers. I would fight for their futures—their children's futures. Because that is who we are."

"Maybe so," I say softly, "but your brothers don't know the full story yet. They won't agree to your war without knowing the truth. You have to tell them."

Duke waves away my concern and captures my lips softly in a chaste kiss. "We'll worry about that later. For now, we'll let Langston talk. Let him spread whatever rumors he conjures up because it will only make him look guilty. And guilty men eventually make mistakes."

He shakes his head, his body tensing. "And that's all we need—a mistake."

It's like he's forgotten I'm here. He's just rambling, his gaze far away.

"That fucker didn't even ask me what documents I was referring to in my email." He shakes his head.

I grin, unable to contain myself. "That's because he knows where our son is! Do you know what this means?" I jump up, my tits bouncing with the energy.

Duke grins. "That I will never get tired of seeing you jump naked?"

I roll my eyes playfully. "This means, Dr. Potter, that I was right! Langston knows where our precious Jude is. We are so close!"

Oh my gosh. "Seriously, what can we do to get this bastard to talk?"

"I'm guessing you're now okay with the possibility of him ruining the Potter name in the process?" My sarcastic husband cocks a brow, and it's not cute.

"Maybe. But what if we could get him to talk without him destroying the Potters?" Because now, I am a freaking Potter, too. "What if we could fight a lie with the truth?"

Duke grins. "I might already have a plan."

Why does he want to die today? "Well, please share with the class, Dr. Potter, because so far, you've been most unhelpful."

I should have known what would come out of his mouth next. "Convince me."

"Dammit, Duke."

I stomp, and when my tits jiggle, he grins. "That was quick. You always did know the way to my heart, Ray."

I cannot keep a straight face. "You're such a shit. Tell me the plan, or I'm getting dressed."

Like a freaking ninja, he springs up and snags me around the waist, pulling me back down to the floor. He slings his legs over mine, pinning me beneath him. "Mm-hmm… This is a much better angle."

I agree, but I'm not telling him that. He needs no more incentive to continue with this behavior while we're trying to have a serious conversation. "The plan," I prompt.

He sighs, pulling in a deep breath. "The plan, my love, is simple."

"I can do simple."

He nods. "Can you also do calm?"

I tip my chin infinitesimally. "Yes, I can be calm when warranted."

"Good," he agrees, "because the person who can help us is an old girl—"

Heaven help me. "Are you serious right now? An old girlfriend is our only option?"

I'm not opposed or jealous—much. After all, Duke endured Langston's and my relationship—but it's important to note he was not calm. At all.

Duke grins, and I swear his cheeks turn the slightest shade of red. "She's not our only option, but she's our best option."

I sigh. "Us against the world, right?"

He nods. "Always."

"Fine, what's her name?"

This time, he does turn red before burying his face in my tits and mumbling, "Summertime Girlfriend."

"Duke!"

He chuckles. "My issues should not come as a shock to you right now."

They don't, and really knowing this is how unattached he was does something to my heart. This man owns me in all the ways it matters.

"I'm assuming she likes to be called something else, though, something a little more biblical."

He arches a brow in confusion.

"Duke, seriously, what's her real name?"

His face scrunches up, and I can't keep the laugh from bubbling out. "We're fucking doomed."

"No, we're not doomed. I'll figure it out before tomorrow, when I have to introduce you." He shifts and wedges his hips between my thighs, already done with this conversation.

"And if you don't remember her name, and she spits in our face?"

I can't even with him right now.

"Then we'll bring wet wipes and go with plan B."

"And what's plan B?"

He flinches. "Telling Vance."

CHAPTER EIGHTEEN

Ramsey

Summertime Girlfriend's name is Kelly.
And not only is she gorgeous, but she's a reporter for a national news network known for its shocking exposés.

"So, you're his winter, huh?"

I flash Duke a glare that he misses since he stepped away to "take a call" that no one heard come through.

"I guess so—though I'm not entirely sure what you mean by that."

Kelly motions to the small bistro table outside the quaint coffee shop, where we met. "Duke's a great guy," she says with a smile, "but his heart was never available. Everyone knew he was waiting for someone else. He was waiting for winter." She pulls out a chair and sits, eyeing the small ring on my finger. "He was waiting for you."

I guess there is no need in denying it. "I suppose he was."

She laughs. "You're just as cagey as he is, but for this to work, you're gonna have to tell me what you know." She pulls out a pen and a notepad like she's ready to start.

"Shouldn't we wait for Duke?"

She grins, and it's savage. I know then that if anyone is going to take down Langston, it will be this woman. "Aren't you tired of waiting?"

Oh, no. This is going to be bad. "I—"

A hand comes down on my shoulder, solid and secure. "Kelly—" At least he didn't call her Summertime. "As we discussed, in exchange for helping us locate our son—who you will not include in this story—we'll provide all the details we know to expose this undercover adoption scandal involving Congressman Ford, Harrison Potter, and Congressman Albrecht."

My breath hitches. "You didn't tell me we were going after our fathers, too."

Slowly, Duke walks around and squats at my feet. "You promised me your future," he reminds me.

I nod, feeling the air change around us to something more suffocating.

"No matter the outcome," I agree.

He nods, pulling a piece of paper and handing it to Kelly.

"What is this?"

His jaw ticks. "The death certificate of our son."

I don't remember Kelly hugging me.

All I remember are the beautifully decorated Christmas trees in the windows of the nearby shops as Duke walks us to the car, closing the door on our past and leaving it in the hands of a stranger.

We told our story—reliving every painful detail like it was merely yesterday and not almost two decades ago.

"Do you think we would know?" I finally ask him as we drive home in silence. "Do you think we would know if Jude was really dead?"

Duke clears his throat, his jaw working harshly. "I've never imagined him any other way."

I can see that. Duke lost hope that night at the hospital.

"How about you?" he asks. "Do *you* feel any different at seeing the death certificate?"

For a minute, I almost say yes. Seeing in print that Jude Potter died the same day he was born at Mercy General Hospital was a shock to my system. That's for sure. But did it make me feel any different? I don't think so.

"I should have checked the medical records," I admit. "That should have been the first place I checked when my mother told me he was alive."

But something tells me, even if I had thought to check, I probably wouldn't have. I wanted to believe he was alive and still waiting for us to find him.

Duke shrugs. "You gave us hope when we needed it the most."

"But what if I'm wrong? What if my mother lied so I would be happy and move on?"

He squeezes my hand reassuringly. "Do you feel like she lied?"

"I don't know what to think," I admit. "I'd like to think she wouldn't spend her last moments lying to her only daughter." But my chest tightens anyway. "Surely her soul had limits."

"And what about your soul?" His eyes turn serious. "Does it long for the life we created, or does it grieve the life we lost?"

A rogue tear drips down my face. "It longs." I let out an agonizing cry. "It longs so very much." Holding my stomach, I start to rock gently. "But what if it's wrong? What if I'm killing your soul by making you relive losing him all over again?"

What if I lose them both?

"Hey, look at me."

"You need to pay attention to the road," I mumble. "I'm okay."

I've resorted to feeling sorry for myself.

"You know what, Ray?" Duke chuckles, and the sound gets my attention.

"What?"

His eyebrows jump as he lowers his voice to a whisper. "We've been here before."

"Oh, shut up." I'm in no mood for his mess.

"I'm serious," he says, pulling over onto the side of the road. "For years, we've been told Jude didn't make it. If you didn't believe that, then this death certificate shouldn't change your mind now."

He's making sense, but… "Why didn't you tell me you had the certificate before?"

He shrugs, not answering.

"Because you thought I was wrong," I answer for him.

He sighs, raking his hands through his hair. "I didn't know what to think. It all happened so fast. I just wanted to protect you."

"And now?"

He grins. "Now, you can protect yourself."

"You're a liar." There's no way he suddenly let all those alpha tendencies go.

"You're right." He grins. "I didn't tell you because I didn't want it to be true. I wanted us to live in this bubble full of hope a little while longer."

My heart flutters. "So, you think the death certificate is a fake?"

Duke leans over the console. "I know it's a fake."

"How?" Those flutters in my chest turn into full-on pounding against my ribs. "How do you know it's a fake?"

This man—this freaking beautiful soul—presses his lips to mine in the sweetest kiss. "Because a mother knows, and I'll trust her intuition over a stranger's signature any day."

"How can you not have a Christmas tree in one of these closets?"

Shockingly, my husband isn't naked. Instead, he lounges on the sofa, watching me with an amused smile as I familiarize myself with his house's eleven billion storage closets.

"I never needed one," he answers, like it's just that simple.

"So, you haven't had a tree since our last Christmas together?" The one where we counted the weeks until our son arrived.

He shakes his head solemnly.

"What did you do Christmas morning?" Since he didn't date in the fall and winter, that had to be excruciatingly lonely.

"Slept through the morning until Astor made us go to lunch as a family."

Ah, Astor. The nicer brother of the two. "How is Astor?"

A smile stretches across Duke's face. "Annoyed but happy."

"Annoyed?" Giving up, I plop down onto his lap, letting him pull me into his arms.

"Yeah." He laughs. "Apparently, his girl has been challenging. But that could just be Vance speculating. You know he thinks anyone is challenging when they don't do what he wants."

Yes, yes, he does.

"Did I tell you Astor is a father now?"

"No!"

He nods, nuzzling my neck. "Yep, her name is Tatum. She's gotta be two months old now."

He speaks of the little girl so reverently that it hurts my heart that he never got to see our son at that age.

"Maybe I could meet them soon? I'd love to meet your niece and possibly smooth things over with Vance."

Astor has always been a big teddy bear. I'm not worried about that Potter—just the hateful one.

Duke chuckles. "Now, the way to Vance's good graces is through Halle."

"His girlfriend?"

"And Astor's assistant."

I laugh. "Sounds complicated." And a much better option than trying to speak to Vance directly.

"It was complicated for a while, but things seem to be finally settling down for both my brothers." He says this like it's a relief—that maybe things were more than just complicated.

"Maybe we should come clean to Vance and Astor about Jude."

His body tenses around me. "No, not yet."

"Why?"

"Because I did something and don't want them part of it yet."

And like his declaration needed proof, his phone buzzes. We both look at the screen, seeing the name Harrison Potter flash across.

I turn in his arms. "What did you do?"

This ridiculously adorable smile emerges. "I was a good son and sent my parents a Christmas card." He shrugs like it's no big deal.

Oh, hell. "What was in the Christmas card, Duke?"

He presses his lips to mine like that's going to distract me. "I can't remember exactly, but I think," he pops the k dramatically, "it was a picture of that Christmas when you and I took a selfie with your baby bump."

My heart sinks. Not only because he still has that picture but because he sent it to the man who is partly responsible for us not taking any subsequent pictures with that baby.

"And," he continues, as his phone buzzes again with another call, "I might have included Kelly's card with a note that said something like: You can tell us where he is or she will. Either way, it'll be a merry Christmas for us."

My eyes widen at his boldness. "I thought we were going to wait on Kelly for more information."

Something flashes in Duke's eyes—something primal. "The season of grieving is over, Ray. It's now a season of war."

And like he just didn't rock my world, he adds, "Now, let's go get a Christmas tree. We have a picture to take."

I didn't realize he meant we would cut down a Christmas tree, but nevertheless, my ovaries are impressed with how he looks in a flannel shirt.

"You know, Potter, I think you might have missed your calling as a lumberjack," I say, appreciating how he wields the handsaw under the fir tree.

Ignoring my remark, he flashes a panty-melting smile instead. "Are you sure this is the tree you want?"

"Yep. This is the one." It looks just like the one we had many years ago.

"All right," he says, his excitement seeming to bleed through his cool demeanor. "Move out of the way."

"What if you need my help?" I tease. "A saw isn't a scalpel."

Those hazel eyes find mine and glare. "A blade is a blade. Now, move."

"Fine." I throw my hands up in a playful gesture and step back. "Someone is sensitive."

"I'm not sensitive." He grunts as he starts sawing at the trunk. "I just don't need your snark when I'm—"

My phone buzzes in my pocket. "Hold that thought," I tell him jokingly. "And don't cut it lopsided. We need it to go in the stand."

I think he tells me to hush, but I can't be sure since I freeze at seeing Vance's name. "Hello," I answer carefully.

"Put my brother on the phone."

This hateful man. "Merry Christmas to you, too, Dr. Potter. It's been a long time. I'm glad to see you haven't changed." At least since I last spoke to him when I asked him to ensure Duke got home safely from Vegas.

Vance sighs like maybe he didn't mean to come off so rude. "Merry Christmas, Ramsey. I hear congratulations are in order."

Duke has stopped cutting and is now standing in front of me, motioning for the phone—which is in vain. Again, I agreed to sit out a round, and that round is over.

It's my turn.

Stepping back, I flash Duke an apologetic smile. "Thank you, Vance. I would have invited you to the wedding if I had known we were having one."

Duke makes a noise low in his throat, and I take another step back just in case he considers lunging for the phone.

"That sounds like something my brother would do."

He swears, but there's no bite behind it, more like frustration, which is understandable. His brother is freaking stubborn. It would drive a person to drink or scream. Vance probably has done both.

"Listen, Ramsey. I don't know what's happening, but I'd like to understand why Harrison is losing his shit, looking for Duke."

He sounds genuine.

"I need to know if he needs my help."

"Duke wants to keep you out of it," I tell him instead.

"Well, that's too fucking bad. Duke doesn't get to keep me out of it. What has Harrison done now?"

I swallow, looking at Duke. Sometimes we have to make hard decisions for the people we love. Duke said he'd fight for his brothers just like they'd fight for him. It's time we gave them the chance to prove it.

Stepping toe to toe with my husband, I hand over the phone. "The season for grieving is over," I tell him. "Bury the past and take the future you deserve."

His brothers are part of who he is.

It's time he removed the barriers between them.

CHAPTER NINETEEN

Duke

"I like what you've done with the place," I say with a smirk, appreciating the full effect of seeing Remington kicked back in a plastic chair just outside Vance's extravagant front entry, smoking a cigarette. "It really brings out the dollar store vibe in the neighborhood."

Remington blows out a ring of smoke and chuckles. "Your brother thinks so, too."

I bark out a laugh. "I bet he does. How many chairs have you been through? Ten? Twenty?" Because there is no way Vance doesn't toss these cheap plastic chairs in the trash on the regular.

"I couldn't tell you." He grins. "I stopped counting after fifty-two." Taking another hit from his cigarette, he adds, "At this point, it's a game between us."

"One Vance loses, I'm sure."

I'm not upset in the slightest that Remington gives my brother such a hard time. One, Vance deserves a little aggravation in his orderly life, and two, I think he enjoys it.

Remington flashes me a devilish look. "Considering I buy these chairs with your brother's credit card, I'd have to agree." Remington chuckles. "That moody fucker is too fun to mess with."

At the mention of Vance's mood, I grimace. "Is that why you're out here? Because he's in a mood?"

He arches a brow. "You mean, am I out here because you pissed off big brother so bad that he broke a vase and needed to bang out his aggression on Halle before you came over?"

That sounds like a yes.

I nod tensely, and it only makes him laugh. "That, and Hal won't let me smoke in the house." He shrugs like neither thing bothers him.

"I thought Halle didn't want you smoking at all?"

She's always hiding his cigarettes.

He flashes me this look of amusement. "Unlike you and your brothers, pussy doesn't control me. Even the sweetest ones."

He might be brash and blasé, but we all know he loves and respects Halle more than anyone. She's been like a mother to him this past year.

"I'll remember that," I tell him, "when—"

The front door rips open, and my brother's harsh gaze finds mine.

"Merry Christmas," I say sarcastically. "I would have brought a—"

"Get inside."

Remington chokes on a laugh, redirecting Vance's gaze to the other problem person in his life. Him. "What did I tell you?" he grits out, snatching the cigarette from between Remington's lips and tossing it to the ground. "This isn't some skeezy motel. We have ordinances in this neighborhood."

"No way!" Remington makes a show of scanning the surroundings. "I felt sure it was definitely a pay-by-the-hour place with how you dragged Hal upstairs."

Without warning, Vance kicks the back leg of the plastic chair, sending Remington scrambling to catch his balance in the midst of his laughter. "Be careful, Vance-hole," he teases, once he rights himself, his voice taking on an edge. "I'm not your fucking brother. I fight back."

Before I can correct his misperception of me, Remington casually lights up another cigarette and waves us off. "Go hug it out before we *all* need therapy."

Good gracious. This kid.

Shaking my head, I take a few steps to the door and pause.

"Don't be scared, Dr. Douche," Remington mocks, noticing my hesitation. "Think of Vance like a big teddy bear—a short-fused, violent bear."

He throws his head back, laughing at his own joke, and I snatch the pack of smokes off his thigh, slamming the door closed and locking it.

"You really shouldn't let him smoke," I say, handing the cigarettes to Vance as Remington proceeds to bang on the door, using colorful expletives.

"Is that Remington?" Halle comes out of the kitchen with a confused look on her face. "Is he locked out?"

Vance hands her the pack of cigarettes. "He's in time-out. You can let him in when he can promise to be a good boy." He says it like he's training a puppy and not raising a teenager.

Halle snorts, already pushing past us to rescue her best friend. "It's Christmas. Give him some leniency."

Vance rolls his eyes and tips his chin in the direction of his office. "Astor is on his way with Tatum. Tell him to wait out here until we finish talking."

Halle nods, her face turning serious. "No. *You'll* wait to talk until we eat lunch. You two are not about to shit on this day with your drama."

I wink at Vance and mouth the word *pussy*.

Never in a million years would he let someone tell him what he's going to do. But here he is, tipping his chin in a tight agreement.

"Good," Halle praises, opening the door and letting in Remington. "Now, all of you will help me in the kitchen until Astor arrives." She sighs. "Then you can yell at each other."

Helping Halle in the kitchen went a little something like this:

I stirred while Vance yelled randomly, when the tense silence became too much for him to handle.

"I can't believe you fucking married her!"

"Do you know what this means?"

"I hope you're happy."

Fortunately, Astor and Halle kept the peace until lunch was over, and we could retreat to Vance's office, where Vance currently passes me a tumbler of bourbon. "To loosen those lips of yours," he growls.

"Such a thoughtful host," I tease, before downing the whole glass and passing it back with a hiss. Vance's mood has only managed to get worse since Astor arrived with the baby. He doesn't want Astor involved, considering he's already dealing with so much with Keagan leaving.

"You need another?" Astor asks me gently, which only earns another growl from Vance, who tries to persuade Astor to leave once again.

"Do you really need to be away from Tatum? What if she needs you?"

Astor, the oldest of us, flashes Vance a patient grin. "Halle is capable of watching Tatum for a little while. Let it go, Vance. You're not in charge here."

The perks of being the oldest.

Vance looks like he wants to argue, leaning back against the front of his desk, but he agrees, respecting the hierarchy. "Fine," he grits out between clenched teeth. "Stay. Add more stress to your plate."

Astor simply grins, ignoring Vance's fit, and looks at me. "All right, Duke. You have our attention. What's going on?"

I held nothing back.

I told them the truth—the *whole* truth.

Their brother wasn't a drug addict.

He didn't run away to get high in an abandoned cabin with his high school girlfriend.

He was a man who tried to honor his responsibilities.

A man who held his lifeless son and prayed as he breathed life back into his lungs.

I told them of the silence.

I shared with them the screams.

And when I got to the end of my story, I stood and begged—for their forgiveness—for their help in finding the boy I lost that winter.

But then the tears started to fall, and things got awkward.

I swipe at my cheeks, drying the unwanted emotion, and try to lighten the tension with a joke.

"Vance, you keep staring at me like that, and it's going to set the record for my longest-lasting relationship."

No one moves.

I'm not sure that either of them breathes until Vance stalks forward and grabs me by the back of the neck, his eyes aflame with something I can't quite place. "I should beat your ass," he says, his voice thick with emotion. "And I will if you ever keep something like this from us again."

He yanks me toward him and… hugs me. It's awkward, but we let it play out all the same. It's not often my brothers and I hug, but this wasn't an easy conversation to have.

"I will kill Harrison," he finally says, letting me go, his gaze flashing to Astor, who, at the mention of a son, had jumped up and started pacing the room.

"Agreed," Astor says, coming over and pulling me in for a hug, too. "I can promise you, we will find your son."

"I've started a war," I remind them, stepping back and taking a seat. "It won't be that easy. Congressmen Ford and Albrecht will do anything in their power to keep this story from coming out. That means destroying Potter's Plastics in the process. They'll go after what we care about."

Vance scoffs, rounding his desk and opening his laptop. "I wish they fucking would. Richard needs something to do."

Richard is our family attorney. He's the one who recently handled Vance's lawsuit.

"Now, this adoption," Vance continues, his focus still on his screen. "You said you had a reporter working on it?"

Relief hits me hard as Vance completely moves on from the concern about the practice. If anyone was going to worry about their reputation, it would be Vance.

"Kelly," I answer. "She's the reporter helping us."

"She's looking into the death certificate, too?" Astor chimes in.

I nod and start to tell him that I have another copy, but Vance cuts me off. "Tell her we'll handle it. Astor, come look at this."

Clearly, being a team player isn't a gene the Potters have.

"You know a Dr. Moroney, don't you?" Vance points at the screen, and I don't bother walking over. I've combed over that death certificate enough to know a Dr. Lance Moroney signed my son's death certificate.

"I know a Thomas Moroney," Astor muses, coming around to view the document on the screen where Vance has accessed the electronic medical records system. "Maybe this is his father?"

"Call him," Vance snaps. "Ask him who the fuck signed this and where we can find him."

Astor chuckles and claps him on the shoulder. "It's Christmas Eve, brother."

"And?" Vance returns. "He's a doctor. He's used to being on call for the holidays."

Something I didn't realize I was missing stirs in my stomach, soothing the ache.

I had been harboring so much pain, so many secrets that I had hidden away from my brothers, that it had worn away at my soul.

"What the fuck are you standing there for, Duke? No one here thinks you're pretty."

Vance's tone snaps me out of my haze, and I blink, bringing my focus back to him.

"Yeah, hello." He waves his hand in front of my face. "Grab your coat. We don't have time for any more hugs, if that's what you're waiting on."

And he's back.

But something has shifted.

This is the brother who bitched that I slept on his couch in college but made sure he left me dinner in the microwave. This is the brother that complained about my late shifts delivering pizzas but waited up so he could study with me.

This is the brother that fought for my education—for my future.

And here he is doing it again with no questions asked.

Like I knew he would.

Because that's who we are.

Family.

"Vance, be serious," Astor tries reasoning once more. "I'll call Dr. Moroney after the holidays." He plucks the keys from Vance's desk, ensuring that he doesn't take off on his own, just in case. "Today, let's just enjoy spending Christmas Eve together—as a family."

Vance scoffs. "Easy for you to say. Your daughter is in the next room. What about Duke? You would have him go one more minute without his son? One more Christmas?"

Talking to Vance is always challenging, but Astor is used to being the voice of reason. "No, I wouldn't want him to miss another Christmas without his son. But"—he looks at me with a fierceness in his eyes—"I can promise this will be the last Christmas you'll spend without him."

Vance narrows his eyes. "Touching," he says, sounding more like Remington, "but that's not good enough."

He ushers Astor to the door, throwing it open. "Go play with the kids," he tells him. "Ask Remington what Santa brought him." He rolls his eyes like it annoyed him to actually buy the kid a gift. "FYI: It's an X-Box so he can play with your dong-hating girlfriend online *at home* and not on the office computer like the shitty employee he is."

Remington is far from a shitty employee. He and Halle run that office better than anyone we've ever hired.

But Vance would never admit it. Instead, he shoves Astor out the door, but Astor catches himself. "Remington talked to Keys?"

Vance looks at me and shakes his head. "Go handle your girl, Astor."

"What are you two going to do?"

Vance turns back at me, and nothing but determination is in his eyes. "We're gonna call Harrison. It's time we had a chat."

CHAPTER TWENTY

Duke

Not unexpectedly, Harrison Potter denied having anything to do with the adoption. He swore Jude died and suggested I seek grief counseling instead of putting my brother through more trauma by lying.

It was a delightful conversation—especially when Vance threatened to hire a private investigator, a former FBI agent and a patient of Vance's, to look into the case. He gave Harrison a week to "remember" what happened and to convince Langston to hand over the names of the parents that adopted Jude before he made the call.

I still don't know what Ray and I will do once we have that information, but at least we'll have a choice—something we weren't offered as teenagers.

And right now, that's all I can ask for.

A choice in knowing my son.

We can't change what happened, but we can change how we move forward. Ray and I have lived in the past for far too long. It's time we heal and move forward.

"You ready?" I ask Ray, who is staring at the packed car with the tree we cut down earlier today tied to the roof.

"I think so."

"Well," I chuckle, "if we forgot something, it'd be a miracle." She packed at least a bedroom full of shit—and it's not even hers. Most of her stuff is still at Langston's, where it will stay until this blows over or Langston grows a conscience. We know which will come first.

But apparently, if we packed a Christmas tree, we had to take all the decorations she bought while I had lunch with Vance and Astor.

"Don't act like I overpacked if you won't tell me where we're going," she snaps.

"I told you it was a surprise." I open the passenger door, ushering her in. Astor thought it would be a good time to get away while he and Vance dealt with the congressman and our father. Not only that, but he suggested my wife deserved a proper honeymoon since I was such a bastard with how I handled the wedding—which I still don't regret. I was marrying Ray one way or another. It's not my fault she's stubborn and forced my hand.

Let that be a lesson to her for the future. There is no escaping this relationship. She is mine forever.

Ray grins, settling into the seat and buckling up. "I think we've had enough surprises to last us a lifetime, don't you?"

Most definitely, but… "We have room for one more."

"If you say so." But the excitement in her voice betrays her. No matter what surprise I have in store, she's in—just like she was all those years ago when we did the very same thing. "Quick question, though."

I groan. "No, Ray. I already know what you're going to ask, and the answer is no. We are not stopping for gas station snacks."

Because I could barely handle it the first time…

"Oh my gosh, Duke, this is so good. You have to try it."

My stomach turns as she dips the stick of gas station jerky into her milkshake and holds it out to me. "No, thanks. You and the baby need the calories, not me."

"I know it looks gross," she tries again, "but it's absolutely divine. Like heaven in a cup."

I snort. "I'll take your word for it." There is no way I'm eating meat—dried or not—from a place that attaches a hubcap to their bathroom key.

"I feel like you're judging me right now." Her eyes water; I'm sure this is round two of the tears since we left our hometown.

"I would never judge you." I reach across the console of the car and take her hand.

"Then why are you looking at me like I disgust you?"

I hold back a laugh. Now is not the time to make that mistake again—even if she looks adorable all bundled up in my flannel shirt with her hair a mess and bottom lip poking out. "You will never disgust me," I admit honestly.

A tear falls down her cheek, anyway.

"You don't believe me?" I say, feigning shock.

She narrows her eyes. "Prove it. Prove I don't disgust you."

My stomach clenches at the thought, but my girl feels vulnerable right now. We're three hundred miles from home with nine hundred and fifty-two dollars between us. If eating this unknown sliver of meat will dry the tears in her eyes, then I'll force it down. After all, we're in this together—disgusting pregnancy cravings and all.

Pulling over onto the side of the road, I snatch the milkshake from her hand, purposely not looking down when I grab the jerky, bobbing in the ice cream, and take a huge bite.

And gag.

"Oh my gosh. I seriously can't believe you actually tried it." She laughs, taking her nasty milkshake from my hands as I choke, forcing myself to swallow.

Gah, I hate vanilla ice cream.

And jerky.

I especially hate them together.

"You look like me in the mornings," she teases, because even at six *months pregnant, she is still getting sick. The doctor at the clinic said it was normal. Some women can suffer morning sickness well into their second trimester. Of course, Ray was the lucky small statistic, but it is getting better each day. I just wish I could do more than hold her hair back and bring her a cold towel.*

"I'm glad it makes you feel better," I say, finally able to breathe when I get the concoction past my throat.

She grins. "It helped a little."

A little is more than nothing. I don't think I can handle seeing her cry anymore—my heart can't take it.

"Ah." She gasps, her eyes lighting up. "Give me your hand."

She doesn't wait before she yanks her shirt up, grabs my hand, and places it on her belly. "Do you feel that?"

I pause, tuning out the distraction of the cars passing by us, and wait. And wait.

"Right there!" She squeals. "Do you feel that?"

Under my palm, a tiny muscle jumps in her belly. "Is that?" I lean in closer and put my other hand on her stomach as the slight fluttering happens again.

My head snaps up, finding her eyes, which are filling with tears. "That's our son, Duke. He knows we're taking him home."

"Duke." A hand grabs my shoulder, and I jump.

"Yeah?"

I turn and find Ray watching me carefully. "You okay?"

"Yep." I blink a few times, clearing away the memory. "I just zoned out there for a minute."

She cocks a brow. "Care to share?"

I almost tease her and say I was thinking of her lips wrapped around my cock. But it was too good of a memory not to share it with her. "I was thinking about that time we felt Jude kick."

A genuine smile emerges. "I remember." She laughs. "He kicked my bladder the whole drive. We had to stop every twenty minutes for me to pee."

"It was that nasty concoction you fed him," I argue. "You upset his environment."

She belts out a laugh. "No, I didn't. He loved it."

"He didn't," I argue. "I assure you."

But I can't assure her of anything because neither of us knows what he would like. We never got a chance to ask him.

We turn quiet, and I use the moment to get into the car.

When I've closed the door and started the car, Ray finally breaks the silence, her eyes staring at her hands clasped in her lap. "Do you ever think you'll want more children?" she finally asks.

I focus on backing out of the garage. "I don't know. It's not been something I ever thought about."

If you had asked me that question last week, I would have given you a hard no. I never wanted more children because I couldn't get over the child I hadn't been able to save. But now, having Ray back in my life, I'm not so sure.

"What about you?" I ask, pulling onto the road. "Do you want more children?"

She frowns. "I've always wanted more, but I'm thirty-six now. I don't know if having more children is in my cards. My eggs might not be as healthy as they used to be."

"Women are having children later now," I tell her. "There's also cutting-edge fertility treatments available."

She nods, but I can tell the subject has brought down the mood.

"We could always adopt, too." I don't know why I blurted it out. Maybe I just wanted to eliminate the sadness from her eyes. "If you wanted another child, we could make it happen one way or another."

She offers me a tight grin. "What if we never find him? What if we never get over Jude?"

Just like all those years ago, I reach across the console and take her hand. "We'll find him," I promise, "and we'll bring him home."

We will finish what we started.

We have no choice.

Because if we don't, neither of us will recover.

Five-and-a-half-hours later, I'm bursting at the seams.

"Ray." I shake her shoulder harder than necessary. "We're here."

And she ruined the surprise by falling asleep midway through the trip.

But at least we didn't have to stop for gas station meat.

"Leave me alone," she groans, batting my hand away like I'm some annoying gnat and not her sweet-as-fuck husband who just listened to her cute snores for the last half hour.

"You're killing me, Sunny Ray." I groan, shaking my head, as I jump out of the car, jogging over to her side and opening the door. She doesn't move, let alone open her eyes, when the cool breeze of the lake hits her.

I look at the water longingly as a ridiculous thought pops into my head.

She won't like it.

But it will wake her up.

Better yet, it will get her naked, and that's always my objective.

Reaching in, I shove one arm under her legs and the other behind her back. "Hold on to me, sweetheart," I coo deceptively.

I almost feel bad when she trusts me to lift her out of the car, keeping her eyes closed.

But I don't feel nearly as bad as when I run down the hill, and her eyes fly open, wide awake in a panic. "What are you doing?" She frantically kicks her legs when I make it to the dock, but we've been here before, and just like last time, I have her in a tight hold.

"Watch out for snakes, Ray. I hear they're everywhere," I warn teasingly, just as I jump into the frigid water.

"I hate you," she yells, coming up for air with a vengeance. Her hair is stuck to the side of her face, and her lips are turning a lovely shade of blue.

"Come here, and I'll keep you warm," I offer, with a playful grin. It's been years since I've jumped off this same dock with her in my arms. Last time, though, it was much warmer.

She splashes water in my face. "Why would you do that?" Her teeth are beginning to chatter as she treads water, looking longingly at the dock.

"Take my hand," I offer, reaching out between us.

She smacks me away, which only makes me laugh. "No."

"Have it your way." I start swimming toward the dock, knowing she's scared that snakes are probably coiled around the posts, just waiting to attack her.

"Fine," she agrees quickly, "but only because I don't want to die of hypothermia."

I grin and swim closer, turning around so she can get on my back.

"I'm still mad at you, though," she says, when her arms are secured around my chest.

"Aww. Don't start this trip on a bad note," I tease. "I've worked so hard on this surprise."

We swim to the dock, and I grab on to the ladder, hoisting us out of the water.

When we're safely on the dock, Ray slides down off my back. "What surprise?" Taking her hand, I pull her, shivering, to the front of my body and wrap my arms around her, directing her attention to the top of the hill where the A-frame cabin we spent our fall and winter sits. "Welcome home, Ray."

"Oh, Duke. It's beautiful. Just like I remember it."

It was supposed to be a temporary memory—a place we could hide until we figured out something more permanent.

But this cabin became home.

The place where we spent nights by the fireplace, reading to our son.

The place where we made plans for the future.

The place where we ended.

Something warm falls onto my hand. "You bought it?" she asks hesitantly.

"I did," I say, tightening my hold on her as if she'll disappear any second. "You remember Mr. and Mrs. Clark?"

She nods. "The couple who rented it to us."

"Yeah." I lean down and kiss her cheek. "They rented it out to me every fall after I finished med school."

She gasps and turns in my arms. "You came back after we left?"

I shake my head. "Not for a while. I tried, but I could never stay through the night. But it didn't feel right knowing someone else was spending their nights in our cabin. So, I rented it every season, even though I could never stay."

"When did you buy it?"

I rub my hands up and down her shoulders to generate some heat. "Several years ago, Mr. Clark fell ill. He told me they couldn't keep the cabin anymore and were planning to sell it."

Ray smiles. "And you couldn't let that happen."

"No. I couldn't." I press a kiss to her mouth. "Because I knew one day, we'd find our way back home."

CHAPTER TWENTY-ONE

Ramsey

"Seriously?" I ask.

Duke grimaces at the peeling paint and rickety steps that lead up to the front of the cabin. "I'm sure the inside rivals an Aspen ski lodge."

I belt out an exaggerated laugh. He is delirious. "Even you don't believe that."

There's no way the inside of this cabin is filled to the roof with luxury. Not with the ginormous spiderweb shadowing an entire corner of the porch.

"Aw, come on, Ray." He throws his arm over my shoulder, pulling me in close. "I thought you were down for an adventure."

I narrow my gaze. "An adventure, yes, a brown recluse bite, no."

"That's not a brown recluse spider."

"I don't recall you being a Boy Scout. How would you know?" A spider is a freaking spider, no matter what kind it is.

He flashes me that panty-melting smile that is the sole reason I'm pregnant to begin with and shrugs. "I do have a general working knowledge that not all spiders are the same kind."

"That doesn't help us at all." I cross my arms and let out a huff of aggravation. "Regardless of the species, that's a big-ass spider, and it's blocking the way in." I let out a whine at the end.

Up until now, I've been a good sport with all the traveling. But now, being cooped up in the car for hours has only made me grouchier. And I have to pee. Again.

Duke chuckles and squeezes me in a gentle hug. "I'll get the spider on one condition."

I pull back and give him the side-eye. If this man wants me to enter this cabin, he will get the dang spider, regardless. One condition... my ass.

"I'm only indulging you because I love you," I say. "What's your condition?"

Those hazel eyes sparkle in delight as he tucks a wayward strand of hair away from my face. "You let me carry you over the threshold."

"The threshold?" I rear back. "But we aren't married."

He shrugs, and it's adorably awkward. "No, but one day, we will be, and you'll be upset that I didn't carry you over the threshold to our new home."

It's so sweet. I can't help but smile and press a kiss to his lips. "You are something, Duke Potter." And that something is so special that I will never let it go.

"Is that a yes?" He sounds way too excited about the idea.

"What if you drop me?" Let's be real. "I'm not as light as I used to be." Growing a baby will do that to you.

"Psh." He waves me off. "You're not heavy."

Gah, I love when he lies to me like this. It's absolutely precious.

"I am. Besides, what happens when we really are married? Are you going to regret unofficially carrying me over the threshold?"

"Will you?" he counters. "Because I can tell you that, officially or not, you are my wife—the mother of my child. And no matter where we are, as long as we are together, we're home."

Again, another reason I am pregnant. The man has a way to my heart.

I smile and run my fingers through his hair. His eyes drift shut at my touch.

This man just left his family.

He grabbed his book bag and made it look like any other school day.

We took only the essentials for what we needed to survive and to deliver a baby.

This cabin is where we'll bring our son into this world in secret.

This cabin is where we'll become parents.

He's right. We don't need to be official to make this moment special. It's already everything.

Because we're together, and nothing, not even a signed certificate of marriage, will dampen the significance of what this moment means to us.

"All right," I say as his eyes open. "You can carry me over the threshold. But," I add quickly, "on two conditions."

"Anything."

Gah, I love this man. "You get rid of the spider, *and when we're married, you do it again—officially.*"

I should have known. He will always honor his word, even if he promised it years ago.

"Come on, Ray, don't be shy." He holds his arms out, and I swear I'm not sure if I love him or hate him more in this moment.

"We're naked." And freezing, but I don't say that. Because he knows it's his fault we had to strip on the deck in the first place.

"And? I'm not seeing an issue here."

Of course, he wouldn't. Naked time is his favorite.

"There's not even a spider," he adds, when I just stand there, shivering, with a stupid grin on my face. This man is so cute it crumbles every bit of willpower I have to deny him.

Not that I want to.

But a blanket would be nice.

"Come on, Sunny Ray," he coaxes, trailing a finger down my breasts.

"You're not going to deny me of performing my duty, are you?" He flashes me a wink. "After all, it was you who requested an official moment."

"I didn't think I would be naked, though." I laugh, and he uses the opportunity to scoop me up into his arms, holding me close.

"Don't blame me that you're naked," he says, walking toward the door. "Had you not needed a swim, we would be clothed and already sitting by the fire."

He opens the door and flashes me a grin. "But you can never just let me do this without an argument."

"That's not true."

He arches a brow.

"Okay, fine. Maybe I've been difficult… at times."

The spider was a serious issue, though. I will always argue about that.

"It's a good thing I know how to deal with your difficult self." He grins, taking the last remaining steps through the door.

"Welcome home, Dr. Potter," I whisper, staring deep into his eyes. This time is different. This time, we aren't on the run and scared. This time, he's officially mine.

"And we're done here. I need to get you warmed up with my tongue." He grins and kicks the door closed behind him, taking off at a trot.

"You are so ridiculous." I can't help the laugh that bursts out of me while I hang on to his neck as he leads us down the hall to the bathroom, which has been heavily remodeled since the last time I was here.

"Ridiculous," he chides, "is the violent way you're shivering. It's not *that* cold." He sets me down on the floor, and I brace for the cold tile, but it never comes.

"Heated floors." He grins.

Why must he be absolutely adorable? I swear, I never had a chance of not falling in love with him.

"Well, I'm sorry I don't run five degrees hotter than the average human like you." It could be twenty below, and this man would still jog in shorts. He never gets cold.

"Lucky for you, I'll always be here to keep you warm." He turns on the faucet, letting the water fill the clawfoot tub, but we both know he isn't just promising a warm bath. He's promising a lifetime of warmth in all the ways he can offer. Duke Potter has kept the trauma of that winter we spent in this very cabin from seeping into my bones. He might not have known it, but he has.

I remembered the warmth of his smile.

The way his warm hand held mine while he whispered my name like a prayer. "Sunny Ray," he would say. "*My midnight sun, the light of my life.*"

I had never been the light of someone's life—never felt so cherished, so precious—until I lay in this man's arms and let him ruin me for all others.

He started as my muse.

The boy that sat across from me in history class.

The one who always needed to borrow a pencil.

He was relentless in his pursuit of my attention.

And I was helpless to stop it.

Not when he asked me to tutor him in chemistry when his GPA was higher than mine.

Not when he bribed my friend to leave me stranded after school so he could be the one to take me home.

And I especially didn't stop him when I found him on the bench that afternoon where I sketched into the evening.

Duke Potter has always known what he wanted.

Me.

And that kind of devotion is unmatched in every area of my life.

He's right. He has, and always will, keep me warm—even if he's the reason I'm literally cold right now.

"I remembered the bath salts," he says, all proud of himself as he sprinkles them in the water. "Just in case you get sore again."

"I'm starting to think you just like me wet and naked."

I know good and damn well he didn't jump in that lake just because I wouldn't wake up. The man is still a rambunctious boy. He wanted to jump in because the lake is his favorite—even when it's too cold to get in. During our last winter here, he spent hours on the dock, just staring at the ripples in the water.

The lake is his peace.

"Newsflash, Ray. I always think of ways to get you wet and naked. My intentions are always two-fold and never as chivalrous as you think they are."

I laugh. At least he's honest. "When you plan these naked times," I tease, stepping into the hot water, "do you plan to get naked with me?"

Because I will be seriously bitter if he leaves me alone in this tub.

"I'm so disappointed in you, Ray." He makes a tsking sound as he drops towels on the stool and steps into the water. Duke insisted if we didn't want to be the next Rose and Jack from Titanic, we should immediately strip and use each other's body heat to stave off the hypothermia.

Again, his way of getting us naked on the back deck so he could carry me over the threshold properly—his words, not mine.

But you didn't see me complaining.

Because I love this man and his creative ways of loving all of me.

"Come here, Mrs. Potter."

The name snaps me to attention as he eases down into the water, his defined pecs the only skin on display.

For a moment, all I do is stare at his hooded eyes and outstretched hand, beckoning for me.

"Ray?" he prompts. "Is something wrong? Is it this cabin?" Concern takes over, and he sits up straight. "We can leave. We don't have to stay here if you don't—"

I slide closer, stopping him right there. "I love you," I admit abruptly, an urgent need taking over. "Sometimes I'm overwhelmed by the sheer vastness of it." Placing my palms against his cheeks, I lean in, pressing my forehead against his. "It's all-consuming—always floating around me."

He groans, taking my hips in his hand.

"I thought I was crazy—that I had issues that I let manifest into my need for you. I tried to let you go."

His fingers tighten against me as if he's prepared for me to run.

"But after being without you for so long, I know now that it wasn't a mental need for you in my life."

I take his hand from my hip and move it up my body, letting it rest on my chest. "This need—this love I have for you—is soul deep. When I'm without you, I'm incomplete. You fulfill me, Duke Potter. You complete me in an otherworldly way."

A tear streaks down my cheek, but I don't stop it. "And I know that sounds cringey, but it's true. I am wholly me when I am with you. I'm not a congressman's daughter or even an artist. I'm simply Ray—*your Ray*—and nothing, not even time or tragedy, has dulled the love I have for you." I press a kiss to his lips. "I am honored to have lived this life with you, Duke Potter—all the wonderful and messy moments of it."

I ease down, straddling his hips. "And no matter what happens next, loving you will always be worth the heartbreaking winters."

It wasn't the sexy words he probably expected, but I needed to say it, anyway. We've been through so much with each other. We've lived apart. We've broken and rebuilt. But somehow, we've found our way back to one another. We've found our way home.

Inhaling, I find Duke's heated eyes. "Let me show you where your heart is, Dr. Potter." I position myself over his cock, waiting.

This isn't like when we were at the hotel, recently married. This is home. This is where our heart is.

The fall and winter were sacred.

A time when we loved.

And a time we lost.

That winter, we found a future.

That winter, we found our hearts.

This winter, we'll breathe life back into our lives.

No longer is this the season of grieving. It's the season of loving.

And I want nothing more than to love this man who couldn't bear to part with any piece of us, even this cabin.

"Love me," I tell him, lowering down, feeling the tip of his cock pierce my center, stretching me with every inch, "so I'll always remember what it feels like to be loved under the warmth of the midnight sun."

CHAPTER TWENTY-TWO

Ramsey

"Do you think he'll take after me and become an artist or after you and become the next Dr. Potter?"

Duke's eyes dance with amusement as he holds my foot, his hand steady as he applies the red polish to my toes. "Who says I'll end up being a doctor? I kind of like being a handyman."

He's been a terrible handyman, but Mr. Clark, the owner of the cabin, helped him get the job. We needed money, and Duke, a man that has always come from money, set any pride he had aside and took whatever he could get.

He didn't care what people thought of him.

He only cared about his family—that we were warm and fed.

So he's been working odd jobs, learning the trade of repairs from a guy named Bill, whose wife sends us leftover dinners.

The people here in this small lake community are incredibly sweet. They haven't once given my swollen belly the side-eye. Instead, they asked if we had everything ready for the baby.

Which, we didn't.

But these people weren't like our parents. They didn't judge the decisions we made. They didn't ask us what we were thinking or how we planned to raise our son. Instead, they supported us with a job and hand-me-down baby supplies that currently sit under the artificial Christmas tree in the corner of the small living room. Mr. Clark said Ms. Clark had bought a new one this year, and they didn't need it.

I'm not sure if that's the case, but either way, we're grateful to spend Christmas Eve with a full belly and money in our pockets. It's not much, and not the life Duke deserves, but right now, we're together and content with knowing this choice was ours.

Shifting to a more comfortable position, I flash Duke a weighted smile. "You're lying. You do not love being a handyman."

He doesn't stop painting my little toe. "Maybe I wouldn't love being a doctor either."

"Your steady hands speak otherwise," I note, pointing out the skill he already mastered for the career.

"Steady hands don't equal happiness," he argues. "If you hadn't gotten pregnant, and gone to Europe as your father planned, painting, but with another man, would you be happy?"

I have to fight back nausea. "No. I wouldn't. Painting without you—"

"Exactly. Just because I love something doesn't mean that I would love it without the person that means the most to me. I'm happy, Ray, as long as I'm with you."

Leaning up as best I can with this ball of a baby in my tummy, I find his lips, pressing a soft kiss before pulling back. "I just want the best for you. I couldn't live with myself if you didn't fulfill your purpose in this life."

"My purpose, Ray," he says, leaning his forehead against mine, "is being the husband and father you both deserve. Having a degree, becoming a doctor, and living in a nice house are tangible things that I could lose. I'll eventually retire, we'll move, could go bankrupt. But my love for you and our son will always remain through it all. I don't worry about what I don't have. Because everything that fulfills my soul is right here on the sofa."

He drags in a deep breath and presses his lips to mine. "I already have more than most people, Ray, and I'd do anything to keep it."

"Even if that means giving up a dream?" *I whisper.*

He pulls back and flashes me a solemn smile. "What's a victory if you don't have anyone to share it with?"

Oh, this man will always have my heart.

"You're right," *I say with a hint of wonder in my voice,* "and I promise to always be there to share those victories with you."

"You sure?" *His voice has a taunting edge to it.* "Because now is the time to back out." *He moves over my body, careful not to put any weight on me.* "You know how greedy I can get."

His mouth goes to my neck, distracting me from where his hands rest on the underside of my thighs. "I'm sure—ahh! Stop—"

"Duke, stop!" *I scream, the memory of the last time we were in the living room fading in my panic.* "I'm going to fall!"

"I won't let you fall," *he promises, not letting me go as he situates me on his shoulders.* "Someone has to put the angel on the top of the tree."

I lock my legs around him and hold on to his head. "I am a grown-ass woman who should not be on your shoulders," *I argue.* "You could have just grabbed the ladder."

"Where would be the fun in that?" *I can hear the smile in his voice.*

"The fun will be when we don't break a bone decorating the Christmas tree." *Seriously, I can't remember the last time I've been this high off the ground.*

"Oh, ye of little faith," *he says, handing me the tree topper, which I grab with one hand so I don't have to let his head go. My balance has never been great, but this is just asking for trouble.*

"I have faith," *I pop back.* "Just not in myself."

I can feel Duke's shoulders shake underneath me. "Then have faith in me. I promise I won't drop you."

"Fine," *I whine. He's never failed me yet, even if I do want to doubt his ability to walk us over to the tree so I can place the angel. I know he would never intentionally drop me, but he could trip.*

"Breathe, Ray." He takes a few steps toward the tree. "We've been here before."

Yes, we have, but that tree was much shorter than this monster we cut down earlier, but that's not what keeps me from saying anything and letting fear ruin this moment for him.

It's my promise that I made many years ago to celebrate every victory with him.

He said he never needed a tree since that last Christmas we spent here.

He's never decorated another tree.

He's waited nearly two decades to celebrate this win with me.

My heart can't even take the amount of love rushing through my veins. This man was adamant that his happiness came from sharing his wins with me. And at the time he made that declaration, I wasn't sure if I understood the magnitude of the feeling of sharing a soul-deep connection with someone. But now, on top of this man's shoulders, as he hums a classic Christmas carol under his breath, his body thrumming with excitement as I place the angel on the highest peak to watch over us all, I realize that he was right. This small, seemingly insignificant moment that essentially only lasts an entire minute was one of the greatest moments I've ever had.

Maybe it was his excitement.

Maybe it was the smell of the real tree with the bright lights and ornaments.

But maybe it was the same reason it was just as magical as it was all those years ago.

Because we are together, sharing this moment.

Sharing this victory of overcoming all odds.

We found our way home and back into each other's arms.

It didn't matter that years have passed, and we were no closer to finding our son than we were yesterday.

All that matters is this moment—this small victory of being together on Christmas as a family—whole or not.

"I got it," I finally say when the angel is secure and not at risk of plunging to the hardwood floor.

Holding my legs, Duke takes a few steps back. He's stopped humming, the house falling silent as we simply take it all in.

This cabin.

This tree.

This love between us.

"It's everything I've dreamed of," I finally say, breaking the silence. "A small victory with you."

Duke makes a noise in his throat as he lowers to the sofa so I can get down and face him.

"A small victory," he agrees as he trails his finger along my cheek, "that will be one of many."

And then he kisses me. "Merry Christmas, my love."

I can't sleep—not even snuggled in Duke's arms.

Years ago, the reason was a wiggly baby growing in my stomach, but tonight, that baby's somersaults aren't the cause of my insomnia.

But wondering about him is.

Pulling out my sketchpad, I curl up on the sofa, turning on nothing but a small lamp on the table. Duke was out in a matter of seconds, which is great. He needed rest. He might act like he has everything handled, and knowing him, he probably has most of it covered, but there's always that small part of him that will obsess and worry that he's done everything he could to ensure our plans go off without a hitch.

But this time, we can't prepare.

We have failed.

And failure teaches us to fear.

No matter how prepared we are, we can still fail.

Kelly, from the network, could come up with nothing.

Langston could burn any evidence of paperwork and die with

the location of Jude. After all, what he's done is a crime. We know it. He knows it, and so do our parents. When that many powerful men are threatened, they will band together and fight back.

I doubt that any of the three will grow a conscience and say they're sorry. That's why it was so important that I found the documents before Langston realized what I was up to.

But that ship has sailed.

Duke and I are in this together—us against the world.

But we both know, even if by some miracle we do find out where Jude is, there is no guarantee that he'll want to see us or that he's even alive. Tragedies happen every day—I know all too well that I'm not immune to hardship. But just this once, I pray that's not the case and that all this effort, all this time we've sacrificed is enough to at least see our son—to see what we created together.

Does he look like Duke, or did he inherit my red hair?

Does he love to draw, or did he turn out to love medicine instead?

The questions I have are endless.

But the most important ones are: Is he alone tonight? Is he staring at a Christmas tree and feeling empty? Or is he surrounded by laughter with a family who loves him more than life itself?

I hope it's the latter, even if my soul aches thinking about it.

I hope he's had a good life.

I hope he hasn't been restless like me. I hope he hasn't been searching for something he doesn't know is missing.

But most of all, I hope he's celebrated small victories with people he loves.

"Ray?" Duke's sleepy voice pulls me from my thoughts.

"Hey," I say, putting my sketchpad down and scooting over so he can sit down and lay his head on my lap. "You should go back to bed," I encourage him. "My lap isn't as comfortable as the bed."

He locks his arms around my waist, a clear message that he's not going back to bed until I do. "What's worrying you?" Just having his arms around me calms my anxiety.

I thread my fingers through his hair, admiring how boyish he looks, all rumpled and sleepy. "I was just wondering what Jude was doing this Christmas."

Duke's arms tighten around me. "We're gonna find him. I promise."

I love this man more than life itself.

I trust him implicitly.

I just hope I'm not killing what's left of him by chasing a ghost.

CHAPTER TWENTY-THREE

Ramsey

"What in the world is that supposed to be?"

Duke rears back like he's offended. "It's a Santa hat."

Blinking like that's gonna make it look any better, I cast one more look at the blob of red icing on his sugar cookie. "It looks like a half circle, half cone."

"Well, we can't all be talented artists, now, can we?"

Someone got up far too early this morning—which wouldn't have happened if he'd gone to bed when I told him. Instead, he pulled me down next to him and spooned me the rest of the night. It left us both with a kink in our neck to start off Christmas morning.

"I'm sorry. Your cookie is the cutest Santa hat I have ever seen." I glance at mine, which is a Christmas tree with ornaments. "It's—"

I chuckle, and a cookie smacks into my chest, sliding down my boobs, leaving a trail of icing in its wake. "Did you just throw a cookie at me?"

I can't believe this man actually threw a cookie. Well, I mean, I can, but still—it's Christmas.

"I dropped it," Duke lies. "But rest assured, I'll clean it up."

He grabs me around the waist and snatches me forward. His eyes darken, and a smirk plays on his lips. "Hold still, Ray. This might take a while." He lowers his head to my chest, his lips lightly brushing it as he nips at the icing, sending chills along my skin.

"You're missing the mess." I groan, my breathing turning shallow as he continues to kiss me. I don't think I'll ever get tired of him kissing me—loving me. I feel deprived of all the years I've missed under his hands.

He pauses, and I almost grab his head. "Well, we can't have that. After all, I'm a man of my word." He lifts my shirt from the bottom, pulling it over my head and tossing it to the floor.

His hands reach around my back, and suddenly, my bra slides down my arms, catching on my wrists. "Ah, that's better," he observes, licking his lips like he's ravenous. "Tell me, Ray. Whose tits are these?"

Oh, dear goodness, why must he drag this out? "Yours." I groan. "Only yours."

"That's right," he confirms with a kiss to my nipple. "No one else gets to see these but me, Ray."

It's not like I went around showing the neighbors, but I agree anyway.

Because hello, he was in the middle of something.

"No one but you, Dr. Potter."

He hums in pleasure, then lowers, taking my nipple into his mouth.

"Mm-hmm..." My knees nearly buckle, but he holds me up until he has me thoroughly worked up and panting when he suddenly stops and steps back, smacking my butt like some football player. "Got it. You're good now."

He waves his hand as if telling me to proceed with decorating.

"Seriously?" I narrow my eyes. "That's all?"

His mouth falls open in feigned shock. "I thought you wanted to decorate cookies?"

"I do," I snap, backing him up against the small island, "but then you had to go and get me worked up. I don't think that's very fair. Do you?" I mean, seriously, how would he feel if I revved his engine and then walked away? "I think you're being a cock tease this morning."

His back hits the counter, and he chuckles. "I must say, that's the first time I've ever been called such a thing."

"And it will be the last, Dr. Potter. I have zero patience for teasing."

The pupils in his eyes widen. "Now, that's not true." He twirls the strand of my hair. "I clearly remember you enjoying my teasing."

Okay, he's right there, but I'll never admit it.

"But if I've upset you, I'm ready to make things right." He seems so freaking cocky—so confident in his ability to melt me into a puddle of mush.

"Okay," I tell him. "You can make it up to me." A sneaky grin curls onto my lips as his cock jumps between us.

"Tell me what you need, Mrs. Potter."

And this is where he goes down. "I need you to put your hands on the counter, Dr. Potter, and don't move them until I tell you that you can."

He smirks, but it falters. He didn't expect to be the one on the receiving end of this game, even if his words say otherwise. "I think I like this bossiness, Ray. It's turning me on."

As it should. One of my favorite things is to play with Duke Potter when he allows it.

He drags his palms against my chest before extending his arms out wide and placing them on the counter.

"You might want to hang on," I warn.

"Oh, yeah?" He sounds excited.

Stepping closer, I press against him and kiss the scruff on his jaw. "Yeah, things might get a little rough."

It's been a very long time since I've taken Duke in my mouth. I hope it's like riding a bike because this girl is as experienced as a virgin.

But if there was anyone who would be a patient participant, it would be Duke, who rolls his fingers around the edge of the granite, bracing himself. "Do your worst, Ray."

I chuckle. My worst he might actually get.

Holding his gaze, I watch as it turns from amused to heated as I lower to my knees, my fingers delicately pulling the strings of his sweats.

"Oh, fuck." He throws his head back like standing still is painful. "I can already see this ending with your ass up over a bar stool."

Meaning, he's indulging me for as long as he can stand it, which, by the twitch in his forearms, isn't long.

"That may be so," I tell him, "but for now, this is beginning with you balls deep down my throat."

"Shut up, Ray," he growls, "before I stop playing your little game. You know my patience is limited when you're on your knees."

Empty threats.

At least for now.

He might be impatient, but he'll wait because this is his favorite, me on my knees, his cock in my mouth as I stare up at him with wide eyes as he uses my mouth for his own pleasure.

Ignoring his impatient tittering, I dip my hands into the waistband of his pants and tug slowly—excruciatingly slow.

"Dammit, Ray. You're playing a dangerous game."

A game we'll both enjoy winning.

Smiling, I keep pace and reach for his boxers. At my touch, his cock jumps against the fabric. "Mmm…" I take a deep breath, flashing one more coy look at Duke before kissing his cock through the fabric.

"Don't let go, husband, or I might stop."

Anticipation is such sweet torture.

"Swear to…" His eyes pinch shut, and he throws his head back once again. "I don't even fucking know what, I swear. I can't think right now. But I can promise I will return the favor, wife."

He's back to threats, which really is all his fault. He started this over a freaking cookie.

"Just relax," I whisper softly, making him snap.

"I can't fucking relax. All I can think of is snatching you up and bending you over a chair."

Poor thing. What a hard life he leads.

"Maybe I can help you," I tease, finally lowering his boxers and taking his swollen cock in my hand.

He grunts, his cock jumping in anticipation. "Please, Ray, I fucking beg you. Please don't torture me." He sounds so helpless, so vulnerable. "Please, just put me inside you."

I smile. This man is never short on telling me how much he desires my body or even my company. He's always been open and honest in that regard. It's the other deeper secrets he likes to keep to himself.

But intimacy—that's always been our love language.

He is the other piece of me. We fit together in perfect harmony.

Together, we're whole.

Opening wide, I take him past my lips and push forward as far as I can until he hits the back of my throat.

"Oh, shit, Ray. You were made to kill me." He tries adjusting his angle to get deeper, but I grip him at the base and take control by sliding him out and licking the swollen vein from root to tip.

He hisses through his teeth, his knuckles turning white against the counter.

But I don't give him time to rest before easing my lips over his tip and swirling my tongue around the head. His knees buckle, and I think that's it. He's done. I might as well bend over, but he doesn't stop me.

Instead, he pulls in a shuttering breath and rights himself against the island. "One more of those, Ray, and playtime is over."

Inwardly, I smile. He acts like he's doing me a favor standing here, enduring a blow job from his wife.

Let's see if we can fix that.

Gripping him, I move my hand in a steady, up-and-down rhythm. When I see his neck muscles straining, I ease the head of his cock past my teeth and suck, bobbing my head in time with my hand.

I take him deep.

Take his groans.

Feel his hands tangle in my hair, moving with me as I work him into a frenzy.

I don't know how long I stroke him, but when I feel him swell inside my mouth, I'm suddenly ripped away.

"Time's up," he grits out, like it pained him. "My turn."

He shoves a bar stool in front of me, and without missing a beat, he presses me down onto my stomach, his breath in my ear when he says, "Might want to hang on, sweetheart. This might get a little rough."

"You promise?" I grin and find the legs of the stool, gripping them hard. There's no way he won't pound the hell out of me now. I have pushed him over the edge—snapped the last of his control.

I love the wild and abandoned side of him.

I love to see him lose control.

To exert his power like he did when he stole me from Langston.

This is the man who owns me, body and soul—and I love to see him consume the very thing he holds above all others.

Me.

"Ray," he says, finding the waistband of my shorts and yanking them just low enough for his fingers to find my center. "I'd be careful taunting me." He slides two fingers in, the delightful stretch pulling a moan from my lips. "I might decide that one is not enough."

Before I can ask what he means, the tip of his cock nudges my entrance, a gentle warning before he thrusts in to the hilt, stealing my breath in one go.

Duke groans, his head coming to rest on my back as I adjust to the intrusion. "Show me my heart, Ray."

And I do, taking his hand and placing it on my chest, where my heart beats wildly for the man who wholly consumes me with an unforgiving passion, taking every thrust, every breath until we're both a spent mess in the kitchen with the smell of burnt cookies in the oven.

It was a Christmas I would never forget.

That is, until the phone rang—a call that changed our lives forever.

CHAPTER TWENTY-FOUR

Duke

"I'm sorry, man. This doesn't mean anything."

Vance's assurance does nothing to ease the pain in my chest. Not after Ray heard the news and ran outside to the dock.

The adoptive mother of our son is dead.

That's all the information Harrison Potter could find. A death certificate of the woman who cared for our boy.

"What about the father?" Ray's mom said it was a couple who took him.

Vance clears his throat. "A politician—he passed a few years ago."

"And they didn't leave any mention of the child? No will that left him any cash or assets?"

I'm grasping at straws, but this can't be the only lead—one that went absolutely nowhere.

Vance sighs. "There's no mention of a child anywhere that we can find. They hid him well, or Harrison is a fucking liar. I'm leaning toward the latter."

I'm not so sure. Harrison Potter would easily lie to Astor and me, but knowing his precious son is upset, I think he'd do whatever it took to get back in Vance's good graces—even if that meant helping me in the process.

"But how could he just disappear?"

This doesn't make sense. None of it does.

I can feel Vance's weariness drift through the phone when he says, "I think you need to accept that anything could have happened with Jude. Paula, the supposed adoptive mother to Jude, died years after he was born. Knowing Langston, his friends couldn't be much better than him." He pauses before he finishes shattering what's left of my hope. "If she wanted the child but then died, it's possible her husband jumped ship and left him with the nanny—or anyone for that matter."

My poor boy, what happened to you?

"How did she die again?" I just can't let it go. We are closer than we ever were before. It can't just stop here.

"Um," Vance hums absently, likely scanning the document before he adds, "it says cardiac arrest."

Well, that could be from anything. I rake my hands through my hair and start to pace. "And Harrison doesn't know these people at all? No family or anything?" Now I'm just thinking aloud, vomiting all the questions until something clicks. "What about next of kin on the death certificate?"

"I checked already. Just a brother who is also dead."

"What in the total fuck?" I yell, allowing my frustration to bleed into the conversation. "Do these people just have bad karma or bad eating habits?"

Vance chuckles. "Well, I'd vote karma, since they are friends with Langston, but the physician in me says it was age and comorbidities that got them in the end. Not everyone has great genes, brother."

If I had only known before.

If I had the same intuition—the same hope Ray did, maybe I would have looked for him sooner. I could have found his parents when they were still alive.

"We'll keep looking," Vance promises, his voice holding a finality to it. "He's a Potter, and you know all too well that Potters can survive anything."

I don't remember what the rest of our call consisted of. I just remember wishing Hal a Merry Christmas and teasing Remington to send me a picture of the stocking with his name on it that he had to open in front of Vance this morning. Then I called Astor and held back tears as I watched him and Keys coo over Tatum, whose face I could barely see under the huge Christmas bow on her head.

But it wasn't until I finished the call that I sat down on the sofa, feeling the weight of the past twenty minutes settle onto my shoulders. What if I can never give Ray the life she deserves? Maybe I was wrong for loving her all those years ago and threatening the other boys in our school for even looking at her.

I've done everything I could to ensure she would always be mine, and look where that's gotten both of us: Ray, out on the dock—risking a vicious snake crawling up her leg as she experiences yet another awful Christmas alone.

What good life have I truly given her? A son she's only held once? A home she's only spent two seasons in?

The only true thing I've ever given her was pain.

And I'm so sorry that I can never fix it. No matter how hard I try, I can't heal the pain I've caused. I was the reason she had to run away from home and have the baby in a rundown cabin. If I hadn't gotten her pregnant at eighteen, she would have never endured the pain of losing a child not only once but twice.

I can't seem to stop making bad decisions.

Should I have let her have a go at Langston to find Jude on her own?

Something swirls in my stomach, and I know that even if I thought that was true, I couldn't risk her more pain or bruises on chance.

I also know somewhere deep beyond the pain that there is nothing greater than creating a life with someone you love. And there was never a doubt that I didn't love Ramsey Ford or the child we created. And that love—that experience—however fleeting, is worth all the pain we've endured.

I just wish I could stop it.

I wish we could be like everyone else.

Sometimes, I envy the wicked ones. Their lives seem so simple—so easy. They do well at work, have more children than they need, and when life's stresses get too much, they jet off to a tropical island for peace and privacy.

I've been fortunate in amassing my wealth.

But it hasn't come easy.

I wasn't handed a silver spoon because I wasn't the same as my father.

I didn't realize why back then, but now, as an adult, I know that the greatest joys in life are free. They aren't earned—they're given.

Ray loved me without conditions.

And I promised her a future without a bargain.

I'd like to think a love as pure as ours deserved the blessing of a child.

And I thought we got that.

But that wasn't the case.

Even now, after everything we've been through, we still don't have the happily ever after we deserve.

And maybe having a child isn't our future.

Maybe our purpose is something other than being a good partner and parent.

I hope not.

Because I'm not prepared to be anything else.

I'm lost just like I was before.

Before I found Ray again.

Before I knew my son survived.

My life before a couple of months ago was nonexistent. It wasn't full of anything but repetition. I was a ghost drifting in and out of each day, doing what I was supposed to do.

Working.
Breathing.
Eating.
Sleeping.

I was a man without a purpose. Ray was on a mission. And now both of us are right back where we started.

In pain.

Sighing, I leave my phone on the sofa, walk outside to the dock, and find Ray trying to skip rocks on the water, just like I taught her years ago.

"You're still holding it wrong," I tell her when I get within earshot. "Lay it sideways between your fingers."

Ray holds up the rock between her thumb and pointer finger, showing me. "Like this?"

"Yep. Now turn to the side." I move behind her and press my front to her back. "Curl your wrist like I showed you and sling it."

She mimics the hand motion and throws. The rock skips over the water twice, and she grins, her voice raspy from crying as she says, "I did it. It's not as good as when you do it, but—"

I turn her and kiss her mouth, offering her comfort in my arms. Which she takes gratefully, burying her face in my shirt as the tears overtake her again. "Did Vance say anything we could use?"

I tuck her head under my chin. "Don't you give up yet," I threaten. "He's out there, and there's not an inch of this earth that I wouldn't tear through to find him."

She nods, seemingly growing stronger as the seconds tick by, and she finally steps out of my arms, wiping the tears along her face. "How many times did you try teaching me to skip rocks the last time we were here?"

I chuckle, remembering all the rocks she just chucked into the lake. She could never quite master the angle. "More than I can count."

"I told you it was the belly throwing my balance off," she argues.

I flash her this look of bullshit. There's no way that happened. "Or maybe you spent all those years in France chucking stones in the Mediterranean."

She laughs. "No, I didn't. I'd have no reason to practice while we were apart."

She swallows, seeming to fight back another wave of emotion as she likely thinks of the same thing I am. The whole reason I started teaching her in the first place. *"You have to learn, Ray, because one day, he's going to be big enough to compete with us. You don't want to be the loser, do you?"*

I shake off the thought of us never standing on this dock as a family, skipping rocks with our son, and pull her in close, lightening the mood. "As competitive as you are, Ray, I wouldn't put anything past you. Practicing and everything."

She gurgles out a half laugh, half cry that nearly guts me. "I promise, I haven't tried skipping rocks since that winter."

Since that winter, when our entire lives were rocked.

I don't know if I can do this—stay here—pretending it's home when something feels like it's missing.

But what happens when I take Ray back to Texas? Is that home? Will we ever be able to call anywhere home when we always feel like home is still somewhere out there?

I don't know.

Everything feels chaotic and jumbled in my head right now. I need peace, and the only way I can find it is here—out here on this dock, where I would spend my days worrying about my girl and the son growing inside her.

Pulling Ray down to sit on the dock, I lean against a post and stare out at the water as she tilts her head up to look at me. "What do you think about when you're out here? It's something I've always wondered when you would sit out here for hours."

I shrug. "Everything."

"Well, that's super detailed. You might want to take a breath there. I don't know if we have enough daylight for you to finish that story."

I belt out a laugh that I really needed. "I don't know. Why do you like to paint?"

"I don't know. I just love it. I find clarity in the process."

"Exactly. When I look out at the vastness of the lake, I find peace."

I reach next to us, grab a stone from the pile she had, and toss it, watching as it skips six times across the water—much to Ray's dismay.

"The water, as you know," I continue, ignoring her annoyed sigh, "is home to many plants and animals." I grin. "Like snakes."

She pops me on the leg. "Don't even start with the snakes."

"And when a storm rolls in, it disrupts the surface of the water, but not the floor." I can feel the tension coil inside my body. "Well, most of the time. Anyway, when my head is full of chaos, I like to come out here and remember that the water is like my skin. It can be scarred and disrupted, but it doesn't affect the floor. It doesn't affect who I am on the inside. When I worried over you and Jude that winter—before he was born—I would come out here and be reminded that all the animals and plants can do is prepare. But they don't worry about survival. They can simply be. The water can rage above them and disrupt their environment, but when it's over, they go on living, surviving. I needed to survive those years after you and Jude disappeared. I needed to remember that my worry was only natural for humans. No other creature does it. They have faith they will be there tomorrow to continue on. Some days, I didn't feel like I could. I couldn't get up in the morning and face questions about my addiction or the disappointment from my family. I found it difficult to even dress most mornings. But I thought about the water here and how the ripples on the surface only affect the environment."

I shrug, feeling silly for even saying the words aloud. But she wanted to know what I thought about, and it's the same thing I think about now when I stare out at the vastness. "The water is a constant reminder to just be. It doesn't matter what disrupts my environment as long as I serve my purpose and prepare."

And that's exactly what I intend to do.

We can find our purpose again.

I can be the husband she deserves, and whether my son is alive or not, I will be the father who didn't quit until he found him one way or another.

I just need to prepare.

CHAPTER TWENTY-FIVE

Ramsey

It's been a few days since we last spoke with Vance. Duke has thrown himself into searching for Jude every minute of the day. The only sleep he gets is with a few naps here and there. He won't even eat unless I—you guessed it—get naked and convince him.

He's not well.

Neither am I.

I'm worried this search isn't good for either of us. There's a time when hope becomes a crutch. Should we keep our lives on pause in search of something or someone we think will complete us? Will we be happy then? Are we happy now?

While we might be in the cabin we called home many years ago, it doesn't feel much like home now, because it's not the future we thought we would share in it.

That's the funny thing about dreams; you never know when you've failed or if it's just another setback that you should power through.

The problem is acceptance. At what point does a dream become a debilitating excuse not to move on?

When it consumes you like it did Duke and I? Do we even know what it feels like to be content anymore? We've lived our entire lives chasing a future we might never achieve.

What does that mean for our relationship?

What happens when we get closure?

Will I still be Duke's ray of sunshine when he has his son? Or will the clouds of despair take him under if he finds out he no longer has a son and must grieve him all over again?

Where does that leave us?

Can we be happy with just each other?

We were once.

Before I became pregnant—when he was the only man in my life.

But now?

When he's buried in online chats and meetings with private investigators… I'm not so sure. His silence haunts me, just like it did before, and I'm terrified this is all ending before I even had the chance to know the man and father that is Duke Potter.

But love doesn't follow a playbook.

It's not easy.

But it *is* worth it.

And as long as Duke is still willing to fight for an unknown future, then I am, too.

Because we're worth the fight.

I drag my finger through the paint on the canvas, smearing the color over the edge. It's not my greatest work, or even worthy of being seen, but I needed a distraction. Duke has the lake, and I have the canvas. But clearly, neither of those escapes are calming the chaos in our minds—especially when I feel a set of arms drape over my shoulders.

"Should I be worried about Langston's safety?" Duke's voice has a teasing lilt to it, which settles something deep inside me.

He's finally broken his silence.

"Depends on him," I say. "He has the power to put a stop to our pain."

But we all know he won't, because men like Langston need to keep their secrets.

Secrets equal power in Langston's world. He won't give them up without a fight—which is hard when you're the underdog fighting blindly in a world you removed yourself from many years ago.

Duke's lips find my neck. "We have the power, my love." His hand trails down my breasts, covered with only a tank top, until he reaches my lap, finding the tube of paint between my legs. "We can silence the screams."

And we can give his silence a voice.

"All we need to do is remember." He hands me the tube of paint, kissing me softly when I take it. "Help me remember, Ray. Show me the way back to my heart."

And then his weight is gone from my shoulders.

I swivel around just as he pulls off his shirt, giving me a clean canvas—my favorite one. Him.

He wants to remember—just like me—what it was like when things were simpler between us.

When he was my muse, and I was his heart.

"Silence your screams," he commands, his eyes red from exhaustion. "Help us remember."

Then he lies down on the floor where we did this so many years before. But this time, his body is bulkier with defined hills of muscles that disappear underneath his sweatpants. He's all strength and power of a wealthy man, but the broken boy still hovers at the surface, waiting to break everything he's built for himself.

Standing, I grab a throw pillow from the sofa and slip it under his head. His eyes close as soon as I place my hand on his cheek. "I promise to remember," I agree, "if you'll promise not to break."

We've come too far and sacrificed too many years to break now.

"Don't let our suffering be in vain."

Never opening his eyes, Duke nods. He doesn't want me to see the pain he hides away from the world. The pain that causes him to grieve every fall and winter.

This man is so strong—so good—pain can't be the only thing in his future.

I press a kiss to his lips, and he makes a soft hum as he takes my hand. "Show me my heart, Ray." He swallows under my touch, his face scrunching under my gaze.

Something in my heart flutters. This is the Duke Potter I know. The one that is obsessed with his heart—obsessed with the artist who holds it. This is the Duke who nestles me in his arms, whispering dreams and promises in my ear. I won't let the silence take him again.

I can't.

I owe him that much.

Reaching back, I remove my shirt and then unclasp my bra, letting it fall to my wrists, watching as his eyes take in the exposed skin before I toss it to the floor.

"Give me your hand, Dr. Potter." He does, and I bring it to my mouth, placing a kiss to his palm. This man might need to see his heart, but I want him to feel it thrumming under my skin, beating erratically every time he comes into my view. He can feel, without a doubt, how much I love him—how much I breathe just for him by merely feeling.

He's the reason I kept going all these years.

He's the reason I still believe in love.

He's the reason I don't scream anymore.

Pulling his hand away, I grab the paint and squirt a dab on his index finger. His eyes follow the slow, methodic movement as I bring his hand to my chest. "Stake your claim, husband."

I can't always be the one who shows him his heart. Sometimes, he needs to remember it still beats right where he left it.

He needs to know that no matter how much he shuts down, I am still here, holding on to all that's precious to him.

With need nestled deep in his eyes, Duke presses the tip of his finger to my chest and draws his heart, reclaiming the space I hold so dear. "I—" he starts, then shakes his head.

"You what?" I grab the paint and squirt some onto my finger, too, holding his gaze as he wrestles with the thoughts in his head.

He swallows, his jaw working. "I feel guilty."

A part of me is excited he's finally opening up rather than holding on to his silence, but then there's another part of me that dreads hearing what he needs to say.

"You have no reason to feel guilty." I swipe down his chest with the paint, creating the outline of the image in my head—a pair of brown eyes.

"Yes, I do," he argues, his eyes closing as I smudge the paint at the corners. "I feel guilty that I didn't grieve with you while you waited—hoping. I just can't—" He fights back the emotion. "I just can't live with myself. I let you down, Ray, and I'm so fucking sorry I haven't been there for you."

As much as his words settle around my heart like a protective warmth, I can't allow him to think I blame him for anything. "I didn't want you to be there for me, Duke."

I grab more paint, this time squeezing it directly on his chest.

He sucks in a deep breath at the cool sensation. "I should have been there for you anyway—whether you wanted me to or not."

I can't help but grin. My white knight who can't take no for an answer. The world's problems are always his burden to carry. "No, you shouldn't have. I couldn't even look at you back then—not up close, anyway. I watched you from afar because it hurt too much to love you up close."

I frown as his hand cups my cheek. "You reminded me of what I could never have. All I saw when I looked at you was a future that the heavens now held. You were the father that gave his last breaths to save his son. You were the soulmate who endured ridicule and rumors to save me from being labeled a teen mom."

Leaning into his touch, I finish confessing everything that stopped me from leaving France and running back into his arms. "You were destined for greatness, and I had already taken so much from you. I wanted you to move on, to have a second chance at the life you wanted."

"But I wanted you." He seems so confused.

"And I you. But sometimes, you love someone so much that you sacrifice your wants for theirs. The world deserved you, Duke Potter, not me. You didn't need to grieve all year with me. You needed to live for all of us."

His face turns serious, and he sits up. "You say true love makes sacrifices." He huffs out this sound of disbelief. "But I didn't. I knew you wanted to marry Langston, but I took you anyway."

He's so cute, trying to paint his actions as the bad guy. "You knew I didn't love Langston," I say, pushing him back down to the floor. "You knew it because you've always known me better than anyone else. You knew I was up to something, so you did like you've always done. You saved me."

"And made things worse." He moves his hands to my hips like he intends to move me off him. And like the understanding wife I am, I lift up just enough to ease his pants to his thighs, halting his wiggling.

"I'll admit," I say, trailing the paint up his thigh, swirling it dangerously close to his thickening length, "you certainly complicated things."

The muscles in his neck tense as I draw a heart on his hip. "But, I'm used to your mess—even if it complicated the plan."

"Please," he begs, his eyes drifting closed. This heart-to-heart is turning into his favorite type of conversation—the naked kind.

"Please, what?" I squirt more paint on his chest, holding him captive. "Put you inside me?"

He nods, his hands gripping my hips. I can feel how badly he wants to grind me onto his cock, but he knows when he's the muse, and the muse is never the one in control.

"Fine," I agree, flashing him a wicked smile. "But only if you show me *my* heart." I place my hand on his chest. "Is it still here?" I ask. "Is it still where I left it?" Inside him.

Something heady passes between us—a bond that formed when we were merely kids. I've seen this boy grow into a man. I've witnessed his gift become a passion—a passion he used to save our son. I've watched him fall in love with me to the point that I fell in love with the girl he loved. I wanted to be the woman he thought she was.

So, I did.

I became the woman he deserved. I fought for her through the grief and pain because I hoped, one day, she would return to his side. I might have wanted him to heal and move on, but I never stopped loving him. I never stopped knowing that the only place I belonged was at his side.

That is the woman he's asking to help remember.

To remember who we were before we broke.

I smear the paint over his chest, making two loops at the top that fall into a V at the bottom. "Are you still with me, Dr. Potter? For whatever future lies ahead?"

It's the same question I've asked many other times, but when you've lived with grief, you understand the power twenty-four hours can have on a person. Some days, you can conquer the world. And others, you simply hope you can get through the next few minutes.

Duke's hand comes up and interlaces with mine as several emotions pass through his eyes, the most significant being determination. "I'm with you, Mrs. Potter. Now and always. Us against the world."

It's all I needed to hear as I guide him inside me, each of us offering the only thing we can give right now, our love and devotion.

With each rock of our hips, we solidify the bond and promise we've kept to each other.

No matter the future, we will endure just as we always have.

Together.

Because a love like ours only happens once in a lifetime.

And ours isn't over yet.

It's just getting started.

CHAPTER TWENTY-SIX

Ramsey

"His cheeks were chubbier."

I glance up from my sketchpad. "How would you know what he looked like? You weren't there that night."

My mother swallows uncomfortably. "I came to the hospital later."

I close my sketchbook and face her. "What do you mean by later? I don't remember you visiting me in the observation room."

"You need to know your father," she starts, flashing me a sad smile, "has his priorities, but he's only ever wanted what's best for you."

Chills break out along my spine. My mother and I rarely have heart-to-heart conversations. This particular night has been off-limits for years. "And what was best for me, Mother?"

Tears well in her eyes. "We thought you both would be better off." She shakes her head. "You and Duke couldn't raise him. You were still babies yourself."

"Mom." I sigh; her memory has been off since going through chemo.

"Jude died." But even if he hadn't, Duke and I were young, but we were eighteen. We were adults in the eyes of the law, and we could have raised him on our own. Maybe not perfectly, but we would have tried.

"He didn't die," she confesses as the tears stream down her face. "We lied to you."

"No," I respond, ignoring the pounding in my chest. "You're confused, Mama. Jude died."

She stares at me, and I know in that moment this isn't her disease talking. She's coming clean on her deathbed, and I don't know if I've ever hated someone—even my own family—as much as I hate her at this moment.

"Don't you lie to me," I plead. "Don't be cruel. You have no idea what I've been through to even be able to say his name."

Her tone softens. "I can't even imagine the pain you went through, Ramsey. It was cruel of us, and if I could take it all back, I would."

My body feels weightless as I look at my mother with urgency. "What did you do? What did you do with my baby?"

Tears stream down my face as her answering sob wracks through her frail body. "Your father and I just wanted what was best for you," she says again, like she's trying to believe it herself.

I fight the urge to lash out—she's sick and trying to make amends, even if it's years too late for being honorable.

"I find that hard to believe, especially now that you're telling me the son who I thought I had cremated is alive! Where is he, Mama? Where is my boy?"

She closes her eyes, the conversation weakening her even more than the cancer. "You had so much potential, Ramsey. So much that I couldn't bear to see you throw it away, not after you told us you would handle the situation."

"The 'situation' was a baby that Duke and I wanted!" I snap, my lip quivering with unleashed emotion. "I still had potential—even with a baby on my hip. Having Jude wouldn't have changed the person I became."

"Maybe not," she says, her voice placating.

It only upsets me more.

"But pursuing that potential would have been much harder for you."

I flash her a stern look. "I don't disagree with you there, but it was my choice. It was my path to alter—not yours or Dad's. Mine."

Duke and I wanted that baby more than anything. We knew it would be a hard and scary road. But we would have figured it out together.

"I see that now," she says, placing her cold hand over mine. "I never meant to cause you more pain. I just wanted you to have everything I didn't."

I scoff. "Instead, you gave me pain and killed any potential I had."

A lone tear streaks down my face. "Do you know what it feels like to be alone, Mother? Where the silence stretches into something you can't bear?"

I swipe at my cheek, not wanting her to see how her and my father's actions hurt me. They've already taken too much. I won't give them the satisfaction of seeing me break again.

"I doubt you know because you've never been alone. You don't know what it feels like when the silence steals your breath, smothering the life you once had. You don't know what it feels like to be scared when the baby you carried for nine months is silent. When he should have cried. When we all should have been crying happy tears."

I shake off her hand and stand. "No, you wouldn't know silence like I have. You will never know that feeling of having to scream just to remember that you are still breathing. That you're still alive when he wasn't."

I let out a disbelieving chuckle. "I hope the potential I had made you and Daddy proud, because all the fancy schools and lavish flats you gave me meant nothing in my prison of silence." I can feel the rage surfacing just looking at her. "You took everything from me. Everything!"

"And I'm so sorry!" she wails in agony. "I regretted the decision as soon as I held him. He was so—"

The moment she mentions him, I tense. I can put my anger aside for the information I need. "He was so what, Mother? Tell me what you know. It's not too late to fix this."

I sit back down in the chair next to her bed and take her hand. "Tell me about my son." I grab the sketchpad and open to a clean page, pleading when I beg, "Help me find him, Mama. Tell me what you know."

I sketch the image from memory. A dusting of fine dark hair, deep brown eyes, and the perfect bow mouth. She had said he was beautiful—more perfect than any baby she'd seen.

But it's still an image I can never get just right. Nothing feels right when I sketch him. He's a muse I can never perfect. But yet, every night, I pull out my pad, and I try. I give him his father's sharp jaw and amused grin—sometimes, I even give him freckles like me. I've tried so many variations of the boy Duke and I created that I have thousands of sketches of him over the years.

If we'd only had time to take one picture.

One memento.

Even his footprints would have been a cherished keepsake.

Anything that I could have held on to would have been better than the one fleeting ambulance ride where it would be the last time I saw him. But instead of a picture, all I have is my imagination and my mother's spotty memory. It's absolute torture not knowing what he's like. All I can do is dream and sketch until, one day, I meet him.

And we have to meet.

Fate can't possibly be that cruel to us.

"Breathe!" Duke's loud voice startles the charcoal out of my hand and onto the bed.

"Duke?" I turn the small book light I was using and flash it toward where Duke is lying next to me, curled in on himself, pulling in laborious breaths.

"Hey," I lightly shake him. "Duke, wake up. You're dreaming."

His body is shaking violently, and the image of this man enduring the horror he tries to forget sends a sharp pain through my chest.

"Duke."

I shake him once more, but it's no use. He's not waking up.

"Breathe," he cries out again. "Breathe, dammit."

Oh, my heart.

The screams—they were mine as I cried and screamed for the

ambulance to hurry. The 911 operator kept assuring me help was on the way, but it didn't feel fast enough—nor was it reassuring when all I heard was silence.

"Duke." I shake him harder, but he's still locked in the nightmare. Running to the bathroom, I grab the hand towel and run it under the cold water and sprint back to the bedroom, where Duke is still curled in on himself, his body shaking as he whimpers. "Please. Breathe."

I place the cold towel on his chest, and immediately, he jerks awake. "Hey," I soothe when he springs up, his eyes wild with panic. "Hey, you're okay. Jude's okay."

Because ultimately, that's all I'm sure he can think about is seeing Jude take that first breath in his arms.

"Jude is okay," I say again as Duke just looks around the room, confused. "You're okay. It's just a dream." I reach out for him, and he hesitantly takes my hand, still trembling.

I don't know what to say—I don't know if there is anything I can say to make it better. We were both there that night; it's not an image you can shake off with a smile. It guts you—splits you in half as you try to come to terms with the guilt. We made a bad call in thinking we could deliver a baby on our own, but we thought our parents would be looking for us, and checking hospitals would have been at the top of their list. So, we thought we could keep the delivery a secret until we were ready to face them.

People delivered at home, or on the way to hospitals, all the time.

Duke was smart enough to handle it.

But then, Jude didn't breathe.

And we were to blame when we were told he didn't make it.

Living with that kind of guilt comes with jagged scars.

For me, it was living a life of solitude, unable to love anything or anyone but the two boys I would always remember, but for Duke—breathing air into his son as he performed CPR, only to know it didn't matter, that his son would still die? I'm no doctor, but Duke's "screams" are really PTSD that he's likely never dealt with.

"Can I get you some water?" I finally ask, as Duke's tremors settle.

He doesn't acknowledge me. He just keeps staring into the darkness.

"I'm going to get you something to drink, okay?" I rub down his back, but he still doesn't answer me. "Stay here."

His eyes never close, but the tremors return. I don't know what to do. All I know is that this is a side of Duke that I only saw once before—and even then, I couldn't be there for him like he needed.

But unlike last time, I have resources.

With a kiss to his cheek, I leave Duke on the bed, grabbing my phone off the nightstand as I go, already dialing the familiar number.

"What's wrong?" Vance answers on the second ring, sounding wide awake in the middle of the night.

"Duke, he had a dream..." I clear my throat and decide to be honest. Vance knows everything. "He dreamed of that night—the one where—"

Vance cuts me off. "I know what you're talking about. What's wrong with him?" I understand his impatience. Vance has always cared deeply for his younger brother.

"He woke up shaking. I can't get him to speak to me. He's just staring."

Vance lets out this frustrated sound. "Take him the phone."

Part of me wants to say no, that he can tell me how to help Duke, but then I think that it's my screams he still hears. Maybe hearing his brother's voice will help orient him back to reality. His brother wasn't there. He doesn't associate Vance with the pain of that night.

"Okay," I relent, walking back into the bedroom where I find Duke still on the bed. But this time, his eyes are focused... on my sketchbook.

"Duke?" His head snaps up at me. He looks wild and unhinged. "I have Vance on the phone." I hold the phone out. "He wants to talk to you."

Duke looks at the phone and then back at the sketchpad just as Vance yells in the phone, loud enough for us to hear. "Duke!"

He takes the phone, his eyes never leaving mine as he presses the screen and hangs up, handing it back to me.

I stand there in shock as Vance immediately calls back. "Are you okay?" I ask Duke, ignoring the call.

He nods. "I'm fine. Go back to bed."

Yeah, like that's going to happen. But I nod anyway as he gets up and shakes his head like he's clearing out the lingering images. "I'm just gonna grab a shower."

"Okay," I answer gently.

Duke pauses when at the bathroom door. "I can't stay here any longer."

"We'll leave," I promise. The memories are too strong here. I get that. The last thing I want to do is cause him more pain.

"In the morning," Duke confirms.

"In the morning," I agree, settling back into the bed, ignoring the next two calls of Vance's as Duke disappears behind the door.

I lie there for a minute when my phone rings again. Poor Vance. He's probably just as confused as I am. "Hey, I'm sorry. I don't—"

"Ramsey?"

The voice isn't Vance's. "Kelly?"

"Yeah." She sounds out of breath. "I'm sorry to call so late, but I couldn't wait to call you." She pauses. "Are you alone?"

I look at the bathroom door. I can hear the water running. "Yeah, I'm alone. Why?"

She sighs. "Because I found something."

My heart sinks to my toes. I don't know if I can handle more bad news.

"Meet me tomorrow at the café." She hurries out.

"What is it? Why can't you just tell me now?"

I can hear the struggle in her silence. "I need you to see it in person."

"See what?"

"Proof."

"Proof of what?"

Suddenly, I'm excited that we may finally have Langston where we want him.

"Proof that," Kelly exhales, "Duke knows more than he's said."

CHAPTER TWENTY-SEVEN

Duke

We didn't stop for jerky or ice cream.

In fact, Ray and I barely said two words to each other when I had her drop me off at the office.

I needed to see my brother. Last night, I was seconds away from rocking in a corner—something I haven't done in many years.

The memory was so vivid that I felt like I was back there. I don't know if it was the cabin or just all the research opening old wounds. But if anyone can understand nearly blacking out from stress, it's Vance. When Logan, his best friend, died under his care, he could barely function from the grief. Astor and I would find him passed out from the anxiety—especially when Logan's wife filed a malpractice lawsuit against him.

Clearly, the Potter brothers don't adapt well to stress, except for maybe Astor. He seems to be holding it together better than Vance and me.

Still, last night was fucked-up—even more so after seeing her sketch. Was that supposed to be Jude? Surely, she didn't mean to draw him with those eyes. What was I supposed to think?

"Yoo-hoo! Everyone off the crazy train."

I snap to attention at Remington's voice, who I find lounging in Vance's office chair, doing something on his computer. "Where's my brother?"

He taps a few keys on the keyboard, never looking at me. "Most likely banging Halle in the operating room, but then again, he did say he had a patient in room five."

I roll my eyes. "So, he's with a patient?" The little shit just wants to get on my nerves.

"I'm supposed to hang out with you until he's done." He shrugs like he doesn't give a fuck since he's paid by the hour. "So, how was your honeymoon? Was Mrs. Potter everything you dreamed of?" He's still engrossed in something on Vance's computer.

"Mrs. Potter is none of your damn business." I toss my bag on the floor and lower into one of the chairs in front of Vance's desk.

"Aww, that's so cute you want to keep her all to yourself. How noble of you, Dr. Douche." He makes this noise and grunts before flashing me a conniving grin. "Hold whatever comeback you were trying to think of."

He presses a button on Vance's phone, leaving it on speaker as he dials the number, a familiar voice laughing on the other end of the phone. "Go ahead, Keys. Tell me what I want to hear."

I smile at the sound of Keagan, Astor's girlfriend, laughing hard. "I refuse."

Remington grins even wider than before. Who knew talking to Keys would excite him this much. "Say it, Keys. You lost fair and square."

Keagan's laughter dies down, and she pulls in a steadying breath as if she's preparing herself for what he's making her say. "Fine," she relents, "a deal is a deal."

"Damn right it is."

Remington is literally thrumming with anticipation when Keys says, "You were right. Dongs rule, and girls drool."

This boy holds out his fist for me to bump, which I do, since clearly, we dongs need to stick together. "Don't you forget it either. Now, go make a game I can't beat. I'm tired of making you feel bad."

Keys laughs. "Will do. See ya later, Rem."

"See ya."

He hangs up, and it takes him a moment to gather his cool composure again when I arch a brow. "So, you play video games? For a while there, I thought you were an adult."

He rolls his eyes. "She's a game writer, dipshit. She asked me to test out a new game she helped create."

Now it's my turn to make things awkward. "That's cute, you being all sweet. Who knew you had compassion?"

"Fuck you."

"Fuck you," I return with a chuckle. Calling him sweet is clearly his kryptonite.

"Fuck both of y'all."

Vance's voice booms through the room, stopping mine and Remington's stupid back-and-forth.

"Get up," he snaps at Remington, who makes sure to take his time rising from the chair, cutting him a shitty look as he slowly walks over and takes the chair next to me.

"Remington," Vance growls impatiently, "can you give us a moment?"

"I could," he agrees, "but you have a therapy appointment in fifteen minutes." He doesn't move from the chair. That's one thing Remington is great at—keeping my brother compliant with his therapy sessions.

"Reschedule it," Vance says, slightly softer. "I have some time tomorrow afternoon."

"You also have time now," Remington notes, a hard edge to his tone. "How 'bout you and baby bro pick this up when you get back?"

I bet Halle is so proud of this kid. Not only does he drive Vance batshit crazy, but he's also a great assistant.

Vance looks at me and sighs.

"I can come back," I say. "I need to go through the pile of mail that I'm sure Remington has thrown on my desk."

Remington flashes me a wink before he stands, dusting off his hands like his work here is done. "Up and at 'em, Vance-hole. Time to ruin Dr. Johnson's day. I'll tell Hal to order an apology gift."

Vance stands, ignoring the teenager with far too much energy, and rounds the desk. "Don't leave. I still want to talk about last night."

I tip my chin just as Remington's nosy ass asks, "What happened last night?" He looks at Vance like he's one to gossip.

"Nothing," I say, rising and taking a step towards the door, when Halle appears... with a guest.

Langston.

My entire body pulls tight as the bastard fills the space like a black cloud of toxicity.

"Aw, hell, Hal. I thought we told you we don't bleach assholes anymore." Remington shivers dramatically. "It makes Dr. Duke's tummy feel weird."

Halle covers her laugh with a cough. "He said he needed to see Dr. Duke," she says, referring to Langston.

"Actually, I came to see all the Potter brothers," the sniveling bastard says with a grin. "But it looks like I'm missing one." He shrugs. "No worries, I'll leave his with you, and you can pass it along to the patriarch of this shitshow." He pulls out several envelopes and hands one to Halle before giving the rest to Remington. "Hand these to your bosses, dear boy."

Remington tenses and takes a sinister step forward, but Vance is there, pulling him back by the collar, plucking two envelopes from his hand, and offering me one while Langston just chuckles.

"You know, kid," he says, addressing Remington, "a worthy adversary always knows when to concede." He turns and looks at me, then at the envelopes in each of our hands. "A peace offering, Dr. Potter. Consider our business here finished."

The envelope in my hand suddenly feels heavy. "Is this what I think it is?"

Langston chuckles. "It's what you and Ramsey deserve."

He turns then but pauses. "One last thing." He eyes Remington with hatred. "During my digging, I found something interesting about your stellar employee here."

Vance has to yank Remington back again.

"Maybe you should ask him why he was on the run for several years." Langston grins like the bastard he is, but this time, it's Halle that steps forward.

"You need to leave," she spits, which only amuses Langston more.

"Dear girl. I wouldn't be so quick to defend someone you don't truly know." He leans in toward Halle, and Remington and I both have to hold Vance back. "Ask him what happened to his mother. I bet you'll be as shocked as I was to hear the answer." Halle backs up and hollers for security.

"No need." Langston puts his hands up. "I'll see myself out." He turns and flashes Vance and me one last look. "I regret not sharing this moment with my ex-fiancée." He snaps his fingers. "That's right, I already have." His face turns to stone, and the evil he keeps tucked away bleeds out when he meets my gaze. "Let this be a lesson to you, boy. Never blackmail someone when you have more demons in your closet than he does."

My heart is pounding as I use every bit of self-control not to chase after him. Instead, I grab my phone and dial Ray.

It goes straight to voicemail. "Fuck!" I yell, pressing her contact again.

Again, it goes straight to voicemail.

"What the—"

I didn't see the punch.

I only felt a sharp sting to my jaw. "What the fuck?" Rubbing my jaw, I stare up at Remington, a vein pulsing in his forehead. "What's your deal?"

He looks at me, then at the letter in his hand, his lip quivering.

He doesn't say a word.

But he doesn't need to.

My gut says it for me. *A mother knows.* His mother knew. His eyes.

Suddenly, last night's confusion comes barreling into my chest like a wrecking ball.

Her sketch.

"Did you know about this?" Remington finally explodes, screaming at Vance, who stares down at the paper in his hand, too. "Vance!" Remington shouts. "Did. You. Know?"

The brother who I've looked up to my whole life looks at me, and it's a devasting blow before he even says, "No, I had no idea. You know I would have told you."

"Do I?" He laughs, shrugging off Halle's touch. "Do I really know any of you?"

"Yes," Halle cries. "You know us. You know we love you. We'd never do anything to hurt you. Never!"

I lower to the floor as if my legs can no longer hold me up. The envelope crumples in my fist, drawing Remington's attention. "Aren't you going to look, Pops? Apparently, we share DNA, or maybe this adoption contract is a lie, too." He laughs, but it lacks his usual humor. "You're familiar with those, aren't you?" He crumbles the paper in his hand and tosses it onto my chest.

"Well, let me save you the breath. Congratulations, it's a fucking boy—Jude, to be specific."

And then he turns and pushes past Halle. "Remington!" Vance shouts, his voice stern and hard. "Don't you fucking think of leaving."

"You see," he turns slowly, "the thing about being eighteen"—he glances down at me—"and on my own for so many years is that I can take care of myself. I don't need any of your guilt-laden parental guidance anymore. Adios, Potters."

He flips us off when Halle snatches him back by the shirt, hugging him to her body. "If you leave, I leave."

If there is a way to Remington's heart, it's through Halle.

"You're staying here," he grits out, trying to pull away without being a real dick. "With Vance."

Halle holds tight. "I'll follow you," she threatens.

"And I'll burn a path through Texas to get to you both,"

Vance assures them. "If I were you, I would stay and work this out, Remington. Only cowards run."

Remington smirks, looking down at me. "Guess it skipped a generation."

I can see it now if I really look hard. He has my nose. My jaw. Even my hair. And while his eyes are wholly his own, his mother knew them before I did.

She drew them without ever seeing a picture. She knew in her soul what her child looked like, and I'd stared at him for a year and never realized he was the missing piece.

A violent sob tears through me. I can't speak. I can't even apologize.

All I can do is stare at my son through watery tears.

Jude.

Our Jude has been here all along, loving my brother like he was his father.

If I thought I had been punished enough, I would have been wrong.

There was always a chance we would find him.

But I never thought he was here this whole time.

A hand comes down on my shoulder. "I need to take him home." Vance's words are clinical, not comforting, but I guess I don't deserve his comfort anymore. I'm a father who couldn't even recognize his own son while his brother cared for him the last year.

"Astor is on his way."

I don't nod or even acknowledge him. All that's going through my head is that my son hates me, and more than likely, so will his mother as soon as she finds out he's been with Vance and Halle this whole time.

Vance claps me on the shoulder, and I watch as he takes my son with him.

I have nothing to say—no excuse I could give would be acceptable. I've spent my life declaring I would never be the kind of father Harrison was. Yet, here I am, on the floor in Vance's office. Alone.

THE SCULPTOR

I've lost my son for good.

And possibly his mother.

Nothing I can do will save this.

Especially when my phone buzzes with a text from Ray, solidifying that fact.

You can have your heart. I don't want it anymore.

This time, I let the screams take me under.

CHAPTER TWENTY-EIGHT

Duke

I don't know how much time passes before I feel a hand come down on my shoulder. "Hey," Astor says, shoving a glass into my hand. "Drink this."

I can smell the bourbon before I even put it to my lips and tip it back, letting the alcohol burn down my throat. "Did Vance tell you what happened?"

"Yep," he clips out, taking the cup from my hand. "And I'm not here to throw you a pity party." He grabs me by the upper arm and hauls me to my feet as if I were still his little brother. "When you're a parent, you have to put your emotions aside for the sake of your child."

I laugh, finally meeting his eyes as I stumble back. "Remington is no child." Getting my bearings, I find the bourbon on Vance's desk and drink straight from the decanter. "I'm no parent, either."

Astor has always had ample patience, but I realize a minute

too late, when he snatches the bourbon from my hands and chucks it across the office, that his ample patience is gone. "You. Are. A. Parent," he grits out, enunciating each word separately as if I'll digest them better that way. "Whether you think you are a deserving parent is a whole different matter." He pushes me down into the chair. "But you are still a parent, and parents do what they need to for their children."

"Newsflash, Astor, my child wants nothing to do with me. He's happy with our brother." Clearly, Remington gets his immaturity honestly.

Astor lets out this long-suffering sigh that makes me feel guilty for adding more to his plate. "Go home to your daughter," I say, trying for a lighter tone. "I'll call an Uber." Where I can self-destruct and drown myself in bourbon in private.

For a second, I think Astor will take me up on the offer, but then he crosses his legs and sits back, making himself comfortable. "I'm sorry I haven't been around lately."

I wave him off. "You being here wouldn't have changed anything."

I still would have fucked all this up.

"No," he agrees, "but we could have talked about Jude—about the pain you've hidden from us all these years."

I shake my head. "It was my burden to bear." I was the one who agreed to the horrendous plan where we thought we could birth a baby alone.

Astor chuckles, but it sounds like a nice replacement for saying I'm an idiot. "Duke, when Vance was spiraling and blacking out from stress, what did you do?"

"It's not the same thing," I argue. "He was suffering from PTSD."

"He was," Astor agrees. "But so were you. Yet, you let Father spread a lie about why you couldn't sleep. Why you couldn't hold down a relationship."

I close my eyes. "The lie kept her out of it."

"Is that what you think?" he asks, like he can't believe I would say something so stupid. "That keeping up a lie was the healthier option than addressing the issue at the source?"

"Don't talk to me like you didn't do the same thing," I snap. "You aren't perfect either."

"No, I'm not. But like you did with Vance, someone intervened and helped me see that holding on to a secret was killing me inside." He adjusts in his chair and puts his elbows on his knees, his gaze set on me. "Humans aren't meant to be alone. We can't do it. We aren't built to sustain ourselves."

"That's bullshit," I say. "We've all been alone and did fine." I don't need my brothers thinking they have to solve my problems. I can handle it just fine.

"Is that what you call this?" He motions to scattered paper on the floor. "Is this your definition of fine, Duke? Because I have to say, I would think 'fine' would be us finding Remington before he developed a smoking habit."

I scoff. "He still would have smoked to spite us." Let's not pretend he's an angel.

"You're probably right, but still. We wouldn't be here—I wouldn't be here, watching my little brother battle the voice that tells him he fucked up."

"I did fuck up. I should have known he was my son." I look up at the ceiling and let out a laugh. "I've had daily conversations with this kid. I've cracked yo mama jokes and told him about Ramsey—his mother. They were so close to meeting." I throw my hands up in the air. "Christmas Eve! He was right there. She was sitting at my house, waiting for the son she longed for." Emotion wells in my eyes, but I fight it off. "All I had to do was bring her over there. She would have known, Astor. She knew! She drew him, for heaven's sake!"

"Let me get this straight," Astor says, his face stoic and calm. "You were supposed to recognize a son that you thought had been dead for eighteen years?"

"I should have been suspicious," I argue. "When I learned he was alive."

"But you didn't know he was alive." Astor cocks a brow. "You knew there was a possibility he was alive, but you didn't know for sure."

I feel exhausted just having this conversation. "I should have known, Astor."

He nods. "I'm sure you're right, because when I was eighteen, I would be able to recall the distinct characteristics of a blue infant that I was performing CPR on. Tell me, brother, did you even get to hold him after you revived him?"

It feels like a knife to my chest. "For a moment, but then I handed him to Ramsey."

"And when Ramsey had him, did you feel anything other than adrenaline?"

"I don't remember."

Astor offers me a patient sigh. "Exactly. You were operating in fight-or-flight mode—you were running off pure adrenaline. Your brain wouldn't have retained small details because in a time of crisis, your brain was only focused on one thing... bringing that boy back." He leans in and puts his hand on my shoulder. "You had one job, and you did it flawlessly. You saved your child. The rest of what happened is irrelevant. *You saved your child.* You did not give up on that boy then, so when I ask you this, know I ask it with love, but why are you giving up on him now?"

Like he could shake me, Astor squeezes my shoulder. "You were a parent when you gave up your life—your scholarship—to have that boy. You then demonstrated what a loving parent you were when you supported him and his mother at the cabin. And if those two things aren't evidence enough, you breathed life back into that baby with every bit of determination you possessed. Most teenagers wouldn't have known how to do CPR or known how to deliver a baby in the first place. But you did. You studied. You prepared."

He drops his hand and exhales. "Duke, you're more of a parent than Vance and I could have ever been. Just because you didn't have the typical introduction to fatherhood doesn't mean you're any less of a father than anyone else. Not being able to recognize a son you grieved is not an excuse to not pursue that mouthy little shit of yours."

I grin, feeling a little better that Astor doesn't think I'm as shitty as I feel. "He is a mouthy little shit, isn't he?"

Astor laughs. "Most definitely. Really, Vance and I should be the ones feeling stupid. We should have recognized that only you could create a child of that magnitude."

"I blame Ray for most of his attitude."

Astor chuckles. "Unfortunately, I don't think she'll agree with you there."

My chest aches as I think of her last text to me. *You can have your heart. I don't want it anymore.* "Yeah, well, I don't think I'll have to worry about that argument. She's done with me."

Guess she'll get that annulment after all.

"Oh, yeah?" Astor laughs. "You think Ramsey Ford, who has waited on you for eighteen years, is suddenly done with you?"

I shake my head. "Don't talk about it like it's not serious. Langston likely gave her the same thing he did us."

"He gave her the documents that revealed Remington was raised with another family until several years ago?" He acts like the evidence is simple to understand.

"There was a picture of him and me at the bottom," I add, "with a closing statement from an investigator." The words flash through my head.

The subject has been living with the paternal uncle for the past year. Subject seems to have a relationship with his father and uncles. Case Closed.

"If Ramsey received the same documents, she will think that I knew he was here all along, and I didn't tell her." I can only imagine the betrayal she must feel, thinking I was trying to keep her from her son.

"Duke." Astor's tone seems incredulous. "Do you really think she believes you would do such a thing?"

"I don't know," I tell him honestly. "If our roles were reversed, and I had been looking for him only to find out he had been living with her and Langston…" I shrug. "People can change in eighteen years."

And I've spent months telling her I wasn't the same man she thought me to be.

"She'll think I married her to keep her away from finding the truth at Langston's." I can feel the blood whooshing through my veins as my heart picks up in a panic. "She'll think back to me taking charge and leaving her out of the plans. She'll remember my visits with Vance." Tears prick my eyes as I bury my head between my hands. "She'll think I wanted to keep him all to myself."

"You know that doesn't make sense," Astor argues, his voice calming but not enough to keep me from lashing out.

"You and I have seen some crazy shit over the years," I tell him. "You know as well as I do that nothing brings out the insanity in a relationship than fighting over a child."

I've had clients want whole new faces just to hide from their husbands. It's not a stretch to think they would do something drastic to hide a child, too.

Astor stands. "I think you're letting fear get the best of you, brother. Ramsey needs time to process it, but I'm positive she'll come to the same conclusion we all have."

"And what conclusion is that?"

He smiles and pulls his keys from his pocket. "That Duke Potter is a good man and an even better husband."

"You didn't mention father," I add, standing up.

"I thought Remington might want to add that part."

I rear back. "You know he won't."

Astor laughs. "You're probably right, but we won't know for sure until we ask."

He starts walking toward the door.

"Are you suggesting we go talk to him *now?*" It's dark, and well, I'm not sure I'm ready to face him and Vance. It's one thing to talk to Astor, who is calm and understanding, but it is another to face off with two of the least patient people in the world.

"I'm suggesting you don't waste another minute away from your son. I think you've earned an audience with the boy you breathed life into."

CHAPTER TWENTY-NINE

Duke

Astor purposely drove slowly, giving me time to think of what I wanted to say to Remington. However, the whole spiel I concocted completely escapes me when Vance opens the door with a nasty scowl on his face.

I couldn't help it. The competitive brother in me rose to the surface. "I want to see him," I demand.

Vance's brows rise mockingly. "So soon? Perhaps you should wait a few more hours. I'd hate for you to spoil him."

Clearly, Vance thinks I should have been here much sooner—which I agree with. I should have pulled my head out of my ass faster than I did. But we all make mistakes.

The point is, I'm here now, and I'm not leaving until I see him. "I will go through you if I have to, brother, but I will see *my son*."

Vance leans casually against the doorway. "You mean *my* son, because I'm the one who's cared for him this past year."

I swallow harshly, forcing myself to take a breath before I drag my gaze back to Vance's. "And I'm appreciative of that but, nevertheless, he's mine, and I intend to make amends."

I can't change the past, but I can change the future. If Remington is happy with Vance, I'll honor his wishes, but he'll hear me out before he decides.

"And you will let him make amends, Vance," Astor responds from behind me. "We all care about Remington. No one wants to see him hurt, but Duke is Remington's father. He deserves to learn the truth of what happened from the source."

How I wish Ramsey would answer her phone.

She's better at wooing people.

And the Potters—all of them, including Remington—will need some wooing.

But she won't answer me.

Because she still doesn't believe me.

Astor told me to give her space and take on one problem at a time. And currently, the most accessible problem is behind my petty-ass brother.

"And if I don't?" Vance taunts. "Are you both prepared to go against me?"

I square my shoulders—I've fought for this kid. Whether my brother believes me or not, I didn't let anyone get in my way of bringing him into this world, and I won't allow anyone to stand between us now.

"Vance." Halle appears in the doorway and puts her hand on Vance's shoulder. "You can't protect him from this any longer."

Vance scoffs. "I'm not protecting Remington. I'm protecting Duke." He grins. "Rem's liable to slit your throat with the mood he's in."

I can hear Astor's sigh of relief behind me.

"Will you search him for weapons?" I ask, only slightly teasing. "I have more groveling to do later."

"Of course not. I like to encourage Remington to express his creativity." He shrugs, a hint of a smirk playing on his lips. "He doesn't like to use his words."

Now he's just being a shit. "Are you done?" I ask, rather hatefully. "Have I passed your test?"

Halle squeezes Vance's shoulder, and it lets me know that behind Vance's jokes, he worries about Remington. And I could never be upset that he's looking out for him—I'm grateful he stepped in when he did. I can't imagine how I would feel if Halle hadn't convinced Remington to move in with them. Langston said he had been on the run. From what? What happened to him after his adoptive parents died? Was he alone the whole time?

I grab my stomach, a pain settling so deep that I double over.

"You all right?" Astor's hand settles on my back, and I nod.

"I was just thinking about what Langston said." I gaze up at Halle. "Has Remington ever told you why he was at that motel?"

She shakes her head. "He doesn't discuss his past with either of us. We didn't even know his last name until we put him on the car insurance."

Wait. "Did it match his adoptive parents' last name?"

Vance clears his throat. "No. It's probably a fake. There's no telling what kind of trouble this kid is in."

And the hits just keep coming. "We'll take care of it." Remington has been through too much. Whatever kind of mess he's gotten into, I'll get him out.

Because that's what we Potters do for each other.

"No matter what," Vance agrees, his jaw clenched in determination. "We'll take care of it."

"Agreed," Astor adds. "Now, let him see his son, Vance. My patience is wearing thin."

A challenging grin emerges as Vance leans against the door. "You hear that, Duke? We've depleted our brother's patience today. Looks like he's on the mend."

I swallow my laughter just as Astor shoves me into Vance. "Get in the fucking house."

Vance doesn't move to let me by. "I'll talk to Remington first." His tone dares me to argue, which, of course, I do.

"No. I want—"

He holds up his finger in that irritating way of his. "And while I *argue* with him, you'll pour yourself a drink and wait for me downstairs."

I pause, waiting for the catch.

"Remington is an adult." He rolls his eyes. "Not a very good one, but he's an adult all the same. If his irrational ass doesn't want to see you, I'll have to honor his decision."

That's not exactly comforting. Remington is a Potter and a Ford. Neither of those bloodlines are rational or forgiving. But there's a chance.

"I understand, but…" I try not to grin. "Just in case… could you take Halle in there with you? She's likely the only one he'll consider."

Vance grins. "You're probably right." Finally, he moves his arm, pulling Halle by the waist. "What d'ya say, Peach? Think you can charm the demon into talking?"

She sighs. "I can, but I'll need a pack of smokes."

It's been an hour, and I'm on my second bourbon when Halle finally comes down the steps, her face red and puffy. "He'll see you now."

I spring up from the chair.

"But—"

I knew there was a catch. After all, this kid shares half my DNA.

"But…" I urge Halle to finish.

She offers me a sad smile. "He'll hear you out. But once you've said your peace, he wants you to leave." Tears slide down her face. "He doesn't want to see you again."

I feel like someone sucked all the oxygen from the room, stopping my breath. "I understand," I manage to say. "I'll respect his decision."

Halle takes the final steps and pulls me in for another hug. "He's just raw and vulnerable right now. He doesn't know how to deal with this, so he's lashing out."

Neither of us says it, but lashing out is how he deals with most things when he's in a *good* mood. Remington in a bad mood is more than just lashing out. Like my brother, he'll shut down.

"Vance is still with him"—she pulls back to look at me—"stitching up his hand."

I rear back. "He's hurt?"

Halle frowns. "Not as much as the mirror he punched."

Ah. "Can I see him now?"

She gives me one last sympathetic look and then takes my hand. "Be patient with him. He'll come around. He has a good heart. He just doesn't want anyone to see it."

Except for Halle and Vance. He lets them see his kindness.

I think of Ramsey with her beautiful morals and kindness—how she gave up her freedom to marry a man that possibly had information she could use to find her son. She was willing to do anything—even endure bruises to find him. And here I am, seeing him before she is.

"Could you do me one more favor?" I ask Halle.

"Sure."

I hand her my phone and unlock it. "Will you see if you can reach Ray? At least tell her he's okay."

Halle nods, a tear slipping down her cheek. "I will. Now, come on. Your son awaits you."

She leads us up the staircase. It's tense and quiet as we go up what seems like a bazillion steps before she stops at the door.

"Thank you for doing this," I tell her. "I know Remington wouldn't have seen me if you hadn't convinced him."

"He would have seen you on his own," she disagrees with a frown.

Eventually.

That's the word she doesn't say, but we both know Remington is a hard ass. He would have made me work for his presence.

And I would do it.

"Well, thank you for threatening him to come back with you from California." I swallow down the emotion, thinking how much worse this could have been. "If you hadn't found him…"

Halle stops and turns around to face me. "He would have found his way back to you." She wipes a stray tear from my cheek. "Because he's a stubborn asshole. He wouldn't rest until he got to confront his father."

That's what I'm afraid of.

She flashes me a grin and opens the door, a plume of smoke hitting us in the face. Halle hangs her head. "The cigarettes came in handy. I couldn't risk chasing him all over town."

I get it. Again, he's grown. He can smoke if he wants to.

She smacks my chest. "Remember that trick when you're in there and want to kill him. He's like his father. He will negotiate with the right leverage."

And like her point needed reinforcement, a shout comes from the en suite bathroom. "That fucking burns!"

Halle sighs. "Good luck, darling. I'm afraid you're going to need it."

She closes the door and leaves me to face my son.

"Ow! Fuck. It's fucking clean, Vance. Just leave it alone. I'm fine."

I follow the bitching, pulling in breaths with each step, until I come to the bathroom door, glass crunching underneath my shoes. Remington sits perched on the counter amongst the glass, a cigarette hanging from his lips as my brother pours antiseptic over his knuckles.

They both turn to me, but Remington breaks the silence. "You have until Vance-hole finishes torturing me to say what you need to say."

Vance sighs but returns to work, pouring more antiseptic and making Remington hiss through his teeth. "Fuck!"

"I would have numbed it first," I say, frowning.

Vance's head rises, and he looks at me, surprised. "I appreciate the consult, Dr. Duke, but my patient is a giant pain in the ass. A little pain reminds him he isn't invincible and is replacing this mirror with next week's paycheck." He flashes Remington a glare. "But be my guest and take over."

"No." Remington grabs Vance's shoulder, preventing him from leaving. "You stitch it up, or it doesn't get stitched."

"It'll leave a scar," I warn, in case he's serious.

Immediately, I regret speaking when Remington's gaze whips to mine, his face hardening into something menacing. "I think I'll live. After all, it won't be the first scar you'll have inflicted."

At that, Vance takes his cue to leave, stepping back and passing me the antiseptic. "There's still glass under the skin," he tells me.

Then he turns and looks at Remington. "Are you going to be a big boy, or do I need to stay and hold your hand?"

"Fuck you," Remington spits, his eyes steaming with fury.

Vance grins. "Attaboy. For a moment there, I thought you were broken." He grabs Remington's shoulder as he tries wrenching away, but Vance holds him still, a silent conversation passing between them before he steps back, patting his shoulder. "I'll bring you back a blow pop."

Remington blows a puff of smoke in his face, grinning. "Don't forget the beer."

Vance rolls his eyes, but I can see the relief on his face. He was worried about leaving Remington and me in the same room. Whether that concern was for Rem or for me, I don't know. All I know is Vance smirks as he passes me. "Just remember you asked for this meeting."

I nod. I did. I asked to see my son.

And even if this conversation results in a black eye, I will have told him everything.

CHAPTER THIRTY

Duke

"Don't even think of stabbing me with that thing," Remington threatens. "I don't care what Vance said. I'll be fine without it."

I push further into the bathroom and take note of the supplies on the counter, particularly the numbing agent. "You don't want me to numb your hand while I suture?"

His jaw locks. "No."

My hands are already balmy.

Relax, Duke. He's the same Remington you've known for a year.

But he isn't really, is he? Can we look at each other the same, knowing we're father and son? Guess we'll see.

I stride up to the counter, pacing my breaths. I need to think of the water, the ripples on the surface. The surface has changed, but the man inside hasn't. I'm still Dr. Duke Potter, who saved his infant son.

"Digging out the glass will hurt," I explain in my physician's voice. "Worse than the suturing—though both are painful."

Like the true Potter he is, Remington lifts his chin. "I'll be fine."

Of course, he will, because the Potter men are stupidly stubborn. I shrug. "Have it your way."

Eliminating the space between us, I take Remington's hand—which is scratched to hell and dripping blood onto his pants—and assess the damage. "Do you hit mirrors often?" I ask, setting his arm down on the counter while I wash my hands.

"Why? Are you planning on making me stand in the corner?"

His sarcastic comeback has me chuckling. "I didn't realize you got off on that sort of thing."

Remington might be my son, but right now, I want to be Dr. Dumbass and create a space for us to talk. I have no unrealistic views about him hugging me and calling me Dad. This is Remington, the man, who's been through more than we know. The best thing I can do is become his friend again.

"I prefer a nice lashing every once in a while," he says dryly, "but you don't have the tits for it."

"What a pity." I grin, drying my hands and grabbing the antiseptic, ignoring how his body tenses when I pick up his hand. "You might want to look away," I encourage.

Miraculously, he does, and I use the distraction to inject the worst gash with the numbing agent quickly.

"Ow! Fuck! What are—" Remington tries jerking his hand away, but I keep him still. This isn't my first rodeo with a patient who hates needles.

"Be still."

"Fuck you. You don't tell me what to do." He tries snatching his hand away again, but goes nowhere.

"I wondered how long it would take for you to say that." While he sits there fuming, I inject him again, which seems to shock him into speaking—or at least growling.

"I'm gonna beat your ass," he threatens.

At least he's talking to me like he used to. I call that progress.

"Yeah, yeah. You've been living with Vance for too long. He's putting pretty little delusions in your head if you think you will beat *my ass*."

He grunts a sound that resembles something close to a laugh, and I inject him again. This time, the area is numb enough that he doesn't feel it.

"How do your patients feel when you ignore their wishes?" He tries a different tactic—one where we're simply avoiding the gigantic elephant in the bathroom.

I shrug, numbing the more minor gashes on his knuckles. "My patients have sense enough not to forego pain relief."

"They sound like pussies."

He doesn't flinch or curse when I grab the antiseptic and pour it over his hand again, looking for embedded glass. "They might be pussies, but at least they didn't cry when I cleaned their wound."

That gets a better reaction from him. "Don't flatter yourself, Dr. Dick. You will never make me cry. When you sold me in an underground adoption ring, you made sure you burned that emotion from my list of amazing qualities."

My body tenses at his reception of the events. "We never sold you."

Remington laughs. "Okay, fine." He taps out another cigarette, puts it between his lips, and lights it one-handed. "You made the ultimate sacrifice and gave me to someone who would treat me better. Spoiler alert, Daddy Dearest, but Congressman Tooney hated me with a fiery passion. Especially when his wife died, and his mistress preferred a house in Tahiti instead of being a mother to his adopted son."

Tooney. The last name of the couple who adopted him. It's burned into my memory. Seeing them listed as his parents. Their deaths. "So, he left you? After she died?"

He makes a tsking sound. "Now, that's not how this conversation works. It's your turn to share."

I nod, beginning to dig out the remaining glass. "Your mother and I were teenagers when we found out you were on the way."

He blows out a puff of smoke. "I'd give you a high-five, but…" His gaze drifts to his injured hand.

"Don't worry about it," I say flatly. "I'd hate for you to put out your cigarette."

He grins around it. "That would be terrible." He takes another drag and, surprisingly, blows the smoke away from me. "Finish my bedtime story, Pops. Daddy Vance likes me to be in bed by ten so I don't walk in on him 'stretching' with 'Mommy' on the living room rug."

I rear back. "They stretch?"

Remington rolls his eyes. "Don't act like you don't have a kink, Dr. Vanilla. Keep on with your story. You're already boring me."

Yet, he hasn't demanded I leave.

He's curious, and curiosity will keep him still, at least long enough for me to finish.

"Your mother and I had influential families," I start, just as he interrupts me again.

"Skip to the part I don't know. Harrison Potter is scum—even the squirrels that raid Halle's bird feeder know that."

Such a fucking smartass.

"Well, since you know about politicians and influential families, you should be able to understand that those families need to appear perfect to the public. When we found out Ray was pregnant, we knew her father would want to do damage control immediately, so we told him."

"And he threw her out of the house? Yeah, yeah. I've seen sadder Hallmark movies."

I ignore his eye roll. "No, he didn't throw her out. He demanded she have an abortion. She disagreed. So, she planned to run away—it was the only way she thought she could keep you."

His face softens at that, so I keep going. "We made a plan to leave before she started showing. We lied and told our parents we had the abortion. Meanwhile, I picked up a part-time job after school and saved every dollar I made so we'd have starter money when we left."

"You left Vance and Astor?" He's staring at me like I'm a stranger. "Why didn't you tell them?"

I understand his confusion. He's always known my brothers and me to be close. "Now you're trying to skip ahead in the story." I pluck another shard of glass from his hand, dropping it into the bowl on the counter.

"Yes." He yanks his hand away, frustrated and impatient. "That's what I've been telling you. Speed the fuck up. I don't have all night."

And he's lying. He wants to know what happened—just on his timeline, like a typical Potter.

I take his hand back, continuing as if he didn't just have an outburst. "No, I didn't tell Vance or Astor," I admit. "I couldn't risk my father or Ray's finding out about you." I don't say it, but nothing is too sinister when holding on to your position in the elite world. Congressman Ford would never allow Ray and me to ruin his image.

"So, we ran." I exhale, dreading my following admission. "And we prepared to deliver you on our own."

I should have known this little shit would laugh. "And I thought you were the smart one in the bunch."

Rolling my eyes, I feel around for any more glass. "Looks like it didn't skip a generation." I nod to the cigarette still in his mouth. If we're going to point out bad decisions and all, let me remind him that he isn't the poster boy for the cause.

"You got me there." He blows out a puff of smoke and grins. "Consider me effectively scolded."

It's like talking to a worse version of myself.

"Anyway." I pick up the suturing kit. "When Ray went into labor, I delivered you in an old cabin we'd rented that fall." The screams hover in my consciousness. I must keep my eyes focused on Remington—reminding myself that those screams are merely a memory. He's right here in front of me now.

"You weren't breathing," I say softly. "You were blue." His hand tenses, and I have to remind him to relax. "We were so far away from the nearest hospital that it took the ambulance thirty minutes to arrive." It feels weird telling him this story—the same one I tried blocking out. "You would have to ask Ray the finer details," I admit. "All I remember is laying you down on the floor and counting as I breathed into your mouth, pumping your tiny chest with two fingers." I shake off the image. "I don't remember how much time passed, but I do remember with spectacular clarity the sound of your first cry."

I feel a warm tear streak down my cheek. I don't even bother hiding it. "You sounded so pissed." I chuckle, but it sounds watery. "I remember staring at you in wonder before I handed you to Ray."

I hear Remington take a long drag on his cigarette like he's struggling just as much as I am with this conversation. "That's my breath in your lungs," I tease, which he counters quickly, blowing the smoke back in my face with a grin.

"Not anymore. Nicotine owns these babies now."

The joke is a welcome reprieve.

"Regardless," I continue, "once we called the ambulance, there was no hiding it from our parents. Harrison and Congressman Ford came to the hospital but not before you and your mother were whisked away, leaving me to answer questions."

Remington's gaze goes tight. "And they convinced you to give me up."

I shake my head. "No, the doctor told us you didn't make it."

The screams bubble up again, and I have to close my eyes and fight back the memories. "Ray said—" I inhale, trying to find the strength to get through the last bit. "Ray said they had taken you to the NICU to check you out and—"

His hand squeezes mine, and I stop, open my eyes, and find him staring back at me. His eyes are glassy, but he clears his throat and masks the emotion quickly. "I get it. You don't need to tell me any more."

I gently squeeze his hand in return, careful of his injuries. "I want you to know that if we had known you were alive, nothing would have stopped us from finding you. Nothing. We would have given up everything. For. You. You were our purpose, and we wouldn't have rested until we fulfilled our promise of becoming a family."

"When did you find out I was alive?" He pulls in a shaky breath. "Was it Ray?"

I nod. "Her mother died several months ago. She confessed to what they had done."

Remington nods, an amused grin emerging. "And Ray figured out Langford knew my whereabouts." Realization dawns on him. "She was marrying him to—"

I grin, filling in the answer. "To find you. She was going to bring you home."

Remington tsks. "And you fucked up her plans. Shame on you, Dr. Dumbass. Next time, let the women do all the thinking."

Laughing, I get back to work on his hand. "Does that mean you're willing to speak to me again? As long as I let Ray make the plans?"

He gives me a long look before he drops the cigarette into the sink and sighs like this conversation is long past annoying him. "I suppose I have to. If I don't, Hal will drive me batshit crazy with lectures, and I endure enough of those already."

I'll take anything at this point. "All I'm asking for is a chance."

He tips his chin. "I can do that," he agrees, "on one condition."

And I know he's my fucking son with that statement.

"What are your terms?"

He looks at me, his gaze raw and vulnerable. "I want to meet my mother."

CHAPTER THIRTY-ONE

Ramsey

The past twenty-four hours have been worse than the last eighteen years combined.

Duke betrayed me.

The evidence was in an envelope hand-delivered to Kelly by my considerate ex-fiancé. I wanted to deny Duke had any involvement with Jude, but I couldn't. After all, the image of my husband laughing with a dark-headed stranger at the bottom of the letter was unmistakable. I would recognize Duke from anywhere. The man he was with, however, I couldn't say if that was my son or not. He was facing away from the camera. But from the note contained in the letter, I was staring at my son and husband, who had been working together for a year.

A year!

And Duke never said anything. He just let me believe that Jude was still waiting for us to find him.

Out of everyone in my life, I never expected this from Duke. Never.

Even Kelly couldn't believe it. *"He just doesn't seem like the sort to lie,"* she had said. *"He's cagey but not a liar."*

But did either of us actually know the real Duke? It had been years since he and Kelly dated and decades since he and I shared a life. Neither of us could say for certain what Duke was capable of—especially when his son was involved.

There was never a question that Duke didn't love Jude. And when you love someone so deeply, you understand the lengths they would go through to keep who they cared about in their life.

But is that what Duke did?

Did he strike a deal with our son?

Did Jude, I mean Remington, know about me? Did he hate me, and that's why Duke kept him hidden?

The possibilities were endless.

I decided to go with my gut without knowing who I could trust for the actual truth. And my gut said to take some time to figure it out before I had another knee-jerk reaction and texted Duke again.

I told him he could have his heart back—I didn't want it anymore. But I lied. I still want his heart—it's still painted on my body—whatever that might say about me.

Maybe I'm toxic. Perhaps I'm naïve. But I can't just turn off decades worth of love I've developed for this man because my mind says I should.

I just can't accept Duke hid my son from me. There has to be a reasonable explanation as to why Duke didn't tell me about Remington. Duke isn't cruel. He isn't like the other men in my life. He's loyal. He's considerate. He's…

A planner.

That's the only one that stops me. Duke plans, and a year with our son indicates a plan I wasn't privy to.

I groan and roll over, burying my head into the motel pillow, where I stayed last night. I couldn't go back home—if Duke's house was even my home to start with. I needed space, and a cheap motel where this all started when we were teenagers seemed fitting enough.

Except someone doesn't realize my need for solitude when they bang on the door—disturbing my cry-fest. "Go away!" I shout. Surely, Duke hasn't found me this quickly. Maybe it's the building manager following up on complaints of sobbing. That's more likely the case. But then again, I never put anything past Duke and his white knight complex. He's already left dozens of texts and messages on my phone.

"I'm serious, Duke." Let's be real. It's him. He's the only one who would keep banging after a *go away*. "I don't want to see you." Or *any* visitors, for that matter, unless you're Publisher's Clearing House. Though, I'd hate to be caught on camera at this particular moment. I've made it a point to look my worst, leaving my hair a tangled mess with mismatched pajamas that look a hundred years old.

But the banging on the door won't stop.

Fine. Screw it.

I throw open the door, ready to act like a complete fool, and fight with Duke in the doorway. "I don't know who—"

Her smile stops me. "Hi," she says, holding out her hand. "You don't know me, but my name is Halle."

Halle.

"Vance's girlfriend?" I ask, vaguely recalling Duke mentioning that Halle was the only way to get on Vance's good side.

She laughs, and it's infectious enough I smile, too. "That would be me."

As lovely as she is, I'm still not in the mood for company, especially anyone close to the lying Potter brothers. "Thank you for coming all this way," I reply, pushing the door closed as I continue, "but I don't have anything to say to—"

Halle sticks her foot in the door. "I know you've been hurt," she says sincerely, "but I thought you might like to know that before I was Vance's girlfriend, I was Remington's best friend."

I stop breathing.

"I think you know him as Jude."

Maybe it was her smile or her saying his name, but whatever the case, I begin to cry. "Yes," I admit through the tears. "I know a Jude."

She pulls me into her arms, letting me cry into her shirt, shushing me softly. "I know you've been through hell these past few months."

I nod, wiping the tears, and pull away. This woman didn't come here to serve as my teddy bear.

"I thought maybe I could help."

Shaking my head, I dismiss her concern. "That's okay. You don't need to—"

"I know I don't. But you see, my friend, well, he can't stand to see women cry." She shrugs like *what can you do when they're stubborn as fuck.* "He also couldn't stand one more minute without meeting you." She blinks back tears. "Just don't tell him I told you that. He has an image he likes to maintain."

I feel a sob bubble up through my chest. *He wanted to meet me.*

My son.

He's here.

"You ready?"

I think of all the reasons I should say no. My hair looks like a bird's nest. My clothes are basically bathroom rags, and my face, well, there's probably no cream in existence that would reduce the blotchiness I have going on right now.

But none of those things matter.

Because it's been eighteen years since I've seen this boy—eighteen years since I've held him in my arms and marveled over his beauty, and nothing, not even the hot mess I am, will stop me from reuniting with my son.

"I've been ready," I tell Halle, with tears dripping steadily down my cheeks. "So, so ready."

Halle offers me a watery smile. "He's really a special boy," she admits. "It's been an honor getting to know him." She doesn't give me time to ask her all the questions that flash through my mind. She simply motions to a parked SUV.

I stop breathing in those moments when the door slowly opens, and a man—not a boy—steps out, his eyes shielded with a pair of sunglasses.

He has dark hair like Duke, but his face… is wholly his own. His cheeks aren't chubby—they're solid and unyielding, like a man who never takes no for an answer.

I can't even form words as the boy Duke and I brought into this world walks toward us so confidently—so healthy that I can't stop the tears from falling. He made it. He really made it.

"Ramsey, I'd like you to meet Remington—your son."

Halle steps to the side, and every lonely night, every tear I've shed, comes to an end.

This boy was the reason I believed.

The reason I suffered.

To have this one moment—of finally seeing his beautiful face as he removes his sunglasses, giving me my first look at those haunting brown eyes I've drawn thousands of times.

My stomach tumbles over as he stares at me, drinking me in as the seconds tick by.

"Hi, Remington," I finally manage through sobs, my hand reaching out instinctively before I catch myself and pull it back. "It's a pleasure to finally meet you."

For a moment, all he does is blink, the muscle in his jaw working just like his father's does when he's upset.

"I—" A cry explodes from my chest, and I'm helpless to stop it as I sink to my knees. "Oh, Remington, I'm so sorry. I'm so sorry we didn't find you sooner. I'm so—"

"Don't fucking say you're sorry," he snaps, startling me by yanking me to my feet. "Don't ever say you're sorry again."

And then he pulls me into his arms, and every tear, every sacrifice, is worth this *one* moment.

A moment where I hug him for all the things we missed together.

I hug him for all the nights I missed rocking him to sleep and the early morning feedings I never got to do.

I hug him for the mid-afternoon snuggles we'll never know.

I hug him for the first steps I'll never see and for the tooth fairy I'll never get to play.

I hug this man, offering every single bit of a silent apology.

We weren't there on the first day of school.

We didn't see him hit a home run at his Little League games. We didn't get to tuck him into bed and whisper in his ear that we loved him.

I simply stand there, holding my son and grieving the moments we'll never get back when I realize how grateful I am just to get the opportunity to have this one moment with him. Some parents will never get to hold their children again, and I can't help but be eternally grateful for this chance.

"You are more beautiful than I imagined," I finally say through tears as Remington pulls back, flashing a smile that melts my heart.

"Let's not tell Dr. Drab that. He might get jealous."

"Dr. Drab?"

He winks, and I know without a doubt that this is Duke's child. "I think you call him Duke," he says with a chuckle.

"Ah, yes," I say, my smile dropping at the thought of his father.

He sighs, stepping back and removing his leather jacket. "I'm only doing this once because I find it seriously cringe." He winces, shaking his head like he can't believe what he's about to do. "But Duke can be convincing when he talks about you."

"He told you about me?"

Remington snorts. "Get a little bourbon in him, and he won't shut up singing your praises."

Somehow, my heart feels too big for my chest right now. Having my son speak about his father, who is telling him about me—nothing feels more like home than that.

"Anyway," Remington continues like he's annoyed with this whole thing. "I'm supposed to tell you that he sent back his heart and—I can't believe I'm doing this shit." He rolls his eyes and pulls up his sleeve, showing me the hand-drawn heart on his arm—the one I'd recognize from anywhere. The very one his father painted on me many years ago.

He drew it on our son.

He sent it back on our boy.

Our heart.

Our purpose.

Our future.

A tear drips onto Remington's arm, and he takes my hand, moving it to his chest, and sighs dramatically. "He wants me to say that he sent back both of his hearts. He hopes you'll find it in you to bring them back home."

CHAPTER THIRTY-TWO

Ramsey

After Remington pushed through my motel room like he lived there and started packing my bag like I never had an option of not going home, I realized we left Halle outside without a thank you. But Remington assured me Vance was parked a few feet away and was on his way home with her as we speak.

I hated I couldn't thank her in person, but Remington waved off my concern, saying Halle would likely text me later because *she's nosy and demanding like that.*

Thankfully, I'm used to demanding.

Seeing that heart painted on Remington's arm, feeling his beating heart beneath my hand… there was no chance I wasn't going home to both my demanding boys after that—even if one of them has a lot of groveling to do.

But my son pleaded his father's case, admitting they both had no idea about each other. *"I mean, it wasn't like I recognized his ass, either,"* he had confessed. "*Nothing felt different when I joked with him. I just felt… comfortable around them all—and that's not something I'm used to experiencing.*"

Yet, he moves around my room, talking trash about his uncles and father, like this is something we do regularly over coffee.

"Be honest." Remington cuts me this adorable smile that I don't think I'll ever get tired of seeing. "Does Duke really say cringey shit like that often?" He snorts. "Out of all of the Potters, I thought he had more game than that."

I'm hoping the ease with which we speak to one another means he feels comfortable around me, as well.

"You're a Potter now, too," I remind him. "Seems like you would have more '*game*' than any of them."

He looks up from a sketch he finds on the nightstand. "I like the way you think."

It's not just how I think. I can tell this boy will be a heartbreaker. I already feel sorry for the woman he decides is his for the taking. Because he won't ask her to be his, he'll demand it.

"What is this?" he asks, bringing my attention to the sketch in his hand. "Is this me?"

I move in closer, still careful to give him his space. "Duke and I never got a picture of you," I explain. "I couldn't bear it." I trace along the edge of the big brown eyes on the sketch. "So, I started drawing you every day." I offer him a soft smile. "I know it doesn't look all that much like you—just the eyes, but it was all I had."

Grabbing the sketchbook from the bed, I hand it to him. "There are hundreds of sketches in here. Pictures of Duke holding you on what would have been your first birthday. Pictures of you smiling up at me." I shrug. "I captured it all—living what would have been our life together."

He pulls me to him when I wipe at the tears accumulating. "I never moved on," I confess. "I couldn't. I had to know you in whatever way I could—even if it was just in spirit."

Remington's chin rests on the top of my head. "We'll fix that, I promise."

His words wrap around me like a cocoon of happiness. "I'd like that."

It's all I can say. I know he's grown and is just starting his adult life, but like any mother, I'll cherish every moment—every conversation and picture—he'll give me.

Letting me go, Remington tucks the sketchbook into my bag. "You ready to go home?"

Home.

I asked Duke to trust me to bring our son home.

Instead, our son is bringing me home.

To his father.

I can't help but ease the emotion coursing through my veins with a joke. "What if I'm not ready to see your father?"

Remington grabs my bag, hitching it over his shoulder. "Then we better get a head start, because your husband is a persistent bastard."

That he is.

"Agreed." I laugh as Remington extends his hand. It's at that moment I worry I won't be able to let this boy go one day. But then again, I've never been able to let him go. At least now, I can cherish his presence.

"Come on," he encourages, stepping closer like he might actually toss me over his shoulder if I don't take his hand. "Show me the way home, Mom."

"So, Duke didn't give you directions?" I finally say when I realize Remington is going the opposite way from Duke's Texas home.

He shakes his head, his fingers drumming along the steering wheel. "Nope. He said you would remember the way."

The cabin.

That's the home he's leading us to.

"Did he happen to tell you the significance of where we're headed?" You never know with Duke and his caginess.

"Yeah," Remington says with a frown, like even he dreads going back there, which begs the question of why Duke would want to go back.

The last time we were at the cabin, Duke couldn't stand it. Why would he want to go back?

Something in the back of my mind tells me I know.

This time, it isn't the same.

Everything has changed. Our future has come to fruition.

"So," Remington says, changing the subject. "I'm supposed to stop at a gas station for beef jerky and a vanilla milkshake." His lip curls. "And try it with you. Apparently, you guys have a bet going."

Oh. My. Freaking. Heart. We did! Duke claimed we had to stop so many times for me to pee because I upset Remington's environment with the jerky and milkshake. I swore he liked the concoction, but Duke disagreed.

Now he's allowing me to find out for myself. Oh, this man knows the way back to my heart.

"Duke really asked you to try it with me?"

Remington chokes like he's fighting back a gag. "I'll be honest; he had to pay me. Beef jerky and milk anything sounds like a bad night."

I don't even care that Duke bribed him—I hear it's one of the most effective ways of convincing children to do what you want. And Duke always needs convincing to do anything. It's no surprise Remington is the same way.

"Well, it's not a bad night," I assure him. "It's a magical experience for your tastebuds."

He belts out a laugh, tossing his head back. "All right, let's do it."

He gags.

Twice.

And then has to dance around to swallow it down.

I narrow my eyes. "You reacted just like Duke did."

He casts me a wary look. "While I make it a point never to agree with Dr. Drab, this is pretty disgusting." He lights up a cigarette and holds up his hands, telling me to wait to say anything about it. "You owe me a cigarette to get this taste out of my mouth."

He makes another face and inhales.

I can't even find it in me to care he's destroying his lungs at the moment. All I can think is that he shared a moment with me—a moment his father told him I needed.

And it was everything.

"So, you ready to smack your husband for being an idiot?" He puts out his cigarette and cocks a brow. "I'm sure he deserves a few. Or I can loan you my belt, if you want to get him as he runs."

"Oh my gosh." I double over laughing. "No. I think we'll be fine just yelling at each other."

He shrugs. "If you change your mind, just know I don't mind holding him down."

"I'll keep that in mind."

For this day to have started shitty, it's sure turned out to be a dream come true.

Five-and-a-half hours in the car with my son wasn't enough time.

"Are you happy with Vance and Halle?" I finally ask as we get close to the cabin.

The question has been weighing on my mind since he started telling me the story of how he found Halle, who was looking for Vance, at a dingy motel.

Remington nods, but it's tense.

"You can be honest," I tell him. "I'm grateful they cared for you for the last year. I would never want to force you from your home. Duke and I are happy to be part of your life in any capacity. Even if you decide it's just as your friend."

He takes the turn that leads to the driveway of the lake house. "It's hard." He clears his throat and tries again. "It's been a long time since I even wanted a friend." He laughs. "Halle was a bully, though, and didn't give me a choice in the matter."

He flashes me a smirk. "She tricked me. I thought she was some helpless tourist that would end up in some alley dumpster without my guidance."

I love to see him smile—especially when it seems like he genuinely cares for her.

"And before I knew what was happening, I had a friend *and* agreed to move in with her and Vance."

"You're Vance's assistant, right?"

He nods, this shit-eating grin on his face. "He adores all the quality time we spend together."

I laugh. "I bet. But someone needed to give him hell."

"Agreed, but Halle does a pretty decent job of it herself." His smile drops like he remembered something unpleasant. "I'll have to remember to threaten him before I leave."

My heart sinks straight down to my toes. "You're leaving?"

Remington's gaze finds mine as he pulls into the driveway, parking in front of the garage. "Yeah, I made Vance a deal to attend college next year in Georgia," he says carefully.

"Oh."

I try to force a smile onto my face. College is good. I want him to go to school. I just didn't realize how finite my time with him would be before he left.

"That's wonderful," I tell him. "I've never been to Georgia, but I hear it's beautiful. What are you planning to study?"

He chuckles. "Well, I guess I'm following the family legacy, though that's not originally why I picked the major."

"You're becoming a doctor," I say, pride seeping into my words.

My heart can't take it all as I reflect on Duke's and my conversation all those years ago. *"Do you think he'll take after me and become an artist or after you and become the next Dr. Potter?"*

At the time, Duke wasn't sure he would become a doctor, but I knew he would. And now, so will our son.

"I mean, at the time, I didn't know I was a Potter," he explains, like he's still not sure if I believe he and Duke didn't hide their relationship from me. "Hell, I never dreamed I'd even go to college. It was not something on my bucket list. But Vance-hole"—he clears his throat—"said I would make a great surgeon one day, and that kind of stuck with me."

I offer him an encouraging smile. "I agree with Vance there. All the Potter men have made great surgeons."

"I enjoy working with them," he admits. "They have always included me in the practice's business." His jaw clenches like he's fighting off emotions. "And they've been generous with sharing their knowledge."

My chest squeezes. How he describes his relationship with his father and uncles sounds like he's never known kindness before. It makes me want to kill Langston.

"The best way to thank them," I add, "is by giving back." I grab his shoulder, wishing we weren't in the car so I could hug him. "Make them proud by showing them how truly incredible you are."

He is a Potter, after all. There is goodness in him, just like there is goodness in his father—and me. I don't need him to become a doctor to make me proud or know how incredible he is. Because a mother just knows—she needs no proof.

"I guess this is it, huh?" he asks, glancing at the cabin door, where his father carried me over the threshold—twice.

I nod, and it takes me back to the car eighteen years ago when I put Duke's hand on my belly. *Do you feel that?* I had asked him on the way to the cabin. *That's our son. He knows we're taking him home.*

But this time, I'm not feeling his kicks in my belly. This time, our son rounds the car, opens my door, and takes my hand, proclaiming, "We're home."

CHAPTER THIRTY-THREE

Duke

Ask me how many rocks I've skipped since I've been here waiting on Remington to bring my wife home.
A lot would be the answer.
But it was either that or text Remington a million times.
And he deserved time with his mother without interruptions.
They both did.
That doesn't mean I wasn't about to lose my mind, waiting for them to return.

"Have a drink before you start crying and make it awkward for everyone," Vance says on the other end of the phone. "I can feel the anxiety from here."

I pace up and down the dock. "What all did you say when you groveled to Halle?"

He snorts. "I didn't grovel. I put her ass in the car and threatened Remington to get in behind her."

"That's not the way I heard it went down." I chuckle, knowing good and damn well my brother begged for Halle's forgiveness. He can try to act all badass, but I know he did what I'm about to do—plead.

"Well, you already know that kid of yours lies. I don't know why you think he would tell you the truth of what went down that day I found them in California."

I would argue that Remington isn't a liar but considering Vance and I just figured out the birthday Remington gave us was not accurate—because I know with certainty when the little shit was born, and it wasn't in the summer—I have no defense. He is hiding something. The question is what.

Vance's SUV pulls into the driveway, and I nearly drop the phone. "I gotta go," I tell Vance with urgency. "Any last advice?"

He sighs like this is the stupidest conversation he's had all year. "Beg—on your knees."

Then he hangs up like he just didn't admit that he begged. Put her in the car, my ass…

Pocketing my phone, I walk up the hill to the driveway, watching Remington open Ray's door and help her out. It feels weird when this sense of pride swells in my chest. That's my son—and my wife. And no matter if I spend the next month on my knees, groveling, I won't let us be torn apart again.

I will do what I must—even if that means tossing Ray into the snake-infested lake she fears until she agrees to give me another chance. I'm not above stooping low.

I reach the driveway and slow my pace when Ray turns, seeing me for the first time since she received that letter about Remington. Her face softens, and her eyes sparkle in the evening light.

"Well," I prompt, "did he like your road trip concoction?"

She fights back a smile when Remington makes this disgusted sound deep in his throat. "He said it wasn't that bad."

I look at Rem for confirmation.

"Don't look at me. I'm not getting involved." He squeezes Ray in a hug and kisses the top of her head. "Remember, all you need to do is holler, and I'll hold him down." He cuts me an amused look. "No one ever has to find his body."

Great, one day with Ray, and she's already charmed him.

I'm not even mad.

"Act right, Pops." He starts walking back toward the door.

"Where're you going?"

He flips me off. "To check out the house—unless you want me to stick around and film the tears for Vance-hole. It'd make for a great birthday gift."

I clear my throat, knowing he's probably serious. "Absolutely. Go check out the house."

He grins like the little demon he is before he disappears into the cabin where we brought him into the world. Just seeing him walk in there is enough to capture mine and Ray's attention for several minutes.

"He's the most perfect boy I've ever known," Ray finally says with a weak voice.

"Eh," I shrug, only half-joking when I say, "you'll change your mind once you get to know him better."

At the mention of me knowing him better, Ray tenses. Immediately, I realize my mistake, and I panic, dropping to my knees just like Vance told me. "I know what the letter said, but you have to know, Ray, I had no idea who Remington was."

I chance looking up and meeting her eyes—her very amused eyes—and pause. "Keep going," she encourages after I just kneel there and blink. "It looks like you've prepared this speech, so you might as well finish it."

Does that mean she knows the truth?

I mean, Remington could have told her, but I didn't ask him to. I wanted his first meeting with his mother to be about them. Well, apart from the whole heart thing and the pit stop for beef jerky. That was for me, but still. That's all I asked him to do. Well, except for bringing her here—You know what? It doesn't matter. She hasn't slapped me or gotten back in the car. That has to be a good sign.

"Okay," I start, hesitating for just a moment. "I don't remember where I was in my speech, but you're right. I did prepare one."

I reach up and take her hand, gripping it tightly. "I'm sorry I failed you. I have no excuse other than I'm a man, and apparently, God did not give us the intuition like he gave women. I should have known Remington was my son. I should have recognized his eyes like you did. I should have felt this nagging sensation deep inside my soul that he was still out there. But I would never keep him from you. *Never.* You know I wanted him just as much as you did. If I had known, I—"

She stops me right there, pressing her finger to my lips. "Do you love me, Duke Potter?"

"More than anything," I reply with a fierceness.

"When Remington goes off to college, and it's just us alone again, will you still love me then?"

I nod. "Without a doubt."

"And if I say I want to spend forever with you and that boy in there, will you—"

I don't know where she's going with this last question, but it doesn't matter. I'm done, and I'm taking Vance's fabricated advice and putting her ass in the house. We're done talking here. It sounds like my dear, sweet son paved the way to forgiveness, and I'm not one to look a gift horse in the mouth.

Standing, I sweep Ray up in my arms, ignoring her squeal, and "What are you doing?" questions as I take the stairs one at a time.

"You know what I'm doing, Ray," I finally say when I'm at the door. "We've been here before."

Her eyes widen.

Yeah, she knows my intentions.

"We've already done this twice!" she argues, though she sounds more excited than aggravated.

"But we've never done it with Remington here. Now, we're officially home."

I yell for the boy, who's likely smoking in the bathroom, until he comes to the door, looking at Ray in my arms. "This looks like something I'm going to need therapy for later," he says, sounding bored already.

"Probably," I agree, "but let's ensure we get our money's worth. Take her left side."

He rolls his eyes and addresses Ray. "Now I know he says *and does* cringey shit all the time."

I swear if I had a free hand, I would smack him, but that would ruin the moment, and I need all the good moments to remind Ray why she fell in love with me all those years ago.

"I think," Ray says as we adjust her between us, "that he's perfect."

Remington gags but then grins when we start walking and he sees Ray's face light up as we carry her over the threshold and into the living room.

He enjoys making her happy.

Just like me.

But then Ray starts crying, and he pulls to a stop. "What? What did you do?" he asks just as we sit Ray down gently.

I pat him on the shoulder and smile bigger than I have in years.

"I left the tree up. We have a picture to take."

EPILOGUE

Duke

"Blow all the smoke out the window."

I cast Remington a concerned look. "Seriously, how often do you smoke in inappropriate places?"

He chuckles, blowing the smoke out the window like I need a demonstration on how to do it properly. "I think the answer you're looking for is more times than I can count." He shrugs. "But that would be a lie. Normally, when I want to smoke, I smoke. I don't give a fuck about cracking a window."

Passing me the cigarette, he cocks a brow to silently ask if I'm going to be a pussy about it. "The only reason I have the window open is so you have a chance of getting laid tonight. If Ray catches you taking a hit off this, you'll spend your honeymoon groveling instead of consummating—which is disgusting enough."

I grab the cigarette and take a long drag. I'm not a smoker, but I had started pacing and sweating a few minutes ago, and it was all Remington had to settle my nerves. I was desperate.

"Well, I appreciate you thinking of my happiness for once," I tease, handing the cigarette back, thinking Ray will likely smell it on me regardless of an open window.

"I don't know why you're so nervous, anyway," Remington notes, adjusting his tie with a frown. "Isn't this the ninth time you've married Ray?"

He's loosened his tie and can't seem to straighten it out without dropping his cigarette.

"For goodness' sake." I snatch him by the tie and level him with a disapproving look. "Who knots your tie at the office?" He wears a suit to the office most days.

He shrugs, unashamed. "Hal."

Ah. Of course, she does. "Well, you need to learn how to do this if you're going to be a doctor."

He chuckles, acting like I'm ridiculous for mentioning such absurdity. "Trust me. When I become a doctor, I never plan on dressing or undressing myself." He punches me playfully in the shoulder. "Perks of that MD behind your name, am I right?"

Heaven help me. I'm about to pay for my past sins with this kid. "You still need to know how to knot a tie." I try changing the subject.

"Sure, Dr. Drab. Keep telling your married self that."

At least he's stopped with Dr. Douche. We're making progress.

"Duke!" Vance yells, interrupting us by banging on the door. "Let's go!"

I flash Remington a grin. "Tell your mama to watch for snakes." Then I snatch the cigarette from his lips and drop it into the sink, walking out to where I'll marry Ramsey Potter for the very last time.

Ramsey

A knock sounds at the door.

"You ready?" Halle looks over my shoulder in the full-length mirror, where I stand in a lace wedding gown.

I laugh. "Is this ridiculous? I mean, I've already married this man once. Now, we're just wasting money."

Halle moves the hair off my shoulder, holding my gaze in the mirror. "You're not wasting money. You're giving your family a chance to celebrate this moment with you." She laughs. "You're also conscious, so there's that, too."

I can't argue with that point, which was the very reason Duke suggested another ceremony.

We'd spent a week in the cabin with Remington, all of us getting to know each other in the home where we dreamed of becoming a family. It was the best week of my life, sitting with my son and husband as we joked and learned each other's quirks.

We spent time on the dock just watching the water ripple and teaching Remington to skip rocks—though that ended with him getting frustrated and saying, "Fuck this," and heading inside to play online with Keys.

It was then that Duke apologized for getting me so drunk I couldn't remember marrying him in Vegas. Honestly, I hadn't even thought about having no memory of that night until he brought it up. We had so much going on with Langston and Jude that remembering the actual ceremony wasn't all that important—finding our son was.

But Duke had to right his wrongs. He couldn't bear me missing another moment in our lives together—unlike our fathers, who remain strangers in our lives and not caring if they miss any moments with Remington. Duke and I have tried to work toward forgiving them for the roles they played in taking our son, but they don't make it easy.

It doesn't matter anyway.

Remington, the Potter brothers, and their women are all the family we need—especially to mark this special occasion at the cabin that started it all.

"Mom!" The banging starts up once again. "Should I start the car, or are we doing this?"

I can hear a hint of concern leaking into his joke.

"Is he not the cutest ever?" Halle grins, walking to the door and throwing it open.

Remington stands there, a distinct frown on his face as he clips out, "What the fuck, Hal? How long were you going to keep me waiting?"

Halle steps back, letting him through. "You're looking sharp, Mr. Potter," she teases, deepening his frown.

"Stop. I can't deal with all your happiness today." He confidently pushes into the room as he heads straight for me, his eyes taking in my dress and flowers in my hand. "You look beautiful." He clears his throat like the words felt awkward coming out of his mouth.

"You look right handsome yourself." He's all broad shoulders and man. Sometimes I still can't believe this man is the baby Duke revived and placed in my arms as he demanded attention with his loud cry.

Duke's and my nights are no longer filled with silence and screams. Instead, this man fills them with laughter and sarcasm.

And the stench of smoke—but we're working on that.

"So," he says softly, "you ready to walk the green mile?"

Halle and I both burst out laughing.

"That is not what we're doing," I scold, setting down the flowers.

I walk up to my little boy and pull him into a hug. "But yes. I'm ready for you to walk me down the aisle."

He tightens his hold. "You sure? I hear there're snakes out there on the dock where he awaits. I think that's a sign to get out while you can."

Oh, this boy is Duke's child, through and through.

"I think I'll risk it," I tell him, pulling back to look at those haunting brown eyes. "That strategy has been good to me."

Remington seems to take a minute before placing a kiss on the top of my head and offering me his elbow. "As you wish."

And then I let the boy I've dreamed of give me away to the man of my dreams.

EXTENDED EPILOGUE

Remington
One year later…

"I'm surprised you asked to see me. I thought you were headed off to college soon."

I pull out a chair and sit, eyeing the expensive drinkware and linen tablecloths, and address the asshole in front of them. "I am," I agree. "Next week."

Langston smirks. "Seems like your life is going better than most nineteen-year-olds."

The fact this man is still alive is a tragedy.

"I hope you didn't think you needed to thank me personally."

Ah, there it is. Exactly what I've been waiting for—an opening.

Grinning, I lean back in the chair and kick up my feet onto the table, sending the crystal dishes to the floor as I get comfortable in the middle of the crowded restaurant. "How could I not?" I ask, aghast, placing my hand over my chest. "You changed my life, Langford."

By taking everyone I loved.

Langston narrows his eyes, casting a wary glance around us. "What do you really want?"

Such a loaded question.

I look up like I need a moment to really ponder the answer before meeting his gaze, letting all the rage and hate bleed into my words. "You know, Langford, a man once told me that a worthy adversary knows when to concede defeat."

I lean down and slap the piece of paper in front of him and whisper, "You should have conceded, Langford."

It's no longer a warning.

"You're a bastard," he grits out, unfolding the paper, his eyes scanning the document.

I grin. "That might be true, Congressman," I chide, dragging my feet off the table, managing to spill his drink in the process, "but I'm not the only one."

He glares at me, his jaw ticking as he unfolds the dorm room assignment—the very one I cut a deal to arrange.

"You know her, right?" I chuckle. "Of course, you do. You know everything about everyone. I guess the better question would be: Does she know you, seeing how she's *your* bastard and all?"

I lean down, my voice dipping dangerously low. "You were right. I did do something to my mother, and that should concern you, Congressman. Because I'm not like my father, I won't turn the other cheek." I tap the paper, feeling the tension grow between us. "Karma is reserved for those who have something to lose, Langford. Vengeance is for those of us who don't."

I grin and take a step back. "I'll tell your daughter you said hi."

Eager for more of Duke and Ray's story? How about Remington? Download this bonus epilogue and enjoy all three!
https://geni.us/Thesculptorbonus

Want more characters like Remington? Check out Theo in *Pitcher* and *Commander* from my *Commander in Briefs Series* or Maverick from *IOU*. They are full of antihero goodness.

The Prodigal, the final book in *The Hands of the Potters*, is coming in early 2023. Don't miss the epic series conclusion with Remington's story.

OTHER BOOKS BY
KRISTY MARIE

21 Rumors Series
A Romantic Comedy Series—All novels are standalone and feature different couples with crossover characters
IOU
The Pretender
The Closer
21 Rumors Box Set

The Commander Legacies
A Second-Generation Contemporary Series—All novels are standalone and feature different couples with crossover characters
Rebellious
Book 2 (Fenn's Story) Coming Soon
Book 3 (Drew's Story) Coming Soon

Commander in Briefs
A Contemporary Series—All novels are standalone and feature different couples with crossover characters
Pitcher
Commander
Gorgeous
Drifter
Interpreter
Commander in Briefs Box Set

The Hands of the Potters

A Contemporary Series—All novels are standalone and feature different couples with crossover characters

The Potter

The Refiner

The Sculptor

Book 4 (Remington's Story) is coming soon!

For more information, visit www.authorkristymarie.com

ACKNOWLEDGMENTS

Dear Reader,

I can't count how many times I've sat here and tried to find the right words to say to make this page mean something to you. But maybe it's not supposed to. Maybe it's supposed to mean something to me.

Just getting to write these sentences to you, thanking you for reading my words and for believing in this series, is a privilege I don't take for granted. You don't have to read this book; you don't even need to read this page, but those of you who do, need to know exactly what it means to me.

I'm so very grateful for the opportunity to spend time with my children and write you a story worthy of your time, money, and attention. Your support, and your love for my books, are a vital part of making all this happen for my family.

I COULD NOT do this without you, and it will forever mean the world to me.

There are billions of books out there, so thank you for choosing to read mine.

All my love,
Kristy

As for the crew who have as much blood, sweat, and tears in this book as me, please stand up and raise your hands high. We did this shit!

In no particular order, these are the heroes of *The Sculptor*.

Sarah P.: Dude. Duuuude. I will never understand why you put up with my mess, but I am utterly grateful for your early morning chats and cheering throughout this process. And let's not even bring up the number of times you had to read this book and hold my hand as I threatened to kill off these characters. You are the damn bomb, girl. You need ice cream.

Jaime: I lack the words to tell you how much you mean to me. I could list a few examples like last-minute editing, dealing with my nonsense, and my lack of time management—I could go on, but let's not. It only makes me feel like spiking my coffee. But more than what you offer me professionally, I cherish what you offer me personally even more. You are my rock. My sister in faith. My best friend. Distance may part us, but I am always with you in spirit. Thank you for enduring my tears, my insecurity, and the days when I hide from the world. You are my girl, and I will be forever grateful for your presence in my life.

Vanessa V.: You are a rockstar! Thank you for reading this book last minute and enduring my millions of questions. I hope you know you are locked into this relationship now.

The A-Team: You guys are named that for a freaking reason. You make all this happen with your brilliant feedback and never-ending patience with my process. I could not do this without you!

Jessica: Can you believe this shit? How many books is this now? We made it through many storms together with minimal tears—just kidding, there were many tears. Thank you for believing in me from the first book and always being there with the umbrella. I love you hard.

Autumn: Thank you for holding the fort down when I disappear and break down from the stress. This isn't an easy job, but you certainly make it a little easier.

Sarah S.: I tried coming up with another hot mess joke since it has become a tradition at this point. But I am sleep deprived and under-caffeinated, so I'm drawing a blank. But just know I would be under the hot mess express if it wasn't for you knowing what I needed when I leave out a million things and can't manage to give you any dates or direction. I now anoint you a hot mess fairy. Congratulations, you upgraded from a fellow passenger to the fairy of the train. I'll find you a trophy because this should be celebrated.

Letitia and Stacy: Here is another beautiful creation by your talented hands. Thank you for always knowing what I need with my limited and scattered input. You both are heroes.

Miriam W.: I truly believe God puts special people in our lives at the right time. He sent you to me at a time when I was questioning what I was doing. But then I received your emails, and your words renewed my spirit. Thank you for reaching out. Thank you for doing His work and encouraging me when I needed it the most. You are truly someone very special.

And lastly, a very special thank you to the real Potter, Refiner, and Sculptor of my life, my Heavenly Father, Jesus Christ. I can only write unconditional love because you showed me what it was. I am forever your clay to mold.

Made in the USA
Monee, IL
27 November 2023